3/21/15

To Ozzo +
John Nolis'

I really appreciate
your friendship

Randy S. Moss

HEARTBREAK TIMES

COLLECTED COLUMNS

DAVID MOSLEY

WITH POEMS BY MARLENE TUCKER

Marlene Tucker!

WINGSPAN PRESS

Published in the United States and the United Kingdom by WingSpan Press, Livermore, CA

The WingSpan name, logo and colophon are the trademarks of WingSpan Publishing.

ISBN 978-1-59594-546-4 (pbk.)
ISBN 978-1-59594-694-2 (hardcover)
ISBN 978-1-59594-882-3 (ebk.)

First edition 2014

Photo and Technical Credits:
Front Cover Graphics: Thanks to Waco Today Magazine, published by Waco Tribune Herald, for use of the Heartbreak logo.
Front Cover Photo: Mark Pepper
Back Cover Photos: Terri Jo Mosley

Printed in the United States of America

www.wingspanpress.com

Library of Congress Control Number 2014955074

1 2 3 4 5 6 7 8 9 10

For Terri Jo and Rebecca,
the two women in my life.

ACKNOWLEDGEMENTS

I MUST THANK SANDRA SANCHEZ OF the Waco Tribune-Herald, who first encouraged me, Clifton Robinson, then owner, who thought I was "the funny man," and Jeff Osborne, my first editor. In particular I must express my appreciation to Ken Sury, my current editor, who has encouraged me and prevented me from looking like a total illiterate for the past three years.

My special thanks to David Collins at Wing Span Press, who never ceased pushing when it was needed. Thanks.

Thanks to my "Council of Crones and Cronies," a circle of friends who have read my works in their roughest forms. This includes my sister Dorothy Spears, my daughter, Rebecca Mosley, and pals Pat Kultgen, Melody Strot, Mark Pepper, and Nita Fanning.

Thanks to Marlene Tucker. She started as a fan, but after showing me some of her poetry, I had to have her on board. Marlene is one of those special finds in life: a perfect lady, a doting grandmother, and an incredibly talented poet with an outlaw sense of humor.

Most of all I must express my heartfelt appreciation for the hours of patience and expertise from my lovely wife, Terri Jo Mosley. She has read and reread my manuscript more times than any of us can count. Although she is a trained journalism professional, she continues to love me despite my propensity to damage the English language.

The mistakes and faults that remain are entirely my own.

FOREWORD

THE STORIES IN HEARTBREAK TIMES
are arranged by story type, and not in any particularly chronological
order. A little math: Janey is 16 when she and Dave arrive in
Heartbreak. Five years of stories later, she is just 19 and off to college.
My fictional characters age at about half the speed of real life.

A constant question from my readers has been, "How much of
this is true?" Many of my stories are based in fact. I really did see
a white kangaroo on my ranch. I suspect he escaped from an exotics
farm up river. An uncle really did fix a fire truck and try to wash off
the front of his house. A cousin really did get in a bar fight much like
the one described.

Many other stories are based on news stories and some others are
wholly imaginary. I've lived the ranching life and birthed and buried
my fair share of goats, God bless their fragile, short lives.

One part of this work of fiction is entirely real: the beauty of
Texas in the spring, the desperate struggle to wrench a living from
the unforgiving land, the unrelenting work of fencing, feeding, and
caring for a ranch, and, of course, the inevitable heartbreak of it all.

TABLE OF CONTENTS

The Tribes of Heartbreak

Holidays

Heartbreak High

Daily Horrors

Elegiac Reflections

HEARTBREAK HISTORY

'BOUT TWO YEARS AGO I MOVED TO Heartbreak with my 16-year-old daughter, Janey. Heartbreak is 50 or 500 miles west of Houston's sushi bars; it's a place where things are still like they always were, or at least as we remember them. Men work hard (well, kind of), women birth easy (well, kind of), and raising cows is such a natural thing for the area, a hard working family can go broke real slow— if they work hard enough.

I gradually learned a little history about Heartbreak. Like most places, after people got to know me, they were willing to talk a little, at least about their neighbors. It's funny how the best stories about a family get buried, and would stay buried, if it wasn't for neighbors. In an African village, a person that passes on these stories is called a historian. In Heartbreak, he or she is called a gossip. I write these stories down. I would hate to know what they would call me if word gets out. So, if you ever meet someone from Heartbreak, keep quiet, would you? I like living here and I don't want my barn to burn.

Originally the area was called "Buried Alive," after a buffalo hunter who made an unfortunate bad first impression on a passing band of Comanches. For a short time after the Civil War, it was called "Sherman's Grave," but that was just wistful thinking aided by a little Reconstruction Era humor. It was renamed "Unmarked Grave" during the cattle drive days (circa 1870). During the 1890's huge ice storms it was first called "Heartbreak," as the cattle died because all the water was frozen, or they froze standing on their feet.

Heartbreak, Texas

During the oil boom of the '20's-'30's, two political groups emerged. One wanted to rename the city "Prosperity" in light of the new found wealth; the other group wanted to go back to "Unmarked Grave" for all the roughnecks that died to bring in that prosperity. Eventually the oil tapered off and then ran out—no one could argue with the name "Heartbreak."

The town always has been decorated with bluebonnets and longhorn skulls. It has a sort of other-worldly beauty tempered with drought, hard scrabble and, well, heartbreak.

Quick Fix is a place (not a town) down the road a few miles south of Heartbreak. Sometimes it's also called "Babel." All the way back to the cattle drives, Quick Fix offered unregulated gambling, untaxed whiskey and rentable women. Local sheriffs tolerated Quick Fix as a necessary evil (and an extra source of income) as long as the games weren't too heavily fixed, the rotgut didn't cause permanent blindness, and the professional women didn't come into Heartbreak proper. Quick Fix would have probably disappeared altogether when the oil boom went bust, but Prohibition saved it by driving up the price of rotgut.

Heartbreak revived a bit during WWII because of an Army base nearby. Quick Fix got another reprieve, but a moralizing sheriff tried to get the area renamed "Headache."

In the '60's and '70's, Heartbreak sort of muddled along, generally doing a better job of it than Great Britain which muddled its way out of an empire and into debt at about the same time. This proves there is muddling and there is muddling. The popularity of marijuana and free love about killed Quick Fix during this era. The only thing it had left was gambling and if a man really wanted a good game he could call a Saturday meeting in his barn. The games were a whole lot straighter and the chances of getting shot were a little less.

Over the last two years, my personal history underwent a few changes, too. My goats kept on birthing about 1.7 times a year, just like my original projections forecast. Unfortunately the coyotes, bobcats and stray dogs managed to eat about 1.9 times a year what my nannies could produce. You don't have to be a math teacher to spot the trend; I was going broke. Also, goats only care about three things in life: eating, reproducing and escaping. Of the three, they're best at escaping. I finally figured out that the best asset I owned was

2

my fences. They were almost good enough to contain a goat herd, so I knew they would keep ANYTHING else in my pastures. Someday I may tell about the day I sold all my survivors at an auction. I'll call that one, "The Day I Got Skinned Alive." But all that comes later.

About this same time, Heartbreak High lost a school teacher. It was early in her second year; she was young, pretty, and had just got married. In no time she was pregnant. Over the years I've seen any number of young teachers choose the "family way" out of a job that wasn't near as much fun as they thought it would be. Why, if my goats were as fecund as a stressed-out young school teacher, I wouldn't have to look for a change. I'd taught for years in Houston, and I knew I could be good, and keep my job going as long as I stayed away from mentioning Evolution.

Finally, Sally Rae and I were becoming good friends. I mean, real good friends. Lord, that woman was hotter than a Texas summer, 'nuff said. Most people don't learn from their mistakes and two years after my divorce I was darn tired of my own cookin'. One part of me just wanted to keep on hiding out in the boonies with my goats, another part told me it was time to start taking life seriously again. As I filled out the teacher application and I seriously looked at Sally Rae's picture, I decided I'd had enough adventures and it was time to change course of a better, if duller future. God doesn't offer Second Sight to fools like me; if I had known everything coming up I might have run. Still, life's sure interesting....

NAMING AWAY

I chose to name my ranch "Ponderosa",
But it seems it had already been done.
I'd thought about calling it "The Tussle",
But then some folks might have wondered who won.
I could have named it for the ground cover,
But who wants a big spread called "Fire Ants".
My wife suggested the name "Love Handles",
After hard laughing I told her "fat chance!"
I realized what we'd always called it.
It's what we wanted to get every day.
Now, remember when you come to visit,
If you miss our place then you've passed "Away".

Marlene Tucker

Getting Started

The White Kangaroo

THE MAIN STREET IN HEARTBREAK HAS
a lot of boarded-up buildings, hardware and feed stores, and you can't swing a dead cat without hitting either a church or a honky-tonk. They both depend on Baptists; around there a hypocrite is someone who has a slice of lemon on their Big O in the optimistic belief someone else might think they're drinking iced tea.

There are two seasons in Heartbreak — Too Hot and Too Cold. Seasonal change is marked by Too Wet, but everyone knows that Too Dry is right around the corner.

BJ Elkert almost ran me down in front of Simmons' Feed. Since he had a 50-pound bag of feed under each arm, I got out of his way.

"Hi BJ," I said, scatting to one side.

"Hey Dave," he replied, "seen any more joeys out at your place?"

"Naw, just the one white one a while back. I figure the coyotes got him."

Several months back, a young white kangaroo had bounded out in front of me about a half-mile from the entrance to my place, just before I got home. I saw him several other times but, dammit, no one else had. Since I was a newcomer, here just two years, and I had traveled some without the Army paying for it, people like BJ eyed me with a bit of suspicion and humor.

5

"I think he must have escaped from that exotics farm 'bout 50 miles north and followed the river down," I finished up lamely. I cursed myself silently. Rule One: If you have to explain or justify an outrageous claim, you've already lost.

BJ slung the two bags into his pickup. "Yeah, well, I saw him the other night. Talked to him, too. Johnny Ruth says I have to give up the Jack Daniels again, huh, huh."

BJ always laughed like he wasn't sure if he was going to growl or burp. "Gotta go, dinner's waitin'."

I knew I'd been had again. Still, I was a little encouraged. BJ wouldn't bother to kid a stranger or an enemy. Southern manners and western hospitality dictated that only friends could be mildly insulted.

I ducked into The Waterin' Hole, Heartbreak's only café. "Sally Rae, got a cold Dr Pepper?

"Sure as skunks got stink, Dave," she replied. Sally Rae had bought a newer car last month and, of course, a skunk had wandered out in front the third day she had it. She was still upset; new anythings were prized here, and dead skunk had overwhelmed "eau de new car" in one stroke of bad luck. "How's that sweet girl of yours doing?"

"Fine, she's just old enough to start making the boys nervous. That includes this boy sitting here."

The one real community asset I had brought with me was my daughter, Janey. Most counties in rural Texas have an average age well over 70. This was a community of breeders, and they knew they needed new blood.

"Say, did you see Miss Scarlet last Sunday? I bet that girl's lost 20 pounds. Getting prettier than a speckled pup." She drew another breath to go on.

"I better get that DP to go, Sally Rae," I interrupted. I was a new single male — a rarity, and a target. Sally Rae was a born matchmaker. Miss Scarlet could lose another hundred pounds and grow another hundred speckles, but it wouldn't help.

"Well, watch out for white kangaroos," she said, firing her parting shot.

I got back into my truck and headed out of town. I liked my neighbors, but small town "community" could get thick real fast. Anyway, I needed to fix another little piece of fence before I could settle down. About a mile out of town, I saw trouble ahead. BJ's truck

6

was spun around and half through a fence. Steam was venting through the hood. I knew he wasn't going to be driving it home that day. BJ was walking around with a hanky on his forehead to staunch a cut.

"Are you all right, BJ?" I asked as I pulled up. He looked shaken.

"I'll live, but he didn't," BJ said.

I walked around to the side of his truck and felt the rush of guilty elation that prophets must have felt when their worst warnings came true.

There, laid out in all its glorious length, lay a white kangaroo.

SWAT A MISTAKE!

Susan was a city girl,
From up New England way.
She married herself a cowboy,
And came to Texas to stay.
"Everything's bigger in Texas,"
Said hubby with a little smirk.
Susan smiled back at him sweetly,
And sent him off to work.

At evening he found her bags packed,
Susan was ready to go,
"I don't like your big o' Texas,
And the mosquitoes take the show!"
She pointed to him the ones she killed,
And some she wanted to clobber.
With a laugh he pointed out
The harmless Texas dirt dobber.

Marlene Tucker

SNAKEBIT LUCK

My NEIGHBOR, BJ ELKERT, HIT A
stray kangaroo with his pickup, an escapee from some exotics ranch
up river from Heartbreak . I felt a little guilty gratitude since I was
the only person who had seen it before the wreck. I was a newcomer
and a city boy, so I was suspect on many levels — from insanity
to (worse) liberalism. I saw BJ in front of Billy's Auto Repair and
stopped to see how he was doing.

"Hi BJ, how's it hanging?" I asked. This was a standard greeting
in these parts.

"My head still has a goose egg, but my truck sure took a beating.
This is the worst damage since I rolled it last year." It was expected
for a man to get torn up on a regular basis and die before the first
Social Security check, but anyone who couldn't get 200,000 miles
out of a pickup was considered sort of sorry. "Still, the joey wasn't
bad."

"What do you mean?"

"Well, it was sort of stringy and gamey 'til Johnny Ruth pressure-
cooked it with garlic and brisket rub." Like many Texans, BJ
spent much of his time a-huntin' or a-fishin', worshipping God by
appreciating His creatures one mouthful at a time.

Billy lumbered up just then. At 230 pounds, tare-weight lumber
was about his only speed. "I haven't got any Chevy radiators right
now, but I can make this old tractor radiator work, or I can spend
another hundred dollars and get you a factory-rebuilt next week."

Billy was a special human: The Great American Mechanic. He understood engines the way a mother understands her child; he forgave it its wear, loved it through years of overdue oil changes. Heartbreak would become "Machine Break" in a week if he and his brothers didn't keep things running. "All I'd have to do is rebore the ..."

My ears blanked out. Billy could talk for 45 minutes about the peculiarities of his craft and I doubted I would understand more than a few words. "Take care, boys."

I walked on down to Sally Rae's Waterin' Hole. It was a beautiful day and, for once, I had a clean conscience. All this made me careless. "Sally Rae, how 'bout a cold DP," I said, dropping on to a seat at the bar.

"Sure, Dave, and anything else for you, Miss Scarlet?" I jerked my head around. Scarlet Hawkins sat on two stools, three seats down. She outweighed BJ by at least 50 pounds. Her Herefords envied her robust figure. She had set her cap for me with the full connivance of Sally Rae. Miss Scarlet was widowed just before I moved to town. Now she raised a nice herd of Herefords all by herself, not counting her four worthless boys. They were easy to not count.

"Nothing for me, deary, but this skinny man-guy looks like he could use a slice of your vinegar pie." She turned the full wattage of her smile my direction. "I've been making steers out of bulls all week. Would you like to come out for dinner? I make the best prairie oysters around." She looked at me with the same sincere love as a snake eyeing a baby chick.

I was on the spot. To decline such a direct invite would be a grave insult; to accept ... I shuddered. "Well, ah, sure, thanks."

"Be sure and bring Janey. I think my boy Jimmy's getting sweet on her. Would tonight at 6 be good?"

"We'll be there, and thanks." Most manners are built on the fabric of righteous hypocrisy. Like white magic, righteous hypocrisy can do no harm, except to the practitioner.

Sally Rae beamed like she had just witnessed the moon landing. She was as much a born matchmaker as any yenta in the Old Country. By the time The Waterin' Hole closed, local gossip would have us marching down the aisle at Cottonwood Baptist.

Back at my ranch, I tried to think of some way out of my disappointing destiny. I threw myself into my work. If work generates virtue, then ranching must produce an inordinate number of saints. I raise Boer goats. They are full of pranks and cussedness, but they have a sort of charm, like a herd of intellectually challenged collies. They only care about two things — eating and making little goats — but even the dullest of the species are escape artists. Fencing in goats is like painting the Golden Gate Bridge; one can get behind, but never ahead.

About 4 p.m. Janey ran to my arms from the school bus. At 16, she was everything that was right and pure about my life. I wished I could freeze this time in history, but at the same time I knew my wish was unhealthy. We don't raise our children for ourselves, but for their own lives.

"Hi Daddy," she chortled, full of life and spunk. "Guess what? Jimmy Hawkins wants me to go out with him! Isn't that great?"

Did you ever dump ice water on a lizard? I turned and walked toward the barn. Time to water the goats, I thought. When in shock or despair, one should stick to normal routines.

As I turned the water spigot, I felt a sharp prick on my hand. Looking behind the post, I saw a copperhead coiled for another strike.

Snakebit! I stepped and shouted, "Thank you, God. You just saved me and Janey from going to Miss Scarlet's!"

THE LAST SUPPER

The old maid lived meekly, catch-as-catch-can,
She had poor ways but never told a lie.
Though she desperately sought out marriage,
She remained single and didn't know why.

She rode her old horse to church on Sundays.
It was the only way for her to go.
She called the bay by the name of Tasty
Because of the way he licked himself so.

A stranger moved in to the area.
He was a widower as gossip went.
The old maid planned on making him supper,
And quickly an invitation was sent.

The guest bragged how the meat was so tasty
"Yes" she smiled and quickly replied,
"When it comes around to church next Sunday,
I'd be pleased if you could give me a ride."

Marlene Tucker

GUNS AREN'T JUST FOR KILLING

THE SUN WAS BEARING DOWN AND sweat ran freely into my eyes. I had smashed my finger with a hammer and decided it was time to knock off and head to town for a cold drink and a roll of wire. Time to be anywhere but here, I thought.

At the hardware store, I spent a while looking through the shelves. There is a special relationship between men and their tools. They learn suckling and love from their mothers, but they learn a special physics from their fathers. Their mothers teach them how to BE. Their fathers teach them how to DO. I've always thought of hardware stores as my special toy store.

Sam Clancy walked up. He owns the place and was a better source of local information than the weekly newspaper. "How's that old run-down Miller place of yours coming?

"Bit by bit, I'm gonna get there," I replied. The Millers sold it to me when they got too old to run it. I guess people will still call my ranch the "Miller place" for at least the next 10 years.

"You live next to Emmitt. Think he's sober enough lately to do a little work for me?" It was an honest question. My closest neighbor, Emmitt Bennett, holds several important positions in Heartbreak. He's the town plumber. Most people say he's pretty good when he's sober, as best as they remember. Emmitt also is the town drunk. That's an important position in Heartbreak, and it wasn't won without some fierce competition.

13

His house is on a hill overlooking my place. It's a very old Victorian monstrosity, complete with fake turrets and way too much gingerbread. He never quite got around to any fancy plumbing in his own home. Lizzy Bennett always is complaining about being married to a plumber and having an outhouse.

"I think he just bought a new 30/30. He's been shooting at cans a lot. He hits some of them, so maybe he's all right." I always try to give my new neighbors the benefit of the doubt.

Like most all men in Heartbreak , Emmitt is at least partly defined by his guns. Texans aren't all gun nuts, but, well, they're like me. I inherited about 10 from my dad, and I only buy a new one every three or four years; somehow they just mount up. I have my snake gun, my car gun, my deer rifle, my coyote gun ... see what I mean? They're just tools, like the dozen or so shovels I also keep.

The next morning, I walked out on the porch with a cup of coffee and heard a loud shot back Emmitt's way. It's always a good idea when you hear shots to check it out. The shot was followed by a "whoosh" sound I didn't rightly place. Suddenly I heard several shots in a row and I realized by their muffled sound they were coming from inside the house. Something was wrong, bad wrong. I headed for my pickup just as the windows blew out of Emmitt's place.

As I bounced over the pasture to get there, I saw something like the unloading of Noah's Ark. Yellow dogs ran out from under the porch. Chickens flew out of the rafters. Lizzy and her eight children followed the dogs. A few dazed, smoldering bats exited the new hole that appeared in the roof. Just as I pulled up, Emmitt ran out with an armload of guns.

"Emmitt, what's happening?" I yelled as I skidded to a stop.

"No time for talk," he yelled. Suddenly he started blazing away again, this time at the big transformer that ran power in toward the city. There was a super white arc and a pop louder that any of his shots, and then the whole transformer sort of shook and shrank at the same time. "Got it," Emmitt said, with the same smile a hunter has looking at his game.

"Emmitt, what in the world is going on?" I asked again. I now had my car gun in my hand; I was fairly sure his pickled brain had taken a decisive trip south.

"Well, you see, I was shooting through my trap door under the house at a possum that's moved in there. I missed the possum but hit the gas line, first shot."

"Yeah, but what about the next nine or 10 shots?"

"I was shooting at the water line next to it so it'd put out the fire, of course." This made some sort of sense, especially if you knew Emmitt.

"But why shoot the transformer?"

"Why, that thing supplies the whole city. There'll be tons of emergency vehicles out here in no time. I couldn't very well call, now could I? The whole house is in flames."

"You could use my phone," I offered.

"Dave, people around here stand on their own two feet. We don't much hold with borrowing and owing and stuff like that." His chin set in a way that reminded me I was new here and on his land at his forbearance. I shut up.

"Daddy, Daddy, come quick. I just saw a flaming possum run in the barn!" one of his kids shouted.

"Don't worry, Jube. Daddy will take care of it." With that Emmitt stalked off toward the barn, stuffing new shells in his 30/30.

I walked over to Lizzy. By now the whole house was engulfed. "I'm so sorry you lost everything, Lizzy," I started.

Lizzy was a fine woman, salt of the earth, and she had a practical streak a mile wide. "I'm not sorry. I paid the insurance day before yesterday. Now I get new everything, and my new home is going to have an indoor toilet in every room!"

A Shot of Reality

Round and round the hackberry tree,
Drunken daddy chased the possums.
He missed what he was aiming at.
Mom's rose bush lost its blossoms.

He chase his prey under the porch,
But saw a long snake by his toes,
He let the buckshot fire away,
And pelted the new garden hose.

Dad took a fall and shot mom's car,
He sobered and felt he must flee,
Because he knew his lovely wife,
Was a much better shot than he.

Marlene Tucker

JANEY

THE PRETTY DAUGHTER

MY SWEET DAUGHTER JANEY JUST
turned into a beautiful 16-year-old. She is at that special point of
freshness and innocent beauty that can leave a father breathless. What
could be wrong with that? Practically everything. I tried many times
to explain to Janey that what might be good for the human herd was
often pure disaster for the individual female involved.

Heartbreak is breeding country, and I don't just mean the cattle.
There are a lot of jokes about fathers and shotguns, but lately if I pitch
a rock over my shoulder it's more likely to hit some moon-eyed boy
hanging around than land on the ground.

The worst of the lot are Jube Bennett and Jimmy Hawkins. Jube is
son of my closest neighbor, Emmitt, who blew up his house shooting
at a 'possum. Jube, on the other hand, likes animals, and he can't
quite get it that everyone doesn't like wild animals as well as he does.

First, he brought Janey a kitten. She loved it, named it Pixie, and
made all sorts of ado over it until the thing peed in my shoes. I exiled
it to the barn. Next, Jube brought her a rough green snake. Janey
didn't like that as well, but Pixie soon ate it. Then, Jube brought her a
robin. She called it Mr. Hood. Pixie called it dinner. I was grudgingly
starting to see a little utility in Pixie, even if I didn't like his concept
of a litter box.

Jimmy Hawkins posed another whole set of problems. Jimmy is built like his mother, Miss Scarlett. Either one can knock a bull down and when it stands up again, it's a steer. I've seen 'em do it. Miss Scarlett is after me, and Jimmy is after my Janey. When they both sit on their front porch, the whole house tilts. Janey says he's just tons of fun. I'm not sure if she was making an observation or developing a sense of humor.

If Jimmy and his three brothers could all get passing grades at the same time Heartbreak would win its state division in football, no small thing around here. Unfortunately, the Hawkins are bred for size, not intelligence. Miss Scarlett's Herefords are more likely to pass the state tests than her boys. Jimmy is probably the best of them. He's fairly clean, has some manners, and he didn't drool until he took up chewing tobacco. Mostly Jimmy just knocked things down, like cows and football players and doorways.

The afternoon sun about chased me out of the pasture. Time to head home. I needed something cool and wet. As I walked into the kitchen, Janey threw her arms around me.

"Daddy, look what Jube just brought me! Isn't he cute? I named him Stinky. Can I keep him, please, please, please?"

I was engulfed in a cascade blond hair, and a milky sort of vanilla smell that announced Janey in all her persuasive glory. I loved her hugs but I have lately learned that, like a boa constrictor, her hugs could have ulterior motives.

"He's sort of like a cat, sir," Jube explained, handing me a baby skunk. "Just pet him and sort of hum at him 'til he knows you."

I petted and I hummed. Holding a live skunk is delicate as stating a liberal opinion in Heartbreak: it's possible, but use lots of diplomacy and keep an eye to the nearest door.

"He is sort of cute," I admitted. The little fella walked like a man with tight shoes. Stinky just fit under the kick board that ran under the cabinets. He was making regular rounds of the kitchen, seeking out stray crumbs and slow kitchen critters. I noticed that he didn't have any odor at all.

"I just love him," Janey simpered. She fed him carrots sticks and celery chunks.

Jube had to brag, he knew he'd scored a hit. "Skunks are really nice; just treat 'em right. They like gentleness. Why, I bet one well trained skunk is better than ten watch dogs." Jube beamed at the scene like he'd birthed that skunk himself.

"I don't know, Jube, if it's the right thing to take an animal out of the wild...." I began, trying for time.

About then Jimmy Hawkins crashed in my doorway. "Hi Janey, do you...Oh My God!"

Stinky heard a new comer and raced to him, happy to meet another nice human. Jimmy stomped twice, and Stinky stopped, did a little dance, whirled around and raised his tail.

Living in Heartbreak has given me good reflexes. I grabbed Janey and dove out the door. Jimmy and Jube weren't all the lucky.

I stopped about a hundred feet out from the house, just outside the main smell. Janey collapsed against me, laughing. Jube and Jimmy staggered out, gasping and half blind. About a minute later Stinky strolled out, all four inches of him. He looked sort of satisfied, having put Nature back in order.

It's been two weeks now. I've painted the kitchen three times and its almost bearable, now, if you're use to it. Janey is starting to smell like milk and vanilla again, with a hint of tomato juice added. Though our acquaintance was brief, I sort of miss Stinky. I guess he did his job and moved on, like The Lone Ranger. You see, Jube and Jimmy haven't been back since.

THE DUST BEAU OF 1955

Daughter, while dusting the furniture, says,
"Mom, the dust travels on our dirt road with the cars
And turns in our driveway.
It rolls slowly towards our house

And comes in through the screen door,
Settling on the furniture,
To waste my time.
In a couple of days it will be here again!"

Mother, while shelling black-eyed peas, smiles and says,
"Your fella comes down our dirt road in his truck
Turning in at our driveway.
He strolls slowly towards our house,

And comes in through the screen door,
Settling on the furniture,
To waste your time.
I feel certain, in a couple of days, he'll be here again."

Marlene Tucker

Summer Love

Two years ago I moved to Heartbreak Texas. Heartbreak is 50 or 500 miles west of Houston's sushi bars; it's a place where all the men expect hard work and hard luck in equal measure, all the women keep pregnant while advising their daughters against the same, and all the cows chew with contented dismay as they watch their humans.

Janey and I were at Cottonwood Baptist's annual ice cream supper. The heat was palpable and the ice cream a welcome relief. Most of the men were telling pickup repair stories and most of the women were retelling their birthing stories. Doubting I would get much useful information from either source, I wandered over the gossips' table. I had Janey on a short tether. My pretty little 16-year-old daughter had poison ivy in several complex areas, and I was taking no chances until the matter was cleared up.

Sally Rae, the village matchmaker, chatted with several friends. I liked Sally Rae — maybe even a lot — but her naturally generous nature led her to regularly try to give me away to the other town matrons. Being her friend was like petting a cactus. Theoretically it was possible, but there were likely to be distractions. Tonight, though, she was talking town history, not romance.

"...and poor Emma just disappeared outta that broken car! Twenty six years and not a word or a trace." Emma Bennett, twin sister of Emmitt, was a favorite cautionary tale. Emma's disappearance was a familiar warning for the young.

21

"Well, if you ask me, it all started with that bunch of skinny dipping teenagers at the Lake," Great Aunt Kathy added. "It wasn't decent then and it's not decent now!"

Great Aunt Kathy was a kindly, if somewhat withered soul who sold fresh eggs to the entire community. She kept peacocks, donkeys, and a large pet monkey that looked remarkably like its owner.

The heat of the evening seemed especially oppressive. There a few things you can count on with Texas weather, but the season of Too Hot was a sure fire thing.

Sally Rae turned her smile on Janey. "Darling, how's life treating you? Goodness, if I could just be your age again!"

"Daddy's just being horrible to me! He's got me grounded; I can't go anywhere or do anything!" Janey complained."

"Why Dave, whatever for?" Sally Rae asked.

"Skinny dipping at Heartbreak Lake," I replied. "I caught her and about a half dozen others."

"Better that than just one," Janey shot back.

"Safety in numbers doesn't apply to dynamite and teenagers," I replied. "Come on, time to head home."

Driving home, I reflected on things. I wasn't so much shocked at Janey's actions as her general direction. Raising a pretty teenage daughter with her spirit and looks was hard enough with a mother to help, but Janey and I were on our own, God help us all. I knew that to train a wild horse you don't break it, you gentle it down with isolation and attention. It worked fine on Janey's horse, Miss Thunder. My personal belief is that kids cause more prayer, worry, and self medication than a malicious disease the doctor names after you. Janey was my 'Dave's Syndrome.'

The next morning, Janey and I saddled up our horses to ride the back fence. My horse, Old Madge, was a dependable nag that had long since learned to go along to get along. Miss Thunder was a sweet little mare that Janey and I had been training for months. To be truthful, she was my bribe to get Janey out of Houston and into the country, where I at least had some clue about the hazards involved in her upbringing.

We rode along at an easy lope along the fence on the back 40-acres. It was one of those glorious days that could make an Eskimo love Texas: the sun wasn't too hot yet, wild flowers gave the air a special perfume, and I felt an optimistic surge. In short, I made the mistake of relaxing.

Just ahead as Janey broke out of a little stand of mesquites, the prettiest little Appaloosa stallion I ever saw raced up on the other side of the old fence. Miss Thunder ran up opposite. For a moment of intense horse romance they stood across the fence, flaring nostrils and breathing heavy. Equine fermones choked the air. I rode fast as I could to catch up, but by then the race was on. Janey held on best as she could as Miss Thunder and the stallion raced down the fence line. Old Madge and I raced along behind, but I knew we were no match for hormone powered horsey love.

"Jump off if you can," I yelled at Janey. Her only reply was a scream born of pure terror. After dragging Janey through some more mesquites, Miss Thunder and her stud reversed and almost knocked me and Old Madge down. I managed to grab Janey just as Miss Thunder cleared the fence.

A moment later a quivering, crying, cut-up Janey lay in my arms as Miss Thunder and the stud consummated their whirlwind romance. I'll spare you the details, but horsey love isn't about shy looks and sharing a carrot. It was nothing if not violent and dramatic.

Maybe there is a special dispensation for fathers I held Janey as she quivered, all a hurt, but she tore her eyes away from the action across the fence and said, "I think I understand, now, Daddy what you've been trying to tell me about boys."

WATCHING FOR THE DRIVE-BY

Picture me on the porch swing
That moans with a creek and crack
Sitting alone on the wooden seat
Rocking gently forward and back

See me in my cotton dress
Barefoot and summer breezy
Chores are done and supper's over
And the sun is setting easy

Look for me as you drive by
Before the dust obscures your view
If you could read my mind you'd know
This girl wants to swing with you.

Marlene Tucker, 2014

JANEY'S STORY

TWO YEARS AGO, DADDY MOVED ME out of Houston to Heartbreak Texas. Heartbreak is 386.2 miles west of all my favorite sushi bars, but who's counting. Worse, it a long way away from all my friends and, well, things, like movies and Starbucks, and flat screen TV's and…well, I could just go on. I was almost 16 when we moved and all my friends were left behind! It was also way, way west of Mommy. I understand why he did it, but it still hurts. Heartbreak is FULL of old people and cows. Yuck!

At first, Heartbreak seemed like living in a Western movie, only with the smells. Yuck again! The old men were the worst. Daddy sure talked a lot about how little it had changed, like that was good, or something. The first six months, my allergies went off like I was making out with a cat! Still, Daddy felt pretty crappy most days, and I didn't let him see me crying. I just did my best, figuring he would give up and go back home after a while. Then something kind of weird happened.

After I got over being the New Girl in town, the girls started coming around, being friendly, and curious. I found out we weren't so different, and that I even knew a lot of stuff they had just heard about. Then, after my 16th birthday, the boys started coming around. Partly, I guess, I just quit feeling so different (well, better and more sophisticated) and pretty soon things just weren't so bad.

Besides everything else, I found out I could tell Daddy just about Anything and he'd believe it. Why, one evening Pepper and John and

Toby and Imma, we all went skinny dipping in the town lake. It would have been nice of them to tell me that the nice clover I laid my clothes on was poison ivy! You can imagine, I don't want to remember.

One of the best nights was at a sleep-over with Pepper. The ranch next door was Old Man Storm's. That old man was just meaner than a snake. Even Daddy couldn't say much good about him, and if anyone could, he would. Anyhow, Pepper showed me the fine art of Cow Tipping.

What you do is sneak up on some old heifer who's asleep standing up. You get 30 or 40 feet uphill, run hard as you can, and push her over. All of a sudden you hear a 1,200 pound "Ouff", and down she goes. Third or fourth one, all those cows woke up at once and started running. Even I knew this was bad news. Pepper made it to the fence first, I was right behind her when I slipped on a fresh cow paddy and landed right on one of those mean old cactuses. Dang, it hurt!

Later on Pepper had to cut my pants off and pull cactus spikes out of my flipside the rest of the evening. She said she learned all sorts of Big City words from me that night. Well, it wasn't her bottom! Anyway, I told Daddy some fire ants sneaked up on me; he never knew.

Another time Pepper and I had a sleep-over and her cousins were in town. Bill Bob was 20 and Eddie was 18, and boy, were they cute! We played spin the bottle out in the old horse barn that night and I got my first kiss! Could have been more, but I'm not stupid, just curious. I learned something that night, though. I'm not ever going to date any boy who chews tobacco! Good looking doesn't mean good tasting.

Still, whenever I get in a horse barn and the smell of old hay and half rotted wood come together on a hot summer night, the locusts are buzzing and the moon's half full…well a girl just has to know when to watch herself, that's all.

Poor Dad just worked and moped. I knew what he needed, but what the heck could I do? One day I was in The Waterin' Hole Café and I saw Sally Rae watching him, and all at once the lights came on. Daddy wasn't the only lonesome soul in Heartbreak.

"Sally Rae, can you come with me for a minute?" I said all sweet and innocent like.

"Sure, Honey," she said.

"Where you girls going?" asked Daddy.

David Mosley

Sometimes I forget that he CAN notice things, just not too often.
"Girl talk, not your business," I said looking down for a moment.
That shut him up, real good.

"Why, what Honey?" Sally Rae said once we were in the kitchen.
"You got girl troubles?"

"No, but you do. You know, you can have him if you want him. I
sure wouldn't mind," I said.

"Why, Janey, what on earth do you mean?" she said, trying to
play shocked.

Adults can be more obtuse than any triangle. "You know what I
mean. You feed hungry men every day! Can't you see one starving
right in front of you?" I said.

"Janey, what even makes you think I might even...." she sort of
trailed off.

"I've got eyes, I see you perk up every time he walks in, and I see
you slump down every time he leaves. I see Daddy slumping down all
the time. Somebody has to do something! Now, pop that top button
open and serve him another piece of vinegar pie. It's time to make a
move."

With that I marched back out into the dining room and checked
out an old rodeo poster on the far wall.

Sure 'nuff, in about three minutes Sally Rae came back out with
a slice of vinegar pie in her hand, still steaming from the microwave.
And yes, that top button was open. A double serving was in evidence.
It was the first time in two years I've seen Daddy's eyes open up for
anything but a cup of coffee.

I could tell you lots more about how I came to stand living in
Heartbreak, but a girl needs to keep some secrets.

Taming the Tomboy

You are my niece and so pretty,
And, being your dad's only child,
Must you always challenge the boys,
And live your life daring and wild?

I know you want to go fishing,
Instead you can go to charm school.
Who cares about some old cat fish,
When learning propriety's rule?

Make sure you're on time for your class.
I'm so glad you chose to wear pink.
But fish hooks don't make good earrings,
And why does your makeup bag stink?

Marlene Tucker

CHILLIN' AFTER A HARD DAY

HEARTBREAK IS SO RUN DOWN THAT
it's downright picturesque. For about two months every spring, the bluebonnets make the air almost painfully sweet. Of course, it takes 12 months of cow plop to get those bluebonnets. Ain't nothing free in Heartbreak.

I'm Dave, I run a little goat ranch on my 80 acres when I'm not substitute teaching at Heartbreak High. Goats are sort of like collies, only they breed slower, die easier and sell cheaper. Maybe I should switch to collies.

Goats have a special charm. They clear land. I needed this because my place was pretty overgrown when I bought it. People say that goats can't have a facial expression because they lack the special facial muscles a human has. I have to disagree. I remember helping No. 22 deliver her twins by a kerosene lantern. First she frowned a lot, had her twins, and then looked up at me as proud and happy as any human mother I've ever seen. Happy mommas just have that look. That night the temperature dropped to 18 degrees and both kids died. Goats can show grief, too. Heartbreak isn't just named for its human inhabitants.

Anyway, Janey sort of took to the country way. Some new goat mommas have a hard time getting their milk right. She could milk out a mastitis-ridden mother way better than I could, and then hold that baby goat and bottle feed it back to health. I always tried my best, but she was just naturally better. I guess it's a woman thing.

29

About this time another woman thing was happening; Janey was growing up. If I had to choose between 91 goats or being a single father, I'd go for the goats every time. I promised her that at 16 she could date. I gave her all sorts of advice, but the goats probably showed her better than me.

I tried to do things right. I bought some castrating pliers and taught her well. I even painted them pink. She could grab a six-week-old male and change his lifetime aspirations quicker than he could say "Baaah?" I bought her a cell phone and gave her clear instructions about which to use first; but young girls are born to have their hearts broken and I couldn't protect her from everything.

Heartbreak High had its own hierarchy, of course. Jeff Fuller was the quarter back of the football team, AKA "Crown Prince." After the Team came the Cheerleaders. After them came the Band, the Heartbreak High Stars. My Janey was lead flute player, first chair, in her freshman year. I was so proud I could almost bust when I saw her marching around the field with the rest of the band.

Now what came next should not have surprised me, after all, I grow out goats for a living. Please don't think me bad for what I have to say now; Janey suddenly grew UP, and Out, and Around. She also grew Beautiful. I suddenly understood the old adage that God blessed men with ugly daughters.

About six or eight times a week, I managed to get into town to The Waterin' Hole Café. The food was good and cheap, but the main attraction was Sally Rae, the waitress. She was as kind and a good woman as I ever met. Years ago, her fiancée got himself killed in a car wreck the night before her wedding, and a few months later she had his baby boy. Most people in Heartbreak understood, but I know she had a hard life.

"Dave," she told me, "I needed diapers, but people kept on giving me Bibles. They were kind, but judgmental at the same time."

I sympathized; we became better friends, started dating and fell in love. Among her other charms, Sally Rae helped me not make to many stupid moves with Janey. I needed all the help I could get.

"If you try to hold her too close, you'll just drive her away; if you don't hold her close enough, she'll give up and just act stupid, looking for love any place she can get it."

Sally Rae was a world of knowledge and inspiration.

Janey had her own sermons. "You treat her with respect."

"When will you be home?" "Don't you dare do anything I wouldn't do."

That part really scared and confused me. I was caught between two women. The goats seemed a lot simpler to live with.

None of this prepared me for when Jeff Fuller, the quarterback, took a sudden interest in Janey. She'd turned 16 and Jeff was on my doorstep to pick up my daughter and squire her off into the night. I tried. I tried hard, but about ten seconds after he came inside I brought up dove hunting.

"Ever use a 12 gauge, Jeff?"

"No sir," he shared.

"I just got a new one. It'll knock a bird down at 75 yards, every time."

I showed him the gun and all its features 'til Janey came down. They left pretty soon after that.

Curfew was 11 p.m. I looked out my window and watched them lock lips for a while. At 11:30 I blew an air horn I had originally bought for the Texas-OU game. Janey scurried right in.

The next week was sort of strange. Janey sort of floated around like she was dazed. I sort of floated around like a drone aircraft hunting for a target with a Hell Fire Missile. Sally Rae found the whole thing hilarious, and that didn't help any. Then Friday came around again.

"What's wrong, Honey? I asked as Janey got into my truck after school.

"Nothing, dammit!"

For once I knew when to shut up. Janey seldom cursed, and when she did, it signified. I waited.

About the time I turned into the driveway Janey said, "I saw him kissing Norma Gene, that slut, between her lunch and biology!" Then she clamed up again.

I kept my mouth shut, as waves of cool relief flowed over me, like a drink of ice water from a tin can on a hot afternoon.

Later on Janey came up to my room. Her eyes were red, but her expression was firm. "Let's go kill something, Daddy!"

I got my pistol and her rifle. We walked down to the river at the back of our place. For all our talk about killing, we really don't kill much. I threw in some plastic Easter eggs. With practiced precision, she split it in halves, then sank both halves. Three shots, total. I took the next one. Three shots, total. I realized that my aim had been good, all along. We stayed 'til dark.

MOMMA SAID

"Don't stand there on my back porch,
Waiting like you've done before.
You can put that charm away,
She doesn't love you anymore.

You hurt her once too often.
You're no better than the rest.
She's dating someone else now,
And she thinks that he's the best.

I hate to burst your bubble,
Or is that your puffed up pride,
But worthless are your good looks,
If there's nothing good inside.

I think you need to leave now,
No one wants you. Is that clear?"
(That is unless her sister,
Realizes he is here.)

Marlene Tucker

ART

I'M DAVE AND I MOVED TO HEARTBREAK
about two years ago with my 16-year-old daughter, Janey. She's the joy of my life, pure as the driven snow, about twice as pretty as I would wish, and a blonde bombshell that I believe I rescued from Houston's evil clutches just in time. She has my mind and her mother's body, and thank God it didn't happen in the reverse.

Lately I've become good friends with Sally Rae, the waitress at the only real restaurant in Heartbreak. I mean, really good friends. Dating is a funny word to use at our age, but most things are sort of funny at my age, so I just let it go. If cows can smell fresh barbecue and not have it put them off their cuds, who am I to complain about repeating a stage of life I thought I left behind in the teenage years. At first I figgered Janey might be put off, but she surprised me. I'd darn near swear she liked Sally Rae better'n' me.

I guess all this sounds kind of idyllic and such, but you have to factor in hours and hours of hard work, my goats dying or being eaten by predators, farming on worn out land, broken fences, bad weather, accidents, and blow flies. Heartbreak isn't Eden, it's about eating. Everything here eats everything else, and it's not the French cuisine like I enjoyed in Houston. Stand still too long and a fire ant will try to put you in its food chain. Country living may look sweet to an outsider, but in real life it's a "march or die" situation. I got so I could whip out my .22 pistol and blow the head off a copperhead so fast he didn't even know I was mad.

34

I bet Adam went through something like this in the Garden of Eden. The Bible is clear he learned about snakes up close and personal; well, so did I. Like Adam, there was a species of two-legged serpent I had not counted on. Heartbreak had an *artist*.

Mac Popper ran an art gallery in town. He painted and sold bad art to tourists when ever he got a chance. Also, Mac was gay. The tolerance level in Heartbreak was pretty high. I mean, Mac was a home town boy that had grown into his own sort of man. Most people, if you asked them, would say the strangest thing about Mac was that he made a living from Art. Gay people are not an urban phenomena. The only real homophobia I had run into was when Emmitt Bennett sold Bill Johnson a bull that preferred the other bulls, leaving his cows barren. It was really about dollars and cents.

I had seen Mac Popper around town several times. He had a little land and raised a few toy cows so he would fit in. Mostly he had a little art gallery on main street with a bunch of old pottery in it, a few bluebonnet paintings on old saws, and a few of his original paintings around on the walls. If you walked in there you could get an honest cup of cappuccino and a lot of tales about how the worn out saddle was ridden by Davey Crockett or the thunder mug that was the original, only used by Jane Long, Mother of Texas. I didn't think him so much a liar as sort of an innovator, even an original business man, in an area not otherwise distinguished by its thoughts. Once in a while he fleeced a Houston or a Dallas tourist and brought in a little money. We're tolerant in Heartbreak; no harm done to us.

Janey popped in to our kitchen as I drank some iced tea. "Hi Daddy, I got a job!"

"That's great, honey. Where you workin'?"

"Mac has a place for me at his gallery," she said. "He says I'm good with customers and I can help all sorts of ways. He wants me to start tomorrow."

Well, in hindsight I can see all sorts of questions I should have asked, but at the moment I saw no harm in it. Mac had always been polite to me and I always figured that Heartbreak could use a little cultural relief. He for sure was no threat to Janey. A small part of my soul even counted the extra time I might spend with Sally Rae, private like, you know. Way too quick I agreed. Janey gave me an extra wet kiss and ran outside into the sunshine.

Well, things happened. Goats kidded, coyotes ate kids, and I was short-handed without Janey. Spring was coming, if you are a stock man you know what I mean. Most years Spring didn't last over 20 minutes, and we were back to Too Hot. I didn't begrudge Janey her part-time earnings, but I was working, right up to the minute I got a call from Sally Rae.

"Hi Sally Rae, how you doin'?" I started.

"Dave, come to town, now, and see to your daughter." She did not have the usual laughter in her voice.

My blood pressure spiked about 30 points. "Is she hurt?" I asked.

"Not exactly, just get here fast."

I got going.

In the front window of Mac's shop was a big new bluebonnet picture. In the middle of the bluebonnets was my Janey, painted as stark naked as the moment I first held her, though considerably more blossomed out since the moment of her arrival on earth. I had underestimated Mac's talent. She looked like Venus sprung full grown from the ocean foam, except Venus didn't have an appendix scar. I had really underestimated Mac.

"Mac, come here, now!" I thundered.

Mac slithered out from behind his cappuccino maker. "$5,000 cash," is all he said.

I considered my options. I knew I could win in court, maybe five years from now. There were no teenage boys drooling around the front window, yet. Janey and I lived here, but a gullible tourist in the next few minutes was too much to hope for.

"Well, can you take Visa or MasterCard?"

THE SCULPTOR

She ordered the likeness of herself,
Chiseled into precious stone.
So she and others could see for years,
Her likeness upon a throne.

The sculptor suffered her vanity,
Her arrogance and her pride.
He struggled with her demanding ways,
And the comments, mostly snide.

Until the artist finally snapped.
It was finished in a day.
The statue was a perfect likeness,
Made of marble-looking clay.

The details were done down to the smirk,
Hard as marble all around.
There were no words at the unveiling.
The woman was never found.

Marlene Tucker

Of Donkeys and Jackasses

JEFF HAMMONDS WAS A BIG-BONED
redneck you never wanted to stand down-wind from. He shambled along like a wind-blown gelding and he never found an English sentence he couldn't murder or add a curse word to.

Most irritating of all, he brayed every thought in a loud, atonal statement. " @#%$# DEMOCRATS DUN RUINED US AND THE @#$^%% REPUBLICANS FINISHED US OFF!" is a typical "Good morning" from Jeff.

He'd pick his nose at a funeral and his only discernible sense of humor either involved black people or female nether parts, or both. He personally inspired a saying around Heartbreak that some jackasses walked on two legs and lacked a tail. I didn't dislike Jeff, but I could get enough of him in about 20 minutes to last me a month. For the last three days, he had been helping me run a new fence, and I dreaded the time it would take to complete the project.

Things out at my ranch were in their usual "too" zone. It was too hot, I was too tired and too broke, it was too dry, and Janey was too 16 for me to get even minimal respect. Sally Rae was too busy and if it hadn't been for my animals there wouldn't be too much humor to be found anywhere.

One night I sat out in my hot tub, sipping a glass of wine. This was my golden hour, when the sky lit up and I could lax down. Most of my neighbors would think it almost unbearably decadent in a citified way to do as I did, but experience had taught me that a hot tub was better than drugs to relax my old injuries and soothe the way into the night.

My hot tub overlooked the pasture and barn to my left, but was set in some scrub oaks just behind my back porch. Bandit, my canine companion, broke loose from some bushes, running and barking joyfully. He was herding three big armadillos back toward me.

I guess he thought them to be scaly toys; maybe that's what they really were. Anyhow, he was a herd dog by instinct, though the armadillos resented the herding. Every once in a while one of them would sacrifice a running mate by hooking his long snout underneath the next one over and flipping him two or three feet in the air. Meanwhile, Bandit was having a fine time keeping them in a group. I guess Bandit didn't have a whole lot of focus, and what he had, he used on herding.

For two or three minutes the dog ran them back and forth in front of me until the whole thing stopped abruptly; Bandit ran full tilt into a scrub oak. He never saw it coming. At first he sort of sank to his belly, but before I could rise to check on him, he stood up and wobbled off. I sank back into my bubble seat in the hot tub and tried not to spill my wine as laughter rumbled through me.

Congress was in one of its usual fights with the President, a Constitutional crisis loomed. Watching Bandit with the armadillos gave me a God's-eye view of what really was going on.

I owned a donkey and a jackass. Although they were genetically similar, anyone around them would quickly know which was which. Jimmy was sort of sweet and liked to be petted; Dick was likely to kick something to prove he like it. (All my donkeys are named after presidents.)

They hated each other, but donkeys are social creatures to the core, so they stayed close enough at all times to torment each other. They reminded me of a number of married couples I've known. Whenever I drove into town they loved to stand next to the fence and bray their discontent after me. If I fed them in two piles they fought over one pile until it was consumed, then moved their altercation to the next pile.

One week Jimmy got out and ran around the neighborhood for four days until I managed to get him back in; Dick was a nervous wreck. When I finally got Jimmy back inside my fence Dick ran around in pure joy, braying and kicking up in the air. After two or three minutes Dick took his celebration a little further and tried to mount Jimmy like a mare. Soon they were both kicking and biting like old times. It's good to see a family reunited.

Anyway, Jimmy was definitely the smarter of the two. Like any animal that figures a way through an old fence, he broke out again and again until I reluctantly hired Jeff Hammond to help me run the new fence. Four days into the fencing I was ready to shoot Dick and sell Jimmy just to get shut of the whole situation. Jeff showed up at sunrise and lingered around the back porch until I gave him coffee and breakfast with Janey and me. He had a gift for souring one of my favorite times of the day.

"…and so the widow says to me, if you believe it, do it…." Jeff hollered across the breakfast table at me, giving me an obscene wink and a nod.

Janey looked down, and looked embarrassed. She wasn't supposed to catch his heavy handed humor, but of course she did. At 16, Janey had at least five years of maturity on Jeff, despite his age.

"Let's go," I said to Janey. We left for school.

In the truck Janey turned to me. "He's so horrible. I don't like him. I want you to get rid of him. He stinks. He looks at me and my skin crawls."

"I know, Janey. I know. He bothers me too. Hopefully, after today I won't need him any more. By the way, I need you to ride the school bus home today."

"Oh, Dad!"

"Yup. It's not punishment, I just got to get this job finished so we can get this jackass out of here," I said. We both knew I did not mean either of my donkeys.

What ever else you could say about Jeff Hammonds (and there was a lot), he was a hard worker. By noon we had the last of the posts in place, and by 3 p.m. we were stringing wire. It looked just possible we might finish, and was I ever glad. Jeff droned on and on with a string of racist jokes that hadn't been clever or funny back when such jokes might have been (barely) acceptable. I guess when someone is really at the bottom of the barrel they need to have someone to spit down on, but still, he grated.

Jeff said, "Did you hear the one about…."

I interrupted him. "I'm going to go get another roll of wire. No way can we finish with what we got."

"Ain't no more wire, this is our last roll," he brayed.

"Keep working, I'm going to town and get it right now." I'd had enough, more than enough. I needed a break.

In less than an hour I returned with the wire. I pulled up where we were working, but there was no Jeff, just some abandoned tools. I threw out the wire and drove on down the road to check on Janey.

The back door hung open and the house was the sort of quiet only an empty place can be. My blood pressure shot up ten points as I ran through the house.

"Janey, JANEY" I yelled, in a half walk and a half run through the house. "Janey, answer me NOW!" I yelled, circling back past the barn.

One of Jeff awful jokes about an Arkansas wedding frittered though my mind, but I determined not to panic.

First I called the bus driver, "I let her off at the gate."

Second I called her best friend, Pepper, "No, I haven see her since school."

Third I called Arney, Heartbreak's only cop. It was time to panic. In the next two hours we search high and low, including Jeff's old shack and nobody could find anything.

I ran back to the house, not really sure why, but getting more upset than I've been in years. I noticed the message light on my phone.

"Dave, this is Jeff. Get over to Mercy Hospital in Picket City." End of message. Jeff was never eloquent and I think phones sort of scared him. Anyway, I called Arney and drove off fast.

Forty miles and 30 minutes later I sat by Janey's bed, holding her little hand.

"A big old rattle snake got me, Daddy. Oh, it hurts." Hot tears rolled down her face and she looked more like 6 than 16.

The doctor spoke up then. "She's going to make it, good thing that Jeff guy was around. He killed the snake and brought it with him. Without his forethought and judgment, we could not have known which anti-venom to use. Most people don't think that far ahead."

"Well, where's Jeff?" I asked, more flummoxed than I've been in a while.

"He went back to Heartbreak, hunting for you," Janey replied.

Quick as I could I called Arney to call off the manhunt. Janey had a bad night, and as I sat there holding her hand I reflected about jackasses and social graces.

It was two more days before I ran into Jeff again. Of course, he'd heard about my wrong assumptions and the manhunt I set on him. He was hurt and righteously so.

"Jeff, it not often a man owes another man such a thank you and such an apology at the same time." I was prepared to eat crow, I deserved it.

After a long silence he stuck out his hand, ready to shake. "Kind of misjudged me, didn't you?" he said.

"Yep, I owe you a lot. Just saying 'Sorry' doesn't quite cover it."

"Well, that's a start. Say, did you hear the one about the blonde and the saltshaker?"

"Yea, twice this week already. I got something for you." I reached in my back pocket and pulled out a hefty little book. "This here's *Wilson's Compendium of Humor*. I misjudged you on a big account. But honest, you need some new material for your gags."

A smile broke his crusty young/old face. "Why, thanks, Dave. No one ever gave me a book before."

That night as I lay in bed, saying my prayers, I thanked God for all his creatures, donkeys and jackasses alike, and asked for the humility to know the difference. I thanked God for the wisdom to know that the best I could hope for was to be a donkey in His sight, and the certain knowledge that more often than not I was another braying jackass.

PUTTING TRASH IN ITS PLACE

Lucy worked in a big warehouse.
She told dirty jokes every day.
Other employees thought her crude,
By the bad words she chose to say.

Every Friday there was a dumpster,
At the end of the loading dock.
Even on days meant for clean up,
Lucy talked dirty on the clock.

One Friday she and a helper,
Carried some trash out to the bin.
When Lucy started her talking,
The co-worker pushed her in.

Marlene Tucker

FAMBILY

A RIVER RUNS THROUGH HIM

SUPERSTITION IS LIVE AND WELL, NOT only just in Heartbreak, Texas, but just about everywhere. The funny thing about superstition is that we see other people's and it seems silly, even funny. We don't see our own. I take a kinder view of superstition. I think it's a combination of warning signals we just haven't processed all the way through.

Take the other night. We had a visiting preacher; O'Riley was his name, who held an old-fashioned tent revival, pump organ and all. He preached against cussin', drinkin', fornicatin',
and cards, all in one sermon.

Clearly, he was a little new to his craft to use up so many sins in one night. Without getting into theology (an area that never tempted O'Riley) I'll just say he reminded me of the worst, not the best in our religious traditions. He wasn't bad entertainment, but what else did he think there was to do in a place like Heartbreak?

His daughter, Lucy, was a saucy little thing about Janey's age, and she played the French Horn real well for some of the old hymns. From almost the first day he seemed to take against me, a single man trying to raise his daughter, and Lucy and Janey spent considerable time running around town together, often with Janey's friend, Pepper. I saw no harm in Lucy spending time with Janey and I didn't take O'Riley all that seriously.

44

Of course, that just made him grouchier. I didn't really mind. You can only pass the offering plate so many times in a town small as Heartbreak, and I knew he'd be moving on soon enough.

After four nights, he announced to the gathered congregation that Saturday had belonged to the devil long enough. Now that was cutting to the bone. Heartbreak was full of good Baptists that need a Saturday night to set their attitudes right for repentance Sunday morning. It had a lot to do with the natural flow of things, especially in a little place like Heartbreak.

Sunday morning, O'Riley started in again.

"You sinners, you heathens, you think you're foolin' everyone, but you're not fooling God, and you're not fooling me!"

Personally, I was perfectly willing to take my chances with God. Many days, in fact, I felt I was on fairly good terms with Him, but O'Riley wasn't likely to hear that, especially coming from me.

"You flaunt your whores in broad daylight, in front of your daughters, and you think you can get off scot free? No way, I'll stay here forever if need be, but I'll never let you get away with it."

He sounded like he had something in particular on his mind, but I couldn't, for the life of me think what it was 'til I looked over at Sally Rae. Her cheeks were a bright red that rouge never touched, and she looked close to tears.

It suddenly dawned on me that Pepper and Janey must have told Lucy about Sally Rae's son, born out of wedlock more than 20 years ago. All of a sudden I was mad. Sally Rae's fiancée had been killed in a car wreck, their baby had been born, and she had lived an upstanding life since the – at least 'til I came to town.

She was mine now, and we were sort of at that spot in life where we were both heading down the same path, a path that had an altar some where along the way. I had half a mind to march down and clock the little prig, but prudence (and Sally Rae's strong right hand) restrained me.

After the service, Sally Rae shook with humiliation and tears.

"Dave, I'll just never live it down, I can't be good enough, straight enough, or ever match up to standards in this town ever again."

"Don't worry, Sally Rae. People who know you understand, and that's most of this town. People that don't, well, like O'Riley says, they can just go to Hell."

45

The next day I caught up with O'Riley. At first he flinched when he saw me, but I just smiled and agreed with everything he said. I've dealt with some other O'Rileys in my life. They want power, power to feed their shrunken little egos, and nothing works like just treating them as if their every word was gold.

Before long we stopped at Johnson Mineral Water Salon. "I can't be seen going in no Saloon, now, you understand," O'Riley said nervously as we stood outside.

"Don't worry, preacher. Everybody in Heartbreak knows that Johnson doesn't sell any alcohol. It's just the natural spring water from right out behind his store, sometimes with a little twist of lime."

The day was hot and we spent the next three hours sittingthere, sipping mineral water as O'Riley set me straight on religion, God, Natural Science, Politics, and Animal Husbandry. For a man whose language said he'd never made it out of high school, he sure had a lot of opinions, especially of himself. We spent the whole afternoon sipping away at Mr. Johnson's Special Water.

I wasn't at the revival that night; I had a few stomach problems. But Sally Rae told me about it later.

"His daughter was playing the French Horn, 'There is a Fountain', I think, when we heard a few sour notes. All of a sudden Preacher O'Riley just got up and started running into the night. After about 30 minutes, people started drifting on home. What do you think happened?"

"I think God takes care of us all," I replied. "He provides everything we need, if we got enough sense to use it. But would you please get that bottle of Johnson's Tonic and Natural Laxative Water out of this house? I don't think I can stand to look at it any longer."

THE PREACHER AND THE WAGES OF SIN

He enlisted the help of a local girl,
To gather offerings after the service.
She was blond and thin; a sweet little thing,
Who could refuse her open hands so nervous?

She was quiet but listened to all that was said,
As the people were admonished to live right.
She also noticed before going home,
The stray women he spent time with at night.

The last act of his traveling revival,
He drove home his message on sin with a yell!
He said money was the root of all evil,
Thus she stole it so he wouldn't go to hell.

Marlene Tucker

HOMER

HEARTBREAK'S A PLACE LARGELY overlooked, but the sort of place that has inspired movies and books. People here are real, even though they have running water, yearling cattle, and (occasionally), streaming Internet. They seem to take all these innovations in stride without losing their values.

After my painful divorce, it seemed the right place for me to find my ground again, and plant my dear Janey on a better path than the rave parties and Tweet culture of her native Houston.

My sorely-tried heart had barely started to heal when I found myself going into town every day to have a Dr Pepper and a slice of vinegar pie at The Waterin' Hole Café. The lady that served me was Sally Rae. She had eyes the color of love, and in less time than is decent I fell into those eyes.

Move things forward a year; Sally Rae and I got engaged. If this doesn't prove that flat worms can learn from experience and humans can't, I don't know what does. But Sally Rae and I were in love, and I popped The Question.

"Will you marry me, darlin'?" I said, wiping the last of the vinegar pie from my lips.

"Are you coming in here drunk?" she replied.

I'm a persistent sort and over the next 12 months we talked and talked (and well, sometimes we weren't exactly talking), but the important thing is we finally agreed. We got engaged.

David Mosley

Love is a funny thing. One I walked through my pasture full of starving goats, with no rain since May, dogged a rattlesnake, and opened a hostile letter from my banker. The whole time I felt incredibly lucky. Love is the closest thing to Heaven any of us ever feel, and I just feel sorry for the cynics that feel otherwise. The closest I ever felt to this pure essence was when I held Janey in my arms for the first time.

I hear trichinosis makes a person blind. Love makes a body blinder, and that's a good thing, overall. Sure, I knew from the start ('cause Sally Rae HAD to confess it the first date) that she had a child out of wedlock when she was 17, that her son was gay, and he had moved out of Heartbreak years ago as soon as he could. She loved Jerry and I promised to also.

Things happen in life and I understood about her dead fiancée who managed to kill himself in a drunken car wreck the night of his bachelor party. As for her son, well, he lived far away and, well, gay just happens sometimes. I'm from Houston and this isn't one of those things I get all revved up about. Besides, Montrose sells fairly good sushi (accepting, of course, that such a thing really does exist).

There were others in The Waterin' Hole every day as I began my gentle conquest of Sally Rae. The three old men sat round the wood stove or the water fan, depending on the season. Miss Scarlet Hawkins came in too often for my taste. She always eyed me like a lean New York Strip until one day at the lake I said some imprudent things to her.

BJ Elkert occasionally took time off from keeping most of the machinery in Heartbreak from quitting, and Old Homer mostly just sat in the corner. He only drank black coffee and stared at Sally Rae, unblinking. Once, I whispered to her, "Is he dangerous?"

She giggled and whispered back, "Not usually."

A place like Heartbreak is full of hidden dangers. One day a semi came through too fast and a local stray cat got mangled. The poor thing got thrown up on the front steps of The Waterin' Hole. It was a sure thing she was dying. We all ran out and just stood there, horrified but helpless. Homer waked to his truck and came back in less than 30 seconds with his pistol. "Bang!" and the poor kitty weren't suffering no more. Homer walked back to his truck to put the gun away, then went back inside to finish his pie.

49

Arney, our policeman, saw the whole thing and he didn't say a word. Poor cat, but Homer had done the right thing while the rest of us all stood and gawked.

A few weeks later another cat showed up at The Waterin' Hole. We all called him "Young Tom", cause that's what he was. Young Tom had a gentle nature about him, around humans, that is. He was a prime hunter, a real vermin assassin that liked to display his talents and then proudly consume them in the presence of humans.

Young Tom was an affectionate sort of guy, except that (like most male cats) he liked to spray his scent around. Cat advertising, yeah, but its sort of hard for us humans to take. Especially, in summer, he liked to dive in open windows of pick up trucks and leave his calling card.

Personally, I'd rather roll over a skunk in the highway than have a male cat leave his scent in my truck. Anyway, rats had been giving me a hard time. Raising goats had shown me lots of ways to loose money, but feeding rats was the one that really irked me.

"I'd take Tom home if he didn't spray everywhere," I said one day while I was in The Waterin' Hole." I was in a rare and fine mood. It was the same day I dropped down on one knee and proposed to Sally Rae. ctually, that's what I did next.

"And Darlin', I'd take you as my lover, my wife, and my helpmate, from this day forward, for better or for worse, richer or poorer, 'til death do us part!" I held Sally Rae's hand and looked up into her eyes.

"I will!" she said.

For the next few seconds we were sort of oblivious. It was love declared, and love accepted, right across the counter top at The Waterin' Hole. We were on!

Behind my back, Homer stalked out of the bar and grabbed a few things from his trunk.

"Come out here," he bellowed in his odd, assertive, tenor voice. Sally Rae and I both walked out, sort of stunned by our boldly stated public pronouncements.

Homer grabbed Tom by his hind legs and swiped his pink stub of a nose with a swab of chloroform. Without pause, Homer put Tom's head in a boot and proceeded to castrate him with his pocket knife. When Homer finished cutting, he rubbed the incision with Preparation H.

"It shrinks the wound," he said.

When Homer drew the cat from the boot, Tom was dead. He was not breathing. He had a rictus on his face that was definitely reserved for the unliving.

"Oops, this sometimes happens," Homer said. Then he put his mouth on the cat's face and breathed out deeply and slowly. After a dozen tries, Tom started breathing on his own. Homer had kitty CPR down pat it turns out.

Then Homer turned round to me. He said, "Take care of Tom and my daughter, Sally Rae." With that, he pitched Tom's male parts into the back of my pickup. The man had a way of getting my attention.

Well, I have taken care of Sally Rae and Tom. He's about seven now. He was sort of brain damaged after the CPR, he has a tendency to stagger a little, but he still catches rats in my barns. All in all, brain damaged in Heartbreak matters less than one might imagine.

Sally Rae still keeps me warm at nights, serves me vinegar pie, and she's taught me that silly old men aren't silly when they go looking for true love. Homer was just one of the first surprises about marrying into a family. Darn. He was the friendly one. More on that later.

SMALL TOWN TEXAS

Small towns in Texas, like books on a shelf,
Hold a story and no two are the same.
They keep their hearts beating by the highway,
And cling to history and a sign with their name.

They would be like freckles on a road map.
Some towns prove to be wide spots in the road.
Not like those who grew larger on cattle,
And whatever help the railroad bestowed.

Age is the beauty in the cracked sidewalks,
Lovely facades and architecture rare.
Store fronts have witnessed time and keep secrets,
That locals are more than willing to share.

Hearts are still beating in small town Texas,
Where living is not considered a race.
The richness of Texas remains hidden,
From those who travel at such a fast pace.

Marlene Tucker

WHOSE WEDDING IS THIS?

A VITAL PART OF THE HEARTBREAK community was its waitress, Sally Rae, at The Waterin' Hole Café. Innumerable servings of Dr Pepper and vinegar pie later I took the bull by the horns and proposed to her. I always thought things between a man and his woman were private, silly me. The moment word of our engagement got out, I began to realize I was a minor actor in a great public drama. I had forgotten that if you take the bull by his tail, it's possible to let go and run. But a bull taken by his horns, well, the bull sets the pace. God help the man who lets go.

The Love Drug, you see, ought to be register as a Class III narcotic. It makes people do all sorts of weird things. At 60, I thought I was past all that sort of nonsense. This just proves how stupid the "wisdom with age" concept is.

Every romance seems to have its own song, its personal background music. For Sally Rae and me. it was *When A Man Loves A Woman*. Don't ask me why, but then love has more unanswered questions than cancer.

When a man loves a woman, he can't keep his mind on nothing else
He'll trade the world for the good thing he's found

I'm a 60-something sort of guy with a fledging goat herd starting to rebuild a run-down ranch. Sally Rae, about 45, was a home grown Heartbreak beauty. Back in high school she was engaged. The morning of her wedding the town policeman, Arney, drove up and told her that her fiancée had been killed during a pickup race that was a part of the bachelor party. She fainted dead away. Eight months later her son, Jerry, was born.

Now Heartbreak is pretty tolerant in its own stodgy way, though Sally Rae got an inordinate number of Holy Bibles gifted at her baby shower. She became the contemporary star of a timeless cautionary tale involving patience and virtue, and the virtue of patience, and she got a job at The Waterin' Hole Café.

"It was sort of like a consolation prize for not getting a life," she told me. The tips were good, but her prospects were not. "I got lots of propositions but no proposals at all, at least, 'til YOU came along."

It didn't help matters that her son, Jerry, turned out to be gay as a day in May. Don't get me wrong, Jerry was far from the first gay fellow in Heartbreak, but it was his misfortune to be born in a generation when acceptance had to be forced, open, and plainly stated. Jerry moved on about 10 years before Janey and I arrived.

If she is bad, he can't see it, she can do no wrong
Turn his back on his best friend if he put her down

To me, Sally Rae wasn't a cautionary tale; she was a gift from God. Did Moses delay crossing the Red Sea until God paved a pretty little path? Did Jonah criticize the beach the whale threw him up on? I may not be the sharpest pencil in the pack, but I do know a good thing when I see it. I'll spare you the flutters and fibulations of a 60-something year old-heart, but it wasn't all that different than when I was 16, except that I knew I had no right to expect this state as a matter of course.

Best I can figure, the Love Drug creates sort of an emotional stampede, like a herd of lightning-spooked cattle. Such an event can save a herd from predators, it can lead it to water, but the most important thing to remember about a stampede is to get out of the way! It's a real commentary on the beauty and perversity of human mating that we all pity a couple that doesn't ever feel this stampede sort of emotion.

It is an absolute truth of humanity (if not a very becoming truth) that when two individuals fix on each other, the last thing on their minds are their prospective extended families. Read *Romeo and Juliet* if you doubt it.

My family was limited to Janey. Poor Janey came to Heartbreak about as emotionally beat up as me. No matter what the circumstances, she had lost her mother. Sally Rae wisely didn't try to fill the loss, but she was there, and sometimes she made things a little better. Sally Rae had good mothering instincts. The first thing I learned about goats was to breed for good mothers; without that instinct, everything else was futile.

Sally Rae's family was, well, more complex. Her father, Homer, was a taciturn sort of old rancher that made a cedar fence post seem sort of gushy and emotionally open. A long sentence for him was, "Yep," or, more often, "Nope." He and Sally Rae's mother, Beth May, had been divorced for years.

Sally Rae had three younger sisters, Penny, Bonnie, and Clyde (old Homer wanted a boy so bad that by the time he got to number four it was Clyde, gender be damned). Collectively I thought of them as "the Furies." What I liked best about them was that none of them lived in Heartbreak.

Of course, as soon as news of our engagement leaked out, they all returned and camped out at the Heartbreak Hotel. From there, they planned what I came to think of as "The Campaign," that is, my wedding.

My first big mistake was thinking that marrying Sally Rae was a sort of private thing, mostly between her and me. Silly me.

As lead mare of the herd, Beth Mae called a meeting in the lobby of the Heartbreak Hotel.

Beth May started off, "What are your colors going to be?"

Penny cut me off before I could compose a dumb look, "And what is going to be your theme?"

Bonnie quickly added, "Who is going to do the catering?"

Clyde, not to be outdone, asked, "What orchestra will you have for the reception?"

Beth May: "Where do you intend to rent your chairs and decoration?"

Penny: "Invitations, I need a list and a printer by tomorrow."

55

Bonnie: "Which flowers?"

Clyde: "I need a list of groomsmen by yesterday, and at least a mock-up on the program."

I dared a look at Sally Rae. My own thoughts had run to a trip toward the Justice of the Peace, or maybe something simple at Cottonwood Baptist. We hadn't even set a date yet. Sally Rae looked like a deer in the headlights. Up to then, we had sort of been enjoying the moment. The next few minutes made it clear that the wedding march had started, and that it was to be a forced march, no side trips allowed.

Now I'm not a complainer, but no one I know ever got rich off of goat ranching. I survived by keeping costs low. It was my intention to publicly take and cherish this woman in front of God and Man, but doing it in front of Woman was suddenly growing more complex (and expensive) than our nation's domestic policy.

Beth May fixed me with her cold, blue, gunslinger's eyes and waited for an answer. I suddenly realized that the Indians were right; every person has a front name everyone knows, and a battle name held between them and God. My prospective mother-in-law was really "Death Ray," the wedding Nazi.

About then, Homer, my prospective father-in-law, walked into the room. Death Ray turned her scorching laser look on him and said, "You're late as usual. So kind to grace us with your presence."

Homer responded, "Still your own sweet self, I see."

That set them off into a bitter sort of exchange so dripping with venom I could tell it had taken years to perfect. It provided enough cover Sally Rae and I could slip away.

"When A Man Loves A Woman", Calvin Lewis and Andrew Wright, 1966

56

THE GUEST

I'm going to a wedding!
I got my invitation.
If I could do things my way
I'd make it my occupation.

Always wearing Sunday best
Attending fancy places
Joined with people expected
To have smiles upon their faces.

With all the lengthy planning
Done well or wafting astray
It is the guests most likely
To be assured a perfect day.

A marriage ceremony
Inviting guests to partake
I'm always glad to attend
And be served some expensive cake.

Marlene Tucker

GETTING HITCHED DESPITE IT ALL

WELL, SALLY RAE AND I SET THE
place as the Cottonwood Baptist Church, chose the local preacher, the Reverend Horace Hollis. His specialty was funerals, so I knew he had the right sort of practice for the job. I mean, when he finished the congregation was grateful to get on with things and the dead were content to be dead; he got the job done.

We chose St. Patrick's Day for the event and, Lordy, we worked. We made lists, ran errands, and answered to Death Ray and the Furies four times a week. (By contrast, a convicted felon only has to report to his parole office once a month.)

When a man loves a woman, spend his very last dime
Trying to hold on to what he needs

My crowd of groomsmen and my best man were all back in Houston. Collectively, they decided to rent a bus and just come up on the day of the wedding. It sounded practical to me. Among other things, they would bring me my rented tuxedo. I knew my friends and, frankly, I didn't want any of them trying to drive back to Houston after the reception.

The down side of having the wedding on St. Paddie's Day was that I doubted that few of my friends could remember much after about 4 in the afternoon on that particular holiday. If the dark side of

Thanksgiving is gluttony and the dark side of Christmas is avarice, then St. Paddie's is, well, self-medication.

Death Ray and the Furies were aghast at my plan.

"No rehearsal?" Death Ray asked, with an expression as if I had suggested an all-nude wedding in a field of snow.

"Let's be honest, Dea, uh, Beth May, all these guys have been married two or three times each. With you and your daughters, we have 40 or 50 weddings experience among us, not even counting the times we weren't the principals involved. What could go wrong?"

Well, Jesus always told the truth, and He highly recommended the practice to others, but you have to consider how it ruined His Passover, too. I tend to tell the truth, like it's a good thing, but it's not always a smart thing.

The Wedding Nazi announced that we were just going to have to have the rehearsal, with or without the groomsmen.

"But who will put out the almonds?" Penny asked.

"Almonds?" I asked, gormless as ever.

"Almonds! People have been putting out almonds since Roman times!" Bonnie snapped.

"And rice," Clyde seconded. Soon they were off into logistics, of moving Sally Rae into position without me seeing her, and a dozen other obscure rules. It provided enough distraction for me to slip away.

He'd give up all his comforts, sleep out in the rain
If she said that's the way it ought to be

Finally the big day came. Couples value privacy above all else. Modern weddings seem designed to minimize comfort, privacy, and, heck, financial security, but like a death sentence, all that planning at some point takes on its own momentum.

We were all supposed to meet at Cottonwood Baptist at 1 p.m. and have the ceremony start at 2 o'clock. I was there early, fresh scrubbed, even dressed in my Sunday suit. We were actually meeting outside, doing the ceremony in Heartbreak's prettiest adornment, calf-deep bluebonnets. This solved an over-crowding problem with the Cottonwood sanctuary, but through some mishap of communication the Rev. Hollis had let his cows into the church yard earlier that day, so the footing was a might chancy. Jerry, Sally Rae's son, arrived with his partner-in-love, Ralph.

The Rev. Hollis started to scowl, but I stepped up and shook Ralph's hand.

"I'm glad you could be here, welcome," I said. Jerry and Ralph were dressed just enough out of the ordinary as to make their preferences known, but this was Sally Rae's big day and I was determined not to let anything ruin it for her. I would not have cared, personally, if they had come in full drag. They were there and as certainly as I love Sally Rae, nothing was going to stop us.

Folks arrived and Janey brought me news that Sally Rae was all ready, but the bus with all the groomsmen, my best man, and my tuxedo had not arrived. People had arrived, were seated, and they were getting fidgety. Grey storm clouds were building up to the southwest. The Reverend was sending me meaningful looks. Homer's face was distinctly more craggy than normal, and Death Ray's eyes were downright poisonous. The hour slipped to 3:30, then 4. Time to get 'er done!

Peggy came running up to me, "Dave, what are you…."

"Peggy, tell Sally Rae we march in five minutes, rain or shine."

"But what about your tux, the best man, the…."

"Five minutes. No buts," I said.

I turned to Jerry and Ralph. "Are you both men?" I asked.

Jerry bristled. "What do you mean by that? Just because…."

"Don't take offense. I need some men. Jerry, you're best man. Ralph, you're a groomsman."

I spied BJ Elkert sitting near the back. "BJ, are you up for a little walk?"

"Uh, I guess so," he said.

"Then walk down the aisle with me. BJ, you take Clyde. Ralph, you take Bonnie, Jerry, you're family, so you walk with your Aunt Penny."

"Uh, Dave, Aunt Penny has always kinda disowned me, won't have nothing to do with me," Jerry stuttered.

"Maybe after the ceremony you can tell me what the trick is, sounds like you got something right. But for now it's time that family pulls together," I said. "Rev. Hollis, assume the position."

60

David Mosley

I nodded toward Great Aunt Katy, who was sitting just inside the church at an open window behind the organ. "Great Aunt Katy, play the wedding march, please!"

Well, it happened. Sally Rae was pretty as all brides are supposed to be, even if she was a little flushed. Death Ray and the Furies all looked at me like I was wearing a skunk-skin coat, but it wasn't about them. Everyone marched through the ceremony. Sally Rae and I pledged "for better or worse, richer or poorer, in sickness and in health...." We looked deep into each other's eyes and we meant it. Life has few perfect moments and many imperfect ones; by my age, I knew the difference and the importance of seizing and holding the perfect ones.

As we kissed I was vaguely aware of a bus pulling up, of a clap of thunder and a sudden heavy rain, but Sally Rae and I really didn't care. We were one.

Yes, when a man loves a woman I know exactly how he feels
'Cause baby, baby, you're my world
When a man loves a woman I know exactly how he feels

"When A Man Loves A Woman",
Calvin Lewis and Andrew Wright, 1966

61

Relative Refreshment

My mother-in-law asked for coffee,
Only after I brought her tea,
I made her mad with two cookies,
Because she really wanted three.

When my wife's Mom came to visit,
We bickered and it was a shame,
Until I came up with a plan,
To keep me from going insane.

I was set to win her over,
With all the kindness of my heart,
And outdo her at her own game,
Until death did one of us part.

I kept food set at her elbow,
And served her drinks until she popped,
She was so full she couldn't fuss,
And so, the bickering stopped.

Marlene Tucker

OLD NAP

PEOPLE IN HEARTBREAK MOSTLY wouldn't win many beauty contests, but most all of them would stop and change your tire if you had a flat, give you a couple of bucks if you looked hungry, or some good advice if you looked confused. As a whole, they are a decent bunch of people.

My Sally Rae had eyes the color of love. Her eyes were brown on the outside; green toward the middle, yellow right next to the pupil....

There is no perception faultier than a man's emotional compass just after a divorce. As a man, I know that. I know that a man's emotions are so wrong just after he has lost his woman . . . but I knew from my first moments that Sally Rae and I were right for each other. After two years of courtin', and a goodly number of slices of vinegar pie, Sally Rae and I got married at Cottonwood Baptist Church.

Cottonwood Baptist is a good reflection of most of the good things and a few of the bad that any small town church can offer. The theology was as homegrown as the choir, but so were the Wednesday night dinners and the food sent to homes of the ailing folks and the bereaved.

Oh, we got regular warnings about worshipping false gods, how true evil was old and practiced while we were all born naive babies, and how sin often sold itself as something else. But honest, I found this sort of sermon sort of soporific. I think one of the best things about most churches is that it gives a good excuse for the natural goodness of most people to show up.

63

Church is also a natural breeding zone for new parents, a place where baby clothes and toys got exchanged and passed around — along with chicken pox and generational advice. My Janey stood out in this congregation as a natural blonde, but I noticed a large number of the Cottonwood kids had curly, ginger-colored locks.

Now I try to stay away from shallow judgments, gross generalizations, and all that sort of stuff. But to put it in short, I'm not real buff. Neither is Sally Rae. We weren't either the sort of people that the word "love" jumps to mind when you first see us. We won't be models for magazines like *Gentleman's Quarterly* or *Playboy*. What we *did* find was a surprising love for each other that defied common knowledge. That love holds to today, tomorrow and on. Let the skeptics say what they may.

Perception is a tricky thing. It's like head lights on a highway. You see what's right in front of you, while missing anything on either side. The Old English word "glamore" shows considerable insight. Although it's the root word for *glamour*, the original word was used to describe a spirit, a special being (usually malign) that sent off shimmers to distract and mislead the viewer through re-direction.

One local character that was never known to warm a pew – at Cottonwood or any house of prayer — was Old Nap, yet he was one of the most popular figures in Heartbreak. He had a way of showing on a body's door step, but he never seemed to push or intrude.

Old Nap was a bee hunter and brewer. Bee hunting is a job as old as the first immigrants to Texas. These woodsy souls specialized in following bees back to their nests and then stealing their honey. The best ones could sweet talk the bees into holding still while the honey gatherer reached down into their hive and pulled out their comb. Old Nap was one of these.

He'd just play his little reed flute and those bees sort of went to sleep. By common consent and custom he could cross any fence, walk any trail, and find the beautiful honey. People let him alone because a few weeks or months later he would turn up with some of his home brew he called "mead."

That mead tasted of bluebonnets and spring days; it tasted like out-lived youth and forgotten joy. It tasted like a fecund moment in a sterile eternity. My first sip put a smile on my face. The second sip reminded me of a cute little girl back in my high school days, and set me to giggling.

Like most folks I had more sips, but the memories slipped into giggles, then drowsiness. My last thoughts were profound insights about the universe that defied my best ability to reassemble into coherence.

When I woke up, Old Nap was gone, the sun was setting, and I had finished one of those rare days that didn't feel so much wasted as used artfully. That was his first visit, right after Sally Rae and I got engaged.

Old Nap was about six feet tall. His hair was snow white with a few streaks of ginger, remnants from bygone days. His long hair fell to his shoulders, and his long beard stretched past his collar-bone, curly, but soft to the touch.

He had a scent to him, like bluebonnets and oak smoke. His eyes were striking, more gold than any other color, and they set off his young-old face that was laced with laugh wrinkles. When he talked, it was smooth, like honey. He was an easy guy to be around.

About a month after Sally Rae and I got married, I was working at the back of the ranch. It was Sally Rae's day off, but I couldn't be puttering at the house with her delightful company when the dang goats were running free — again. Fencing goats is like fencing the wind. The darn things were not only escape artists, but they had a way of breaking down new fencing, so I never quite caught up.

"Dave, you work too hard," Old Nap said.

I jumped a little; I hadn't heard him coming up behind me. "No harder than I have to," I said, wiping sweat from my eyes.

"Well, I didn't make your wedding," Old Nap said, "but I have a little something for you anyhow." He unplugged the stopper on his famous mead skin and poured me a tin cup of his special home brew.

It would have been un-neighborly to refuse, despite my work.

"Sure, I'll have a cup, but just one. These goats aren't letting up," I said.

Half an hour and three cups later, I sat back beneath a mesquite tree, just for a little breather, and began to doze off. My dreams troubled me, a sort of obscure insight that seemed, well, just off. I might have slept 'til dinner but for one of those pop-up summer storms that sent a bolt of lightning to a tree too near me for comfort.

I didn't so much wake up as get blasted to my feet.

At the same time, a truth that seemed obscure suddenly became crystal clear. I ran back toward the house. When I reached my truck, I grabbed my pistol from my pick up and charged into the kitchen.

ure enough, Sally Rae, my new bride, was almost passed out in a stupor. Old Nap was still talking in that same honeyed voice as he unbuttoned her blouse.

"Stop right there or your honey-stealing days are over. We don't need any ginger-haired young'uns in this house."

Of course he looked surprised, but he kept his calm.

"Dave, this isn't what it looks like, I'm just...."

I put my pistol site smack dab on his on his lying mouth and said, "Old Nap, or maybe Old Pan for all I know; I see you for what you are. Now git!"

He gat.

"And leave that skin of mead, right there on that table."

"What? You're robbing me, too?"

"Yep. Call it rent against my silence, or I'll tell everyone around about the real size of your family."

Now he looked really stricken. "Imagine all the hurt, busted families and disowned children you'll cause! All I ever done was help women who want children and men who want relaxation from their labors for a while!"

"So maybe we'd all be better off if I just shot you now?" I asked.

He considered it for a moment, and walked out of my kitchen.

Sally Rae and I enjoyed that mead for a long time. We used it cautiously, just a little at a time, and only inside with the doors locked.

THE TIP

"Ma'am the food here is just delicious,
And the service is better than great!
I go right past where your husband works,
Would you like me to take him a plate?

I think you're the prettiest waitress,
And a person I might like to know,
And I guess that's partly the reason
Why I sit and eat my lunch so slow.

Your husband works the longest hours.
I bet you miss out on having fun.
If you'd like to go to a movie,
I'd sure be glad to take you to one."

"Sir, you could star in your own movie,
Probably not what you had in mind.
My husband will be the director
If he sees your hand on my behind."

Marlene Tucker

THE NEW KID

SALLY RAE AND I WERE LOOKING
toward a quiet sort of marriage. Acceptance from Janey was coming.
I couldn't hardly blame Janey if it took a little while for her to catch
up. After all, when we fled Houston she lost her friends, her school,
her clothes, and, well, darn it, her mother, too. She wouldn't be human
if she didn't feel a few bumps in the road.

Thank God Sally Rae was a born mother. She understood the
pouts, the moodiness, and even the downright disrespect from Janey,
but Sally Rae always came back with pure love. I could sense Janey
was being won over, one step at a time.

I envied those children's stories that always ended, "And they
lived happily ever after..." Truth was, I still had a mortgage, my goats
still died about as fast as new ones were getting born, and if Sally Rae
hadn't kept her job at The Waterin' Hole Café, there were some nights
when Janey and I might not have had much to eat. Rich ranchers are
all Republicans and poor ones are all Democrats, and there were a
whole lot more Democratic ranchers than Republicans. Financially, I
was darn sure a Democrat.

About 8:30 one evening, we were just sitting down for dinner
when a knock came at the door. It was my cousin Buck, an oil patch
redneck of the highest caliber. He'd risk his life for six months straight
to bring in a rich man's well, and throw away all his earnings for a
bottle of whiskey and a loose woman to drink it with.

"Are we too late to come visiting?" Buck asked.

"Not at all, come on in," I said. Truth is, I didn't know how Buck ever found my place, I'd almost as soon find a skunk in the yard, and I was tired. Still, hospitality had its rules and truth and hospitality had little in common.

"Have y'all eaten yet?" I asked. "We're just sittin' down. Will you join us?"

Buck and his slutty girl friend walked in.

"Actually, we're about half starved. This here is Puella Easley, my one true love," he said, pushing his dishwater blonde girlfriend forward, "and of course, Li'l' Billy."

Li'l' Billy was the more interesting of the two. I knew of his existence from some Facebook birth announcement four years back.

"I believe in love, and all its mighty courses,
And I believe in you, my mighty hostess true..." Li'l' Billy sang in the pure soprano of the very young.

Buck said, "Li'l' Billy don't exactly speak, but he sure copies good."

Sally Rae got busy and "stretched" dinner for two and a half more.

Puella went straight to the bathroom and stayed until we were forced to eat our dinner without her presence. Her only offering for the evening came through the bathroom door, "I like cold food, go on, don't worry about me."

Li'l' Billy entertained us throughout the meal. *"This here is good grub, pilgrim,"* he announced at one point.

It was a good John Wayne impression, done in his child's soprano, and it set us all laughing.

After dinner, Buck got down to business. "I got the best job of my life waiting for me in Canada, you know, where the oil shale is comin' in. I can make some real money there. Puella is up for it, but it's no place for a child. Could you handle Li'l' Billy for a while?" he asked.

"Well, I don't know about that," I said, "after all, Sally Rae and Janey and I are trying to set up shop here, well I just don't know. Let me talk to Sally Rae. I don't really see it, though.

"Just sleep on it," Buck said.

Not long after that we set up Buck, Puella, and Li'l' Billy on couches and a pallet in the living room. Sally Rae and I went upstairs and Janey went to her room. That's all I remember 'til dawn, when a screech like a mating banshee split the dawn's early light.

"I got my little pee pee stuck in the goddamn zipper! Help!" a clear soprano pierced the morning.

Sally Rae, bless her heart, hit the floor, bare feet slapping down the stairs. Somewhat slower, I pulled on a robe and came after her. She grabbed Li'l' Billy's zipper and pulled it straight down. She was immediately rewarded by a shot of hot little boy juice in her face.

She grabbed a towel, and asked, "Finished, little booger?"

Tearfully Li'l' Billy said, *"Yes, for now. But tomorrow and tomorrow, who know what shall come?"*

I looked in the living room for Buck or Puella, but only bed sheets remained crumpled on the floor. I ran to the window, in a panic, but Buck's pickup was long gone.

"Where are they?" I asked, panicked as any man with a sudden child thrown into his midst.

"They're half way to Canada by now, I expect," Sally Rae said.

Janey poked her head out her door and asked, "What's happening? I can't sleep with all this racket."

Sally Rae turned around to and me and said, "There are four of us now. I hope you see that."

Then she took Li'l' Billy upstairs and put him in our bed. I don't claim to know a whole lot about women, but one thing was apparent to me that morning: newlywed or not, Li'l' Billy was sleeping in my bed between me and Sally Rae. She was a born momma and no one else was there for that child. I could be the sperm donor (not!), the occasional guest, the optional creature. With Janey and Li'l' Billy, Sally Rae was prepared to see them to adulthood. To stand in the way of motherhood was to stand in front of a train.

It took me a pot of coffee and a little introspection, but when I was all thought through it, I knew Sally Rae was right. It was time for me to man up. I marched up those stairs and snuggled up with Sally Rae next to our new son. It takes nine months for most people to make a new son, but it only took Sally Rae and me one night of simple of hospitality. Many Western men have a problem with Fate; I decided not to be one of them.

David Mosley

All too soon, the alarm went off.

"What do we do now?" I asked.

Sally Rae said, "Let Li'l' Billy sleep 'til he wakes up, then feed him. Teach him the goats, how to use his zipper, and how to be a man. I'll be home about 6."

I realized I was in Heaven. I had a new wife, my beloved daughter going high school, and I had a new kid. His biological parents may have shunned him, but as I looked at Li'l' Billy sleeping there, I knew I was lucky—mortgage, dying goats, and all.

Janey, of course, was angry. She was at the age where she was angry often. Events hadn't helped much, but she saw Li'l' Billy as the last straw.

That night, at dinner, she looked at Sally Rae and I like a viper deciding between two trapped mice. "You think you're going to put him in my bedroom? Why not the barn?"

Sally Rae and I solved the bedroom problem by doing a quick clean-out of the pantry behind the kitchen. It was big and old fashioned. Much of it could be moved out to the barn. In two days, Li'l' Billy had a room of his own, even it did look like a broom closet off the kitchen.

"My kingdom, my kingdom, stuff the horse!" Li'l' Billy said when he saw it.

I took it that he liked having his own room.

In the following weeks and months I cussed Buck a lot, but later on I started thanking God for my son. I knew Sally Rae had it right from the start. A mother protects children. It may take men a little longer to see it, but we're up for the task if we're real men. I have never regretted Li'l' Billy.

We wanted Li'l' Billy to feel like part of the family, so we took him to church. We had him "dedicated", a Christian sort of ceremony where the whole church pledges to accept a child and help raise him right. We wanted Li'l' Billy to feel like he had a real home. As we were driving off Li'l' Billy broke into tears.

"Why, what's wrong, Li'l' Billy?" Sally Rae asked in her sweetest voice.

Heartbreak, Texas

"They said back there that I was going to get raised by a Christian family, right?" he asked.

"They sure did," Sally Rae said.

"But, I want to stay with you guys!"

DAD. A VISITING PHILOSOPHER

*"It's good to see company come
And good to see company go."
I'm sure Dad wouldn't have said it
If events hadn't proved it so.*

*Stopovers by the relatives
Were a pleasure and time well spent,
But if they stayed three days or more
Dad contemplated charging rent.*

*If the neighbors lingered too late
Sometimes dad would feel pressed to moan,
"Momma we need to go to bed
So all these people can go home."*

*When it came to saying good-bye
Dad's heart carried a happy tune,
"Y'all come back to see us, ya hear?
But just not any time too soon."*

Marlene Tucker

THE MUSEUM

BLESSING IS SORT OF COMPLICATED.
It takes a person being *blessed*. It has to have knowing that one is *blessed*. Hopefully, one returns the *blessing*. Whole religions have been based on less, and whole cultures have fallen for missing this simple truth.

The Heartbreak Museum is a museum of misdirection. Nobody wants their own local history told, unless it's so far back you can brag on a rustler or the odd great-great uncle who was hung for stealing a horse. Problem is, everyone wants a piece of it. It is a center of social climbing and bickering.

Heartbreak Museum was no exception. It features a real Billy the Kid's grave (of course!), a broken-handled rifle (Davey Crockett's?) and a listening horn used by Deaf Smith. There is a thunder mug from Jane Long's hotel (her personal one?) and a birthday card signed by Youra Hogg to her father, the Governor. This is all about the politics of small town's social climbing.

I didn't care much one way or another about them, but they were kind enough to make Janey a Heartbreak Belle. She got all dressed up in a big satin dress with a low-cut top and rode in a parade. Janey loved it and so did Sally Rae! All this was outside my ken but it made my womenfolk happy, so I was all for it, too.

When Sally Rae, Janey and I arrived at Cottonwood Baptist church the next Sunday morning, we really had not expected anything new. I have been a constant attendant at my church for about two years and I was seriously thinking about joining. I was already on the "House and Grounds Committee" mostly because I could fix things like plumbing and fallen trees. I tried to tithe, but 10 percent was often an elusive point when I was losing hand over fist with my goats.

I clapped to the beat of the songs as best I could, and Sally Rae was a member from birth. The current pastor had actually been to a seminary for a few months. I think if we, as a congregation, had a few more months to work on him that we might have brought him around.

That Sunday there were a couple of visitors. They were Special Visitors (not folks like me who sort of crept in on the back bench) but some real bold visitors who obviously wanted to be noticed.

The man wore an Army uniform with lots of hash on it. His wife was decked out in several layers of pink; they sat on the front row and at the end of the sermon they went right up front and joined the church (first visitation!). He was Brigadier General John Ashford Miller Forrest, Ret. and she was Mrs. Brigadier General John Ashford Miller Forest, Ret. (but just call her "Millie"). They chose us and they were Somebody! We were there to be honored, and we were.

The General and Millie bought a big run-down Southern mansion sort of place, and Millie got busy spending the General's money fixing it up. Millie joined the Heartbreak Museum and instantly got herself elected President. As her first move she renamed it Le Beaux Arts Metropolitan (known to its detractors as "BAM"). Millie declared that she was going to bring "life" back into Heartbreak. Darn. I sort of liked it as it was, but that was just me. I didn't mind, but then Sally Rae put her name up for membership at the museum.

The lowest social strata in Heartbreak was the Cedar Choppers (except for their mothers, the working girls out in Quick Fix, but that a different story for another day). Anyway, Cedar Choppers worked hard for little pay, drank hard for little pleasure, and seldom stayed around to raise the numerous children they sired. For a short time they attended the local Methodist Church but as soon as they discovered a few "liberal" beliefs, they split off to their own church, "The Mighty Tabernacle of God's Right Arm." They met in and rented from the Local Cedar Choppers Union Hall No. 1 for some obscure tax advantage, but most of the members complained that union dues and tithes amounted to double taxation. They had *lots* of issues.

Meanwhile, Millie brought Le Beaux Arts Metropolitan Museum back to life. She dedicated several of her own paintings to the museum. She gave a Monet to the Museum, then a Clearsemot, then a Chileat. Never mind that we had never heard of most of these artists, but what did us ignorant country hicks know? They all looked like mud through dark glasses to me, but I would never admit it out loud. Millie announced a wine and cheese opening for next Saturday.

The night came when Sally Rae was to be voted into the Le Beaux Arts Metropolitan Museum. Sally Rae hand-sewed a beautiful black satin dress for the occasion. Sally Rae, Janey and I were dressed to our tops. I even washed my old pickup truck. We pulled up outside and started to walk in. Mayjune, the greeter, met us outside. She couldn't meet our eyes. She was grim.

"Sally Rae, I can't say this any easy way. Millie blackballed you. You have a son out of wedlock and you work as a waitress. Most of us wanted you, but Millie wants something else. Sorry". With that Mayjune walked back inside the Le Beaux Arts Metropolitan Museum and closed the door. The door went BAM!

As we drove back home in stunned silence, I started to say something, but Sally Rae held my arm and said, "Don't".

The next day was Saturday, Grand Opening for the Museum. I got up to The Waterin' Hole Café early; I wanted to show Sally Rae my support. The place was packed with the Local Cedars Choppers Union Hall No. 1. They were a rough-looking crew. No one had whiskers less than three days old. Several were starting to swig on hard drink (never taxed) at breakfast time.

Sally Rae was hard pressed to serve all the fried pig and fried eggs and fried potatoes they demanded, but she was holding her own.

"Are you OK, Honey?" I asked as she sloshed a little coffee into my cup as she ran by.

"Just hush. I got it,'" is all she said.

Once she served free coffee, Sally Rae came out with an old tin frying pan and she banged it loudly until she had the attention of every cedar chopper there.

"Something big is happening in Heartbreak tonight!" she announced. "There is going to be a big opening at the old museum. Free booze and food for anyone who shows up. Yeah. They said that if they lied, why burn 'um down!"

There was a pause and then a collective roar came back, "We'll all be there!" the Cedar Choppers yelled.

RAIN FALLS ON THE JUST
(And the maladjusted)

Marlo seemed most worried about
What other people thought.
It influence everything she did
And most of what she bought.

When she was on the sidewalk
And got caught out in the rain
She threw such a conniption fit
Some thought she'd gone insane.

She pointed to the Heavens
The details of her dress
The water on her leather shoes
Was adding to the stress.

She screamed about the high cost
Of having her hair set
I was so relieved to know
That all I got was wet.

Marlene Tucker

Li'l' Billy and Sabina

AFTER ENOUGH TIME SALLY RAE AND I
got married, much to the relief of Janey. She has a hard time ignoring, righteously, (of course!) her father's courting. Courting at my age is complicated enough without a 17-year-old daughter hanging around like a Puritan gargoyle. Things were just settling down to normal when one of my stray cousins abandoned his 4 –year-old son on us. Li'l' Billy started as a liability, but he quickly grew into our hearts.

Have you ever looked at a Bluebonnet? I mean really looked at it? In the fall and winter it looks like a hairy weed, but it cups every small bit of dew towards its main stem, conserving its tiny moisture to its core. In spring it jumps up! It uses its short life to sweeten the air and announce hope and beauty for another year. It spirals in a perfect Fibonacci sequence that gives it sort of a Ferris wheel view when looked at from straight above. Its seeds are patient. They can wait a century or more, but all they want to do is make more of the sweet scent that tells anyone with the sense to listen that the air is perfumed, life has meaning, and hope will prevail.

Raising young humans is a lot the same. Sally Rae and I had just married when Li'l' Billy got dumped on us by his father, Buck, who took off to the oil shale jobs in Canada. Li'l' Billy was always his own kind of person. He seldom spoke, but when he spoke it was almost always a quote. Maybe he made them up, but this Li'l" kid always spoke like Charlton Heston defending guns, or Shakespeare defending some king I had never heard of before, or Paul Harvey

79

talking about farmers. He had accents and inflections, heck, he had *voices* all his own.

"Li'l' Billy, quit playing in the mud!" Sally Ray exclaimed.

"We are all sprung from Earth and Water," Li'l' Billy replied.

"Li'l' Billy, leave my cookies alone! I made those for school," Janey warned.

"If God had not created yellow honey, men would regard figs sweeter than now," Li'l' Billy replied.

"Li'l' Billy, get your hand out of your pants," I told him.

"Know thyself," he said.

"Li'l' Billy, some knowledge is private. At least check it out when you aren't in the kitchen," I said.

Sally Rae and I took Janey and Li'l' Billy to Cottonwood Baptist Church every Sunday. The first time Li'l' Billy was unusually silent for a long while. I asked him what he thought about it all.

He said, *"No man has existed, nor will exist, who has plain knowledge about the gods. For even if someone happened by chance to say what is true, he still would not know that he did so. Yet everybody thinks he knows."*

"What the heck does that mean?" I asked again, somewhat aghast at my son's incipient agnosticism.

At that point he lapsed into silence, filled his pants, and began to cry like any 4-year-old boy might do if pressed. I was mightily impressed, and I changed his clothes as Sally Rae fixed Sunday dinner. I'm not real bright, but I knew the time for discussion of theology had passed.

I have studied all sorts of ways of describing children. I was a teacher, way back in Houston, but now I was a rancher, ready to learn, anxious as heck about the new crop of kids from my goat herd. I had a new kid, a warm, special human, and my first survey placed him in the savant category. This is a broad, largely undefined category, and I felt shaky about my diagnosis. I knew that the people who studied this sort of behavior were about as confused as I was. I made a decision: Li'l' Billy was mine; I would keep him, send him to school (if possible) and do some homework of my own.

Every morning as I shaved he watched me with worshipful eyes, and made motions that pantomimed my own. When I took my high blood pressure pills he dutifully took his vitamins. For all his strangeness, he desperately wanted to please, and to belong to our family.

"All men think they know, but all men are guessing," Li'l' Billy thundered as he ran in and ate our lunch.

I ate lunch too, but slowly, and with a lot of thought.

"I think Li'l' Billy needs some grounding," I opened, when he had left the room and Sally Rae was cleaning the dishes.

"Yep. No offense, but Janey sure isn't the one."

I agreed. Janey had her first serious boyfriend. She was doing well in school, band and drama. She was doing well at Heartbreak High School and this was no small feat. Heartbreak High sports was probably a bigger religion than Cottonwood Baptist in this little town. Best friends here went back to grandmothers, along with some grudges, too. Janey was doing well. She looked like Barbie, but she had brains, and she had a sort of core, a grit, I secretly admired. Taking her time away to babysit for Li'l' Billy would be asking more of her than I thought wise.

"Maybe Li'l' Billy needs a babysitter, just someone special for him?" I notioned.

"Sabina McDaniels. She'd be perfect. Also, she'd be cheap enough we could afford her," Sally Rae said. As usual, she was a step or two ahead of me.

"Isn't Sabina one of those Cedar Choppers?" I asked. I'd been in Heartbreak long enough to get a little local lore. The McDaniels were part of a local tribe that mostly centered down in Quick Fix, or Babel, as our preacher called it. Quick Fix was where dope was openly grown, home brewed licker was openly served, and ashes got hauled when there was no fireplace present.

"Sabina is different. She's just 15, she's trying hard. She hasn't had a chance. Somebody needs to give her one," Sally Rae said.

I was skeptical. Cedar Choppers were an odd sort of clan, even for Quick Fix. The men were noted for violence, their women for good looks and early fertility. They all considered marriage a sort of unexpected event, and reproduction as inevitable, without much regard to such matters as cohabitation or degrees of kinship. Some people thought them short a few genes, other thought them cross-bred with pit bulls. I figured that most of them had just gone cruising for chicks at family reunions for too many generations.

Cedar Choppers were a special subgroup of white trash. They lived almost universally in older, single-wide mobile homes; these homes were landscaped with dead appliances and plumbing fixtures, and animated with children, dogs and chickens. First time grandmothers averaged about 30 years of age. The men worked hard and still managed to stay poor. They brewed copious amounts of moonshine that was used, variously, for antiseptic, mouthwash, mood enhancer, motor fuel and fertility booster.

They had their own spiritual leader, Brother Ralph, who preached a sort of Old Testament Christianity. His sermons featured especially vivid descriptions of Hell, a reality that the Faithful and Hung-over communicants believed in as certainly as fleeting youth and looming mortality.

Despite my own misgivings, Sally Rae was all for Sabina's caring for Li'l' Billy. I went along, intoxicated with the powerful love drug of early marriage.

So Sabina was hired to look out for Li'l' Billy.

Sabina, at 15, was temptation made into flesh. She was the reason for all those child protective laws. Her figure was movie star quality and she could have given Mona Lisa lessons on smiling.

Li'l' Billy's only comment was *"Desire doubled is love; love doubled is madness."*

Wow.

At first, Sabina and Li'l' Billy seemed to work out well. She got him to playing like a kid, even got him making some simple sentences that weren't pre-manufactured.

Then one day I turned into my driveway and I saw Sabina punch Li'l' Billy in his stomach. I sped toward my home, panic rising, when she hit him again. Poor Li'l' Billy just turned my direction and threw up all over Bandit, who was a little slow moving out of his way. Bandit barked his concern, Li'l' Billy upchucked, and I was mad and yelling at Sabina. Through it all she kept her calm and washed Li'l' Billy's mouth out with a garden hose.

I took her arm, and not too nicely, either. She was hitting my boy!

"What do you think you're doing?" I asked in a tone of voice that didn't much ask a question as announce a war. I'm sure I added some intemperate things, too, in the heat of the moment.

"Listen to me, just listen to me, Li'l' Billy ate the goat medicine," Sabina wailed.

That stopped me cold. Goat medicine is poison. It kills worms; give a goat too much and it will kill a goat. About then Li'l' Billy threw up on my boots. He was sure doing his part.

"Let her rip, Li'l' Billy" I encouraged.

I learned several lessons that day—that an admiring boy who saw me taking pills would do the I same, that if I looked for abuse, that is what I would see, that even a pretty girl could become a monster if monsters were all I sought.

That night at supper, Sally Rae said, "You know, Sabina won't be coming back."

"What?" I asked, "Didn't I apologize?"

"You did, it ain't you. Sabina's getting married, we're invited."

CALLING FOR A BABYSITTER ON A BUSY DAY

My plans were measured for the day,
A sitter new would come and stay,
'Til I came back from errands done,
With ample cash promised to pay.

My children hoped for someone fun.
It seemed their wishes had been won.
She came on time complete with smile,
As cheerful as the morning sun.

I must admit I liked her style.
My children had fun all the while.
I gladly added to her due,
And put her number on speed dial.

Great sitters found are far and few,
And though reliable to you,
They sometimes sit for others too.
They sometimes sit for others too.

Marlene Tucker

.

SABINA'S WEDDING

AT 18, JANEY WAS READY FOR COLLEGE
— or at least some place other than Heartbreak. I loved her enough to let her go. I had found some foolish fate of my own that felt great, but I knew my happiness wasn't some sort of inheritance I could force on Janey. Soon, she would leave to find her own way but I cherished every day she was still at home.

Contentment is what I felt, but domestic bliss can make a person easy to sneak up on. I forgot that I was part Cherokee, the civilized tribe that had been getting "snuck up" on for 300 years.

Because of Janey's restlessness, Sally Rae and I had hired a part-time baby sitter for Li'l' Billy. Her name was Sabina. Sabina was from Quick Fix, a place of low repute that was located in the river lowlands just south of Heartbreak.

Recently, Sabina saved Li'l' Billy after he ate a can of worm medicine; after a period of initial confusion where I yelled at her for punching the child in the stomach (to make him vomit), she quit. Actually, though, it wasn't just me. She quit to get married.

Sabina was just 15, but she was four months pregnant. In Quick Fix that meant motherhood for sure, and a marriage if one was lucky. I thought it a peculiar sort of luck, but I wished Sabina well.

"Well, Mr. Dave, I sure hope you and Miss Sally Rae come to my wedding this Saturday," Sabina said.

"We'll be there with bells on," I said. Next to me, Sally Rae shuddered but kept her peace.

When Sabina was gone, Sally Rae said, "Well, we better leave the children at home."

I didn't know what her point was, but I bowed to her superior knowledge of local ways, and I agreed.

Everything thing about Sabina's wedding seemed wrong from the start. At only 15, she was smart, loving – and she looked like Marilyn Monroe. I silently grieved that she had not lucked into just a few more years to enjoy life before her femininity was harvested. This kid had brains and beauty both, but she came from the Cedar Choppers. They never looked at a woman's potential at 25 or 30; at 15, Sabina was a full woman, at least by the way her tribe saw things.

Sabina showed up before the wedding, dressed in her mother's white gown. She was "showing", that is, her tummy was visibly rounded. I didn't fault her any, but I again felt sorrowful for her loss of opportunity in her life.

Sally Rae, another very young mother back in the day, hung on my shoulder. One thing I loved about her was how she could read my thoughts.

"Don't grieve, Dave. She'll find her way, or not. Being a young mother isn't the end of the world, especially in this family."

I had my own opinion, but men, when confronted with femaleness, need to know when to shut up. I shut up.

The wedding, mercifully short, was performed by Brother Ralph. Like many before him, he had felt the "call" of God. In the normal course of events he might have been given a few trial sermons and eventually even found his way to a seminary for formal training, to emerge "Reverend Ralph." But along his path he also developed a particular taste for rotgut moonshine. This taste shaped his career, but by no means curtailed it. It took a special sort of person to live among the Cedar Choppers, and seminaries did not, perhaps, provide the specialized training he had acquired.

"...and so, by the power vested in me, I pronounce you, Man and Wife," Brother Ralph grandly pronounced.

Sabina kissed her new husband, a scraggly sort of boy with a wisp of a beard on his chin. I sincerely doubted either of them had a clue what they were getting into, but the human race is built in numbers by the fertile clueless, and managed by the more experienced, jaded survivors.

Sally Rae and I proceeded to the reception line. The boy's family was not represented, but there sat four generations of Sabina's female fore-bearers.

Sabina's mother, Ima Gene, 32, had mental issues. The common opinion was that some of the moonshine she drank might have been more methanol and acetone than honest hooch. Her favorite pastime was directing traffic in Quick Fix when she was naked as a jay bird. Arney, the policeman, hauled her in the first few times, but since this was Quick Fix he soon concluded this was, at heart, a family problem. After all, people in Quick Fix were good at living with family problems, almost as good as creating them. Plus, with Ima Gene, any sign of mental activity at all, illness included, was considered a plus. I extended my hand and we shook.

Sabina's grandmother, Sara Gene, 45, was the outlaw of the tribe. She worked as a research librarian in Heartbreak's Public Library. Most of the tribe claimed to distrust her for her bookish ways, but the truth is, without her input for everything from snake-bite remedy to land tax law, the others wouldn't have lasted long in the modern world. I extended my hand and we shook.

Sabina's great grandmother, Maida Beth, 60, was a full time gardener. Her fresh vegetables and canned fruits staved off scurvy and even outright starvation for the extended tribe. Rumor had it that her marijuana harvests were the main cash crops, competing even with the tribe's moonshine for financial dominance; but then, I tried to avoid rumors. I extended my hand and we shook.

Sabina's great, great grandmother, Jimmy Lynne, 74 was something of a local legend. In the Summer of Love, 1968, she had been one of the Flower Children in San Francisco's Haight Ashbury district. I extended my hand and she bit me, **bit *me hard*!**

In the next minute a big, raw-boned redneck, the biggest mud-sucking cedar chopper of them all, stepped out of the shadows and grabbed Sally Rae by her hips. He planted a huge smack on her lips. Both his hands rose toward Sally Rae's upper parts in a universal way that even a citified flat-lander like me could identify. In a flash I stepped forward and hit him on the point of his chin with all the strength I had.

Sally Rae was no wilting rose. With equal speed she raised her knee in another universal gesture guaranteed to change any man's channel, especially if he was tuned into lust.

The giant went down, went down hard, and he stayed down.

At that moment Arney stepped out of the shadows and slapped handcuffs on me. "You're coming with me, Dave," he said in a tone that allowed no argument.

Maida Beth walked up to us, all of a sudden, smiling a big smile. Arney reached inside her blouse. To my astonishment he pulled out a straight razor. "Not this time, Maida Beth," he said, pushing her backwards. "The Law is claiming this here guy, now all you just back off!" I hadn't ever heard that tone from Arney before, though I knew his job wasn't just returning little lost dogs and writing parking tickets.

Arney pulled me to his car and we sped off, into the night. I barely had time to pitch my truck keys to Sally Rae.

"Arney, can you tell me what the heck was going on back there, and why I'm under arrest?" I asked.

"Dave, you're lucky to be alive. Great great grandmother Jimmy Lynne bit you. You were the chosen one. Did you notice that you were in a fight less than a minute later?"

"Uh, yeah. That big redneck was putting his hands on Sally Rae," is said defensively.

"Well, from the moment she bit you, you were a marked man. If you stayed you would have been in one fight after another until you were either dead, or wished you were. On the odd chance you survived, you would be one of them. You don't know how lucky you are to have your initiation canceled."

Arney pulled in next to our driveway, opened my cuffs, and said, "Get out. Get some antiseptic on that bite, or maybe snake-bite medicine. Stay away from the Cedar Choppers, if you got any sense."

I got out, a little shaken, and I got in the truck with Sally Rae. Home never looked so good.

ONE SHOT AT HAPPINESS

The wife-to-be looked beautiful,
Her father wore a crooked smile,
The groom, dressed in a barrowed suit,
Sweated at the end of the aisle.

The preacher brought the short version,
And was ready to do his part,
There were no guests and no flowers,
No music to signal the start.

The bride waddled down to the front,
Dad's "Promise Keeper" was in view,
It was brought along to make sure,
The groom came across with "I do."

Marlene Tucker

THE AGE OF PLAGUES

JANEY AND I ARRIVED IN HEARTBREAK almost three years ago like refugees. I was fleeing a painful divorce and about all I had besides Janey was a broken-down pickup truck and a bad attitude.

My, how time heals! Now I was married to Sally Rae and a struggling goat ranch. We had sort of inherited Li'l' Billy, an overly bright 4-year-old and who loved being Janey's little brother, and now Janey was ready to go off to college.

Janey was my special pride. She had grown prettier and smarter every day she was there. I managed to cobble together some special state loans and soon she and Cricket, her best friend, were going to go off for their education. I was thrilled for her.

That all changed the afternoon I came in and Janey gave me her special look.

"Daddy, let's talk," she said.

I knew the tone well enough that I took her seriously. She had my complete attention.

"Ok, let's talk," I said.

"It's not just going to be just me and Cricket," she said. "Jimmy Hawkins is going with us."

"Fine, fine, some education could help out that boy," I said. Despite the intense summer heat I felt a sudden chill start around my ankles.

90

"We are all going to get a house together," she continued. "It just has 2 bedrooms."

"So you and Cricket are going to be roommates? Good deal."

"No, Cricket is going to be by herself," Janey replied.

I remembered that Janey and Jimmy had been dating since Christmas. I did the math. The chill rapidly spread upwards. I was massively underwhelmed.

"No, no way," I said. I'm still not sure if I was denying the situation or permission, but "NO" was the only word I had.

"Look, I'm 18. I don't see how you can stop us."

She had me there. At 18, a father has little moral suasion; that Janey considered me to be much above a babbling idiot was testimony to our good relationship. Actually, as a father I only had one real card to play — the money card.

"It just isn't going to happen, Janey. Push come to shove, I won't sign the papers."

At that moment she turned to tears and rushed out of the room. If it hadn't been for my years, I might have cried, too.

That Sunday at Cottonwood Baptist Church, our preacher started a rare two-part sermon on the Children of Israel breaking free from the awful old Pharaoh.

When Israel was in Egypt's land,
Let My people go!
Oppressed so hard they could not stand,
Let My people go!

I'm not dense. It did not escape me that Janey sang loudest (and sweetest) of all. Daughters have got a way of making their presence felt, bless their little hearts. Indeed, in my limited but robust experience, if God and a daughter believe in something, it will come about. If only Daughter believe in it, God tends to shift positions. Nobody said parenting was easy.

To make matters worse, Sally Rae didn't automatically back me like she usually did.

"Dave, she's going to grow up no matter what you want. Did you think Nature gave her all that prettiness for your benefit? She's going to go her own way."

"I don't want to hear it," I said, sharper than I meant to; my reward was that Sally Rae looked away from me, all hurt.

Call it happenstance if you will, but that week crickets got into an old feed sack in our kitchen storage room. We suddenly had hundreds of the things hopping around the kitchen. At night when I closed my eyes to sleep they would jump on my face. About the third day I found the feed sack, and fed the grain and the crickets to the goats.

Next, as I brushed my teeth, my mouth began to burn. I spat and to my horror I saw little black things crawling out of the toothpaste tube. I looked at my toothbrush and ants were all over it. I went to the kitchen and ants were all over the counter. I spent half a day spreading Borax behind the counter and furniture.

As I sat reading for an hour in my small library, I thought I saw a blur near the corner of my eye. As I lay drowsing near sleep I heard a rustling in the pantry. I hoped it wasn't Jimmy Hawkins getting an urge for a late night snack. House rules exiled him at 10:00, rain or shine. A boy that size could starve the whole household come mid-winter. But as I listened I had my suspicions it was something much smaller.

On the third day of the ant invasion, as I began to clean up the millions of little carcasses, I noticed that many of them were sort of oval-shaped. I put on my glasses and sure enough, they were mouse pills. I opened the pantry and what wasn't eaten had been wasted by these furry little pillagers! If I could grow goats as fast as I grew mice, I'd be the richest rancher in Texas. Unfortunately, that was not to be the case.

Of course, with the mice came the fleas. I don't know why, but fleas prefer me over a new-born puppy. They just love to sting and torment me something fierce.

Wednesday night I dragged my family down to Cottonwood Baptist Church. I needed a little fortification and I chose spiritual over spirits. I didn't want to give away any turf in this fight with my little blonde Puritan. True, I had the moral high ground, but we all know that satisfies about as much as kissing your sister. It might be pleasant, but there's no future in it.

Sure 'nuff, in no time we were back to darn old Moses. With the pre-sanctified look of a martyr, Janey sang:

David Mosley

No more shall they in bondage toil,
Let My people go!
Let them come out with Egypt's spoil,
Let My people go!

Thursday morning Li'l' Billy said, "Daddy, can I run outside to the swing?" I was real pleased he'd asked so nice and in plain English, too. "Sure Li'l' Billy, go ahead."

Moments later I heard his shrieks. Any parent has a fine sense of when a child's cry is nagging, sleepy or just a lung exercise. Li'l' Billy's cry was sheer pain and terror.

I rushed outside and saw instantly what was happening. A dozen big red wasps buzzed around his little head, diving in for a sting whenever they felt like it. I grabbed him and ran for the back door. For the next hour I gave him antihistamines, ice packs, and a heap of prayer. He finally settled down to a troubled nap. Despite his swelling he breathed easily.

I don't usually get mad at nature, but I was mad at these wasps. They had hurt my child! I made a torch from rolled up newspaper and walked out to his swing set. I felt murder in my heart. I wanted to commit insect-icide with extreme prejudice.

Sure enough, there was the nest, right under his swing. I lit my torch and held it right under the nest that grew on the bottom of the swing.

A breeze sprang up and blew a spark in my eye; I dropped the torch and backed up. It took me a minute to get clear, and I was blinded. Darkness at noon! I groped my way over to the faucet and felt for the hose. In my blindness I got it off, and washed my eyes. When I could finally see again I didn't like what I saw at all. The torch I had dropped had blown over to my lawn mower. To my horror the gas tank exploded.

The first casualty was Sally Rae's favorite rose bush. This burning bush brought me no wisdom. It was next to the front steps. It didn't take a genius to figure out that the next casualty was likely to be the whole dern house. I screwed the hose back on and got to squirting. It was a close call, but I saved the homestead.

About then I heard Janey's clear, high, soprano voice,

93

Heartbreak, Texas

You need not always weep and mourn,
Let My people go!
And wear these slav'ry chains forlorn,
Let My people go!

For the first time in my Judeo-Christian heritage, I started to sympathize with old Pharaoh. Maybe he had more of a case than I had given him credit for. Rulers, even minor despots like myself, are often misunderstood.

I walked the long walk up to my mailbox. I was in a plain, mad funk. On the way, a skunk crossed my path. I held real still until he was gone. I wasn't feeling too lucky that day.

When I got to my mailbox, I had eight letters. One was from the County Ag agent warning about increased wasp infestation this year. The second was a flier from BJ's Hardware about a mouse trap sale. But three were from the county and three more were marked "State of Texas." The tenth plague had arrived!

I'm a big enough man to know when I'm licked. I had decided that deNile wasn't Pharaohs' private creek. I had all I could take.

"Janey, come on down, darlin'. It's time we talked."

Your foes shall not before you stand,
Let My people go!
And you'll possess fair Canaan's land,
Let My people go!

DREAMS BE TWEEN
(Circa 1963)

She stands up on her tippy toes,
To hang the laundry in three straight rows,
Underneath the clear blue Texas sky,
Dreaming while the clothes get dry.

Daddy treats her like a baby,
Momma says she's a little lady,
Not woman or child but in between,
She can't wait to be fourteen.

Sweeping with an old corn straw broom,
Dancing her chores in the living room,
Her imagination swings and sways,
Lost in thoughts of future days.

Thinking of boys and young desire,
Are certain signs of a building fire,
Daydreams are useful to quench in part,
The yearnings of a young girl's heart.

Marlene Tucker

MY WOMAN

MY WOMAN, MY WIFE, SALLY RAE,
gets up every morning at 5 and drives into Heartbreak Texas and
fixes breakfast for about a third of the town. She cooks so good that
if Heartbreak had two restaurants, the other one would go broke real
soon.

Anyway, Sally Rae married me despite her whole family saying I
was short of prospects. I was, true enough, but I work hard and clean
up fairly good on Fridays. Many times I put more money into a goat
than I sell her for, but when you see the new crying baby about to
bleat out her short life for lack of $3 of colostrum milk, or your best
lead female nanny's caught in bob wire, with cuts that have to have a
vet's attention, what can you do?

Many times Sally Rae's pay check covered the mortgage when
my end fell short. She never begrudged me a cent; we were in love, a
special gift, and that was all that mattered between us. Love forgives
all sins, cherishes each other, remarks on the good and is forgiving
to the bad, just like it says in Chronicles II. We had it said at our
wedding and it is our Constitution, our way of loving each other.

Over time our relationship had grown from my driving my old
broken down pickup truck into Heartbreak and getting a Dr Pepper
about 4 in the afternoon. Sally Rae and I had both picked up a few
extra pounds over the years, but we loved each other. The rest of it
really didn't matter. People age. I found beauty in my darling, and if
others did not, so what? Our love was private.

So were some other things. Sally Rae had birthed a child out of wedlock more than 20 years ago. Her fiancé had died in an accident the night before her wedding, and most people in Heartbreak didn't hold her son's mistimed birth against her; but it did sort of take her off the marriage market until I came along. I saw Sally Rae as a treasure; I loved her passionately, and I had no apologies for her past behavior (or my own).

Anyway, I had a hard day that day. I'd had half a dozen things make me mad. My lead billy had died of nematodes. His first symptom was putting four feet into the air and biting his tongue. It was hard luck for him, but a $1,200 loss for me. The goats had found a new way to break out (normal), but they had run into a pack of coyotes, and I lost four more.

Li'l' Billy had just discovered his special man thing and maybe developed his first testosterone; anyway he had peed in all four corners of the kitchen. I took it as symptomatic of his special brightness that he marked his territory in the most important room of our house.

"Li'l' Billy, why are you peeing on everything?" I asked.

"*Offer the Gods no wine from an unpruned grapevine,*" he responded.

Oh my gosh, he had gotten into my Pythagoras again! At 4-years-old, Li'l' Billy could read most anything, but his interpretations often made sense only to God and to him. Increasingly, I feared even God was a little bewildered with some of Li'l' Billy's musings.

It was a tough day, but not unusual in a town called Heartbreak.

So I left off Li'l' Billy with Lizzy Bennett, next door, for a few minutes and I went into see Sally Rae at The Watering Hole Café. It was just like we were courting again. Darn it, I was fed up and I needed a break.

I walked in and ordered my Dr Pepper and a slice of cold vinegar pie. Sally Rae treated me like any other customer at the counter, served me up, and we both glowed a little bit. Arney, our town policeman, was on my left and I took an open seat beside him.

The cedar chopper on my right smelled like a man who hadn't taken a bath in a week. His cheeks had a gristly three-day beard and I'd bet he didn't own a washing machine. I decided to tolerate him and ignore him; maybe he'd endured a hard day, too.

"Here you go, sir," Sally Rae said, setting my afternoon sugar fix down in front of me.

"Fill me up with hot coffee, you lazy, fat whore," the cedar chopper next to me said to my Sally Rae.

What happened next was sort of automatic. Sally Rae's face went hurt. My honey, my darling, looked like a hungry 6-year-old that had been slapped for begging for a cookie.

I went into overdrive. I raised my glass straight into his face so hard he fell off the stool. A part of me knew he out-weighed me by 70 pounds, mostly youth and muscle, and a bigger part knew I didn't care. I picked up my bar stool and I had hit him at least three times when my lights went out.

I woke up with a heck of a headache. Old Doc Bailey was shinning a light in my eyes. I saw bars, and a part of me recollected that I was in jail.

Arney, the local policeman, was looking down at me, but there were two of him. Gosh, it felt like Saturday morning, but I knew it was only Thursday.

"What happened?" I asked Arney.

"I broke my new flashlight over your head before you killed that guy. How're you feeling?"

I could tell from the sound of his voice that Arney was real concerned about me, and I got to feeling embarrassed about putting Arney out. "I'm fine, I guess. You mean you broke your shiney new black one over my head?"

"Yeah, that one."

"Well, sorry, Arney. I know you were right proud of it."

Arney got all official then. "I have to write you a ticket, then. Pay $5 or spend five days in jail."

Sally Rae came into my vision then. "Here's $5. It's my whole tip jar for today."

I wanted to tell her that Arney had just given me a heck of a deal, but things went a little foggy again and I shut up. Sally Rae had saved me again.

Arney got all official and said, "Don't go brawling again in a public place. It won't be $5 and a headache next time."

I took a warning and went on home. I will put up with whatever happens to me, but if something cuts my lady, that same something cuts me twice as deep. Sally Rae has earned her respect. I mean it.

I do love my darling. I do love my whole family, period. I know I can't be there every time someone hurts them or disrespects them; I know I can't use a bar stool and beat some senseless cretin cedar chopper half to death every time it ought to happen, but a part of me wishes that I could.

Later that evening Sally Rae and I took our special time together on the front porch. To us this was the most special time of the day, our recounting. It kept us close.

"Did I make a damn fool of myself today?" I asked.

"Naw, but you're no hero either. Don't go gettin' in bar brawls, Dave. It don't build the reputation you want."

We talked about the whole thing 'til Sally Rae said she had to go to bed, if she was going to get Heartbreak up in the morning. I kissed her and she went to bed.

It's a funny thing about a head injury. That night, I couldn't sleep at all, but I kept on looking over at my Sally Rae, her face all angelic in the moonlight, and I had no regrets about a hard day in Heartbreak Texas.

THE ANCHOR AND THE CHAIN

Lord, help me to appreciate
The fine woman that I've got.
She does her part in our marriage,
And doesn't ask for a whole lot.

She runs the house and keeps the yard,
Never once does she complain.
I count on her when times get hard,
She's the anchor for this old chain.

So, Lord, please send a reminder,
When she fixes up real nice,
To stop and take time to notice,
And mention it once or twice.

It seems so corny just to say,
"Honey, I'm glad you're my wife."
But Lord, it's You and me that know,
She's the best part of my life.

Marlene Tucker

THE WORST 10 MINUTES

I JUST HAD THE WORST 10 MINUTES OF
my life. I've had my share of bad experiences; the day my momma
died, the day my daddy died, the day my first wife told me she loved
someone else. I had the day a chain saw reared up, and I looked
down at my shoulder bone and my rib cage on display like Grey's
Anatomy. That day I dropped the saw, got in my truck, and I drove
that old truck a half mile to the nearest help. It hurt, but it never hurt
like today.

Heartbreak is a little off the maps and it's a little weird, but most
people here are real, real in away the talking heads on TV sorta miss.
People in Heartbreak wake up facing a long hot day of fixing fences,
slopping hogs, washing dishes by hand, and they *smile*. Work in
Heartbreak is not some sort of life sentence; when we wake up every
day it is a new opportunity to be alive, to establish one's integrity
before God and everybody, to do work that says, "I AM!"

I sort of understand the people of Nepal. In the United States, we
talk a lot about Gross National Product, or GNP. In Nepal, they are
more worried about GNH, or Gross National Happiness. I have no
clue how they can measure it or promote it, but GNH sounds pretty
good to me. I expect Heartbreak may be a little short on GNP, but we
have lots of GNH.

Since I moved to Heartbreak my GNH has gone right up. My
beautiful daughter Janey has gone off to college. She has a right good
chance of making a good life for herself. I met Sally Rae, the main

101

lady at The Waterin' Hole Café; we fell in love and married. A stray cousin on his way to the Canadian oil fields dropped a savant little boy on us. To our mutual surprise, Li'l' Billy filled a void in our lives we didn't even know existed!

Anyway, I picked up Sally Rae late at night on Saturday at The Waterin' Hole. Of course, Li'l' Billy was strapped into his seat, and I called ahead to Sally Rae. We started home.

"Dave," Sally Rae started, "you know I serve drinks, and there's always some fool who thinks he's so drunk no woman can resist him. Anyway, there was a kid tonight that topped all the charts! I finally had to cut him off from buying more drinks, I threatened to call Arney, but he just went out to his truck and I bet he had more there. Then he....*Oh, God, he's right behind us coming up fast!*"

"Watch out, we're....we just got hit!" I said. Arney wasn't in sight, and I make a decision. It's a bad time to get out of my truck. We got a jolt, but Rosie, my pickup, ran fine and we kept rolling. Home was close.

The drunken idiot behind us followed too close for a while, and then he commenced to showing off. He ran back and forth between the left and the right lanes, only topped the hills in the on-coming lanes, and then he would stop all of a sudden just in front of us. Beside any of his other stupid antics, I could not afford a doctor bill, a truck repair, and most of all; this drunk, aggressive moron was trying to kill my family!

I pulled to the side of the road and I waited for him to drive off. Of course, I got optimistic after a while that he passed out. I tried to drive on home; instantly his lights snapped on and he kept harassing us. So much for passive tactics. My anxiety for my family topped my anger at his stupidities. Yeah, I was ready to fight, but my family came first. For them, I would take anything.

It isn't that far from Heartbreak to my ranch, and eventually me and my family made it. Stupid drunk as he was, he wasn't stupid enough to set foot or tire on my private property. We Texans got our ways. Another foot on my property and I would have announced a contest where there could only be one winner, somebody would die, and some mother would be weeping in the corner. I was there in the moment. I was that spiked. This was my family. I'm a gentle enough sort of guy, but if he had followed us down our drive, one of us would had died pretty quick. I'm a Baptist, I have my limit.

At the same time, I knew this was some alcohol-poisoned kid, too full of testosterone and youth to know limits. I knew odds were that if he could survive the night that he would probably be a good man. I guess, looking back, the most important thing is that we all got out of it alive.

That evening I carried Li'l' Billy inside, scooped all close to me. My other arm had held Sally Rae's, and we grasp each other with the knowledge that life was short, often unfair, but sometimes love could happen. We knew the high side of blessing: We *knew* we were blessed. We were all home and safe.

Anyway, we reported the whole incident to Arney and he said he would keep a watch out. I switched out my .22 mag. for a .357 engine busting mag., carried it around for about 6 months, and then I got tired of the weight. That is about how long I was mad, too. I swear, I hated that guy, but hating takes a lot of work. It's harder than fencing, tougher than cornstalks, and meaner than a teenage skunk; hating is a lot of work. Holding a grudge takes a lot of effort, especially against an unknown face in an unlikely situation.

Sometimes at night I wake up. Sometimes at night I worry. Usually I go right back to sleep. Sometimes I put my leg out next to Sally Rae's long, silken leg, then I sigh, feel her warmth, and then I sleep.

DRUNKEN DNA

He came passing against the yellow line.
He had a drunken grin on his face.
He pulled his truck right in front of me,
Let off the gas and closed up the space.

He veered near to the edge of the bar ditch,
Weaving crazy on the shoulder a while.
He waved his beer bottle out the window,
Then sped up in the wrong lane for a mile.

O'l smiley didn't make it much further,
He jumped the median and flipped his truck.
I could hear him wailing when I got out.
His being alive took more than good luck.

The drunk went off in an ambulance,
The cop said "Don't worry about that fool.
People who drink and drive have their own way,
Of taking stupid out of the gene pool."

Marlene Tucker

THE TRIBES OF HEARTBREAK

HEAT

I've never heard a Texan complain about the end of the heat. Every summer, some kid makes the news by frying an egg on a sidewalk, no other heat needed. Natives feel something similar with their brains every afternoon about 3. Feeling the heat break is a cause of universal rejoicing.

Of course, not everyone makes it. Old Man Johnson died last week, just two days after his air conditioner went out. He was too tight to fix it. Nobody questioned the cause of death. All his life Johnson was a thorn in everyone's side. He'd stomp out of church in the middle of a sermon if he didn't get his own peculiar brand of theology. He sued neighbors, beat his dogs, and once cussed his milk cows so hard they gave sour cream for two weeks.

We all stood at the Cottonwood Baptist Cemetery, sweating in our dark suits. Mitty Johnson, his widow, was about as sweet as Johnson was ornery. Preacher Horace Hollis droned on and on, "…and God, you know all our ways, and judge us fair and right, as I know you will this good and kind man."

Remarkable how saintly a man can get by dying.

"…and love him well, until the Resurrection. Amen" Rev. Hollis finished. We all said a loud "Amen" before the Preacher got any more inspiration.

About then Mitty struggled to her feet. "Open the coffin once more," she said in a surprisingly strong voice.

"Mitty, is that wise?" Reverend Hollis asked. "I mean the heat and all...."

"Open it, Reverend," she demanded. "I've always done my duty and I won't be stopped now. Either you got the wrong sermon or you got the wrong man in that coffin!"

The heat about had me. I stopped in for a cold drink and to see Sally Rae at The Waterin' Hole Café. Truth is, Sally Rae looked better and better the longer I knew her. Like most everything in Heartbreak she had a little wear and tear, but she also had two tone green and blue eyes my Janey described as "the color of love." Sally Rae just loved serving things to people. I was glad she'd stopped trying to serve me up to Miss Scarlett who, as usual, sat on two stools just down the bar.

"...and Sally Rae, look what I got at that garage sale for just $2.98!" Miss Scarlett held up a two piece bathing suit that almost made me choke on my vinegar pie. It wasn't so much so small in size until you compared it to all the area it had to cover. I mean, imagine Rhode Island trying to clothe Texas. Strippers got arrested with more on than all the fleshy acres that little wisp could hope to hide.

I quickly hit the road before I said something intemperate. As usual, my truck's air conditioner was out. My burying suit was about to bake me! I felt dizzy, then nauseous. Heartbreak Lake was just off to the left. All native Texans have faced heat exhaustion at one time or another. We take these symptoms seriously as an Eskimo guarding against frost bite. On an impulse born of great discomfort I pulled off to a secluded little spot locally known as "necessity point." In no time, I struggled out of all that black cloth and dove in. Ah, sweet relief! Cool water washed away my impending melt down. Texans endure the heat, but nothing can make us love it.

I was about ready to head home when I heard a snicker from the bank of the lake. There stood three local women and Miss Scarlett in ALL her glorious wonder. Acres of milky flesh bulged out around a few wisps of fabric.

"Dave, you ain't decent," she yelled. "You could get arrested, running around like that."

I was well and truly busted. "Any chance of a little privacy while I get to my truck?" I asked, dropping to my neck in the murky waters.

"Heck no!" she said, and all her friends laughed again. "What you gonna do about it?" More laughter deepened my humiliation.

Don't ever embarrass a nekkid man. There are limits. "In a world where the dead are all saints and those hankies you're wearing count as modesty, I may be nekkid but I know damn well I'm decent." I walked to my truck and drove on home.

That night, Janey giggled several times for no apparent cause. I finally broke down.

"Darling," I asked my daughter, "what IS it?"

"Why, Daddy, the whole town's just wondering why you went running down Main Street in your birthday suit."

The story was already growing its own legs. Rule One: If you have to explain you're already lost. I sighed. "I guess my brain just got fried like an egg on the sidewalk."

A Few Words at Fred's Funeral
some spoken, (some muttered)

Here he lies
(He always did)
And when he's buried
(He'll be hid)

We will mourn
(His rotten soul)
For who he was.
(And what he stole).

The friends he had
(He had my wife)
Will think of him.
(His lousy life)

This man has died
(What a relief)
He was called home
(He was called a thief)

He enjoyed life
(He enjoyed my wife)
We wish him here
(So he'd die twice)

Let's say a prayer
(Yes, bow your head)
To thank the Lord
(That now Fred's dead.)

Marlene Tucker

Food on Fords

ABOUT TWO YEARS AGO I MOVED TO
Heartbreak, Texas with my 16-year-old daughter, Janey. Heartbreak is a century behind Houston in technology, and a century ahead in general decency.

For one thing, people in Heartbreak really care about one another. One way they proved this was by feeding their shut-ins, their old and the cripples. They called themselves "Food on Fords" — not wanting to presume on any other organization's name. It's just natural that they meet at Great Aunt Katy's house. In it she has raised 11 children of her own, five strays, and several grandchildren. Now her old house looked older than Great Aunt Katy, but, like her, all the important parts still worked.

Inside she had a State of the Art Propane Powered Kitchen (circa 1940). Just behind her house she has a wood fired summer kitchen (circa 1900). Behind that was a chicken house, next to a year-round garden, and the whole batch was fenced by a stand of live oaks that were mighty trees even when Great Aunt Katy was a pretty 16-year-old girl herself. Her front porch is the serving station and three times a week the poor and the needy get a meal that money couldn't buy.

Of course, she didn't work alone.

The Lunch Crew met at Great Aunt Katy's. Chipper, her ancient monkey, helped by bringing in a newly-laid egg every few minutes. He marched along on his old spindly legs, poker faced, like an old soldier marching into battle. Most times he carried a single egg. He

109

had a unique way of spurring egg production along, though.

If he couldn't get an egg he'd be likely to yank off a leg or a wing instead. Great Aunt Katy's chickens knew this and generally produced for all they were worth. When he brought in two or more legs or wings Great Aunt Katy would have a few curt words with Chipper, after which he would crawl into his favorite tree and sulk until dark. Great Aunt Katy next had to go to the hen house and commit a little euthanasia on the maimed hen; then she'd add Chicken-a-La-Chipper to the menu. Everyone who ever tasted it commented on its freshness.

Olive Green had married into Heartbreak. She just arrived from Dallas. Most people were willing to forgive that, but of course she brought a lot of other issues that made it difficult for her to fit in. Once she washed Great Aunt Katy's cast-iron skillet in soap and water!! Can you imagine? And then she used mix to make cornbread!! Great Aunt Katy forgave her, of course, because she must forgive in order to keep on being a Christian, but it was hard to overlook such ignorance in action. Still, Poor Olive was doing the best she could, bless her heart.

By anyone's standards, this was not an easy group to fit into. One day a state regulator of the food police variety breezed into town in a new sedan that he left parked in front of Great Aunt Katy's. He announced that everyone had a compulsory "Food Health and Standards" meeting right darn NOW!

His name was Rufus Toby, a deficiency he tried to make up for by standing tall and speaking in a tone of voice better reserved for drill sergeants than one addressing his elders. He had a six-hour food safety course the State of Texas required he present verbatim, and he loved to present it to any audience he could ensnare.

Underlying his verbosity was a deep seated belief that all things from nature were a biological threat to his very existence. Rufus was powered by fear, and, like all truly petty men, he thought his fear must make him the only enlightened human present. He even had a paper certificate from the State of Texas to ratify his fears, so he knew he must be right.

Young Rufus would have been a lot easier to take if he didn't go out of his way to look silly. Nature made him prematurely bald and wider at the hips than his shoulders, but it was Rufus Toby himself who choose to take most of his public speaking cues from a Bantam rooster.

Everyone lined up and sat down. Like many people, he confused Southern Politeness for subservience. He commenced to speak for an hour and 45 minutes about hair nets, temperature danger zones, and four-hour pathogen blooms.

Great Aunt Katy is 91, and three of the other women are older than her. Odds are that at her age she has a fairly good working knowledge of an older person's needs. Still, he wound on:"…and an older person has special needs, and these are…."

I glanced over Toby's shoulder and saw Chipper slipping into the new state sedan through an open window. Chipper didn't speak English, but he understood Emotion better than a hound dog. First, Chipper peed on the front seat, knelt over for something I couldn't see, and emerged with a large stack of papers. He began to throw out his gleanings one at a time.

A stray hen walked by and Chipper grabbed its feet and threw her in the window. A few papers were ejected, and then he reinvented the Frisbee with a stack of CDs. I caught one. It was labeled "Adverse Findings on the Elk Hill Meals on Wheels group." I quietly crumbled the disk in my pocket. Meanwhile Chipper sent more discs in all directions.

The captured hen ran in panicked circles around the interior of the car. Like most panicked birds, the poor hen started marking up the place pretty bad with high nitrogen chicken by-product.

Finally, Chipper threw one CD with particular vigor, catching Mr. Toby behind his left ear.

"Of course, a pathogen bloom is invisible and offers no initial taste…." and *whack!* The CD connected. Mr. Toby turned round and for once he had nothing to say, to the considerable relief of his audience.

He first stared in disbelief at the chicken, and then dodged another CD from Chipper. Mr. Toby just sort of inflated. For once his chest got bigger than his hips. He spun in midair and exclaimed, "Who did this? There's laws against harassing and assaulting a public official! Someone's going to go to jail for this!"

Great Aunt Katy jumped up and yelled, "Run, Chipper, run! You're a criminal now! I've tried to raise you right for 40 years and

111

I've failed. Run or the Texas Rangers will git you! No one escapes the Food Police."

Suddenly Parker House and Ginger Punch took up the cry. "Flee for your life, Chipper. The State Food Police will rub you out like a blooming bacillus! He won't care if you are a fungi or not!

Old Sloppy Joe ran out with a sandwich in his hand. "Eat this if you dare, Chipper. Its twenty minutes into the danger zone, so you might as well end everything. It's better than letting the Food Police get you."

Curley Endive had to get his two cents in as well, "Run Chipper. Them Food Police want to sterilize you first! It's no way for a good monkey to go!"

Rufus Toby looked around him in disbelief. His expression could not have been more shocked if his audience had morphed into werewolves.

"You're crazy, all crazy. I wouldn't let you crazy people wipe my windshield, much less prepare my food!" With that he hopped into his state sedan and began rolling down FM 454 toward the highway.

About two days later Great Aunt Katy got a call from the head Food Policeman in Austin, Texas. "Ma'am, I just got the strangest report about harassment of one of my inspectors on some kind of monkey business...."

Great Aunt Katy cut him off short, "Don't listen to a word that idgit says. He's not only a supercilious dang little fool; he's a chicken thief, too. Just look at the inside of his car."

A Petty Incident

Mr. Petty, the mayor-appointed,
Neighborhood trash can police,
Canvassed the total four streets of the town,
With citations ready to release.

He pulled up in front of the Jones' place,
Waiting for a crowd to grow.
He pulled out his pen and began to write,
Putting on a pompous show.

"Your two trash cans are in violation,
No lids, and look at the flies!
I'll have to write you out a citation."
The owner watched with despise.

"The flies belong to the city," Jones said,
"It's them, I didn't do it."
"You tryin' to make a fool of me, son?"
Jones replied, "Naw, nature beat me to it."

Marlene Tucker

The Age of Information

In Heartbreak I hoped to find a more basic, natural sort of human, a place with sweet air, honesty, where a man's reputation still meant something. Well, Heartbreak is all that, but I overlooked something crucial; Eden had its snake and Heartbreak had its humans. I could quote scripture or just curse, but it would all come out about the same.

I had the internet, or course. Nowadays a fella better know the price of slaughter goats in San Saba, Goldthwaite, and New Holland, Penn., or he can get skinned faster than his goats. Of course, I also used the Internet to keep up with old friends, and a surprising number of new ones in Heartbreak. In my milder moments I thought of this as a sort of emerging national conversation. Silly me. I forgot that the bow that first brought food to the tribe became a crossbow for hunting humans, that cars became tanks in less than a generation, and barely 10 years after the Wright Brothers flew their first airplane, humans were shooting each other down over the skies of France.

Anyway, I did my morning chores, checked my emails, and went to town to get a Dr Pepper at The Waterin' Hole Café. Sally Rae was the waitress; Sally and I had "reached an understanding" as the saying goes. Of course, Anyone, male or female, who has ever had any sort of romantic attachment knows that "understanding" between the sexes is almost always better described as "misunderstanding." True understanding, like Heaven, is a reward better sought in the far distant future and most romance is about trying to minimizing the damage.

"Hi, Sally Rae," I ventured as I walked in The Waterin' Hole. Silence screamed back at me. A wise man would have just ducked out and tried again in a few days, but I was trying to be "good," a very different goal indeed.

After about 20 seconds Sally Rae said, "Hi, yourself."

More deafening silence. She slammed a Dr Pepper down in front of me and walked off.

I quickly realized that I had been promoted to the bomb disposal squad. "Something wrong, Honey?" I ventured.

Her eyes flashed. "If I'm such a disappointment to you, you could at least be man enough to tell me up front, not hiding behind your darn old computer machine."

"What?" I asked.

"Just drink up and get on out. I don't want to even talk to you." With that, she teared up and ran out the back of the counter.

In retrospect, I see I should have chased her and settled things right then, but like I fool I tried to do what she said, and I left.

I ran into Miss Scarlet just outside, on the boardwalk. "Hi Dave," she smirked. "Feeling your oats, are you?"

I stood mystified. I looked over my shoulder and I swear she wiggled her rear end as she walked off. Given her proportions it looked like an earthquake in the Rockies.

Next, I ran into Emmitt Bennett, my neighbor who had the dubious distinction of being the only man in Heartbreak that managed to burn his house down while shooting at possums. He stopped loading feed long enough to say, "If you need it, well I wouldn't think much less of a man for taking it. Personally, Jack Daniels is good enough for me." He kept chuckling as he worked.

BJ Elkert walked up in front of me, and just stood there, looking me in the eye, and walked off without any greeting at all.

I always thought of Heartbreak as the soul of normal, but I suddenly had my doubts. Another part of me remembered when I was a school kid during the Cuban Missile Crisis. The teachers had us hide under our desks with our hands behind our heads for protection. Even in the fifth grade, we were smart enough to add "...bend down, way down, and kiss your rear goodbye." I didn't have a clue what was wrong but "bend, stretch, and kiss" was feeling like my likeliest option.

I picked up Janey and we drove home. She was silent and a little red faced. At times I would swear she was giggling. Some latent survival instinct kept my mouth shut.

Like most people when confused and needing information, I went to the Internet. I had about two dozen new mailings. They varied considerably in content, but eventually I realized that I had somehow downloaded some sort of robot-virus that had e-mailed all my friends, relatives, and business contacts the following message: "I've tried this new Viagra and boy, howdy, it's the Real Thing. It sure changed my life! There's also a Viagra Pink for ladies and I know it works." My name was signed below with a link to Canadian Pharmacies.com.

I immediately began opening the responses and sending personal apologies to one and all, while disclaiming responsibility. This is good training for a politician, but kinda hard on me personally.

The last message was from Great Aunt Katy. It said, "You were right about the Viagra Pink. Haven't had so much fun in years."

Way, way too much information.

Now I know why people call this the "Information Age." It sure isn't the "Age of Wisdom."

FACE BOOKED

No sooner said then words are spread,
On social media sites.
It's unnecessary gossip,
That sometimes comes back to bite.

Sandra dated a married man,
And then told her friend, Earlene,
Who accidentally posted it,
Complete with details obscene.

She could not hide on her device,
And no longer dates that guy.
In their small town the wife found her,
And gave her a big black eye.

Marlene Tucker

BEATING A DEAD HORSE

MY DAUGHTER JANEY AND I LIVE IN Heartbreak Texas, located 50 or 500 miles west of Houston's sushi bars. In Heartbreak women are strong, men are stronger, and children smell strongest of all. Heartbreak is a place that's still like it use to be, even if it never was.

Old Frank holds an auspicious position in Heartbreak society: he is about the orneriest old cuss of a rancher to be found in the whole area. Once when I visited he was milking a cow and steadily cussing it hard enough to curdle the milk before it hit the bucket. Most people agreed his happiest day of the year when he was castrating the yearling bulls. Old Frank is a direct ancestor of the type of Scots-Irish settler descended from a long line of bachelors that out fought Comanches, Mexican raiders, and anyone else they could get to play. Of course, Old Frank is a little more conservative than King George III, and maybe a little crazier, too.

Doc Sam is the county vet. He's about the same age as Old Frank, but no body has nerve enough to ask either one their age; most of us just say "older than God but not near as nice." He has several distinctions; he's even ornerier than Old Frank and he's the town Liberal. Somehow he keeps up with all Liberal views, never letting one go unless the Conservatives adopt it. I've heard him myself repeat William Jennings Bryan's speech about free silver and not crucifying farmers on a cross of gold. When Doc Sam accepts a point, he sticks to it.

Doc Sam and Old Frank are neighbors. Most Saturday evenings they stand on either side of the fence separating their property shouting insults and political slogans at each other. In their earlier years they ran against each other for a series of different offices until no one would vote for either one of them. Theirs is a peculiar relationship, peculiar in the sense that slavery was described as a "peculiar institution," but I always suspected that when one of them died, the other would feel a real sense of loss.

It transpired that Old Sam had an old, really old horse, Excelsior, whose final day had just about come. As Doc Sam put it, "His final day came and he missed the appointment; now I got to be an executioner because of his sloppy behavior."

"That's about what I expect you're good for, I sure never would take an animal to you if I expected it to survive," Old Frank complained. That, of course, was a whopper. No rancher could live long without the services of a vet. "Í raised that horse from a colt, but I can't see him suffer no more. I doubt he'll make this next cold snap, anyway. Will you do it or not?"

"Meet me tomorrow at our usual spot. Bring your backhoe, lets do it right," Doc Sam said. Saturday afternoon I drove in to Heartbreak. A sure 'nuff blue norther was heading our way. Most people who think about Texas think about the heat because there's so much of it, but our cold can match anybody's. It's a matter of record that most Texas weather records date back to about 1895 when one of these blue northers gripped Texas for weeks. Cattle froze standing up, even cattle in barns died. It wiped out more than one rancher and it put a real hurting on all the rest. It's just plain human to put off things until they're necessary; and I was like all the other ranchers, buying up excess hay and circulating heater pumps for the livestock.

Driving back home, I noticed Doc Sam's pickup on the hill that separates his place from Old Sam's. I saw the back hoe, but I didn't think too much of it.

Well, I had my hands full the next three days. Ice closed the roads; I steadily built fires in my barn stove and dripped water from the faucets. All my goats and my two donkeys looked at me with hurt in their eyes, as if to say "You're God, how could you let this happen? Make it stop!" Janey wasn't much better. The first morning I saw her sitting on the couch, all wrapped it blankets.

119

"Janey, darlin', why don't you fix us some breakfast while I make coffee?"

"NO. You fix me breakfast! I'm going to be a parrot. You fix it and feed me, or I'm just going to sit here and say words you'd swear you never taught me!"

So much for being snowed in with your loved ones.

After three days, I was tired of my goats, tired of Janey, and just a little bit crazy myself with cabin fever. I drove toward Heartbreak without even offering to take her; we needed milk and eggs but we didn't need each other about then.

As I neared the summit of the little hill just outside Heartbreak I noticed Doc's pickup and the back hoe, still out in the pasture. I almost drove on, but a tingle in the back of my head said something didn't look right. I pulled to the shoulder and jumped the fence.

First I heard two old men giving each other a cussing that would have expanded the vocabulary of most sailors. As I got closer I saw a sight that explains more human nature than I care to explore. Doc Sam and Old Frank were in the bottom of a hole over 8 feet deep. Old Frank was sitting on a dead horse's head and Doc was beating the late Excelsior's neck with a 2X4.

"What are you two old coots doing, beating that dead horse?" I yelled down to them.

"We figured that if we could get his head around, one of us might be able to step up high enough to get out," Doc Sam ventured. "You see, just as I gave him the shot he reared up and knocked us both in the hole. Probably we'd both froze to death that first night if Excelsior hadn't landed on us."

Frank picked it up, "Then we had to skin him to get warm. Sad way to treat an animal I raised from a colt. Anyway, we're about frozen to death, ready to try anything," Old Frank added. "We've been stuck here 3 days and I don't think either of us could last much longer."

They both looked up at me, eyes so pitiful I suddenly flashed back to my poor goats.

"OK, here's the deal. I can go get a ladder and in an hour you'll both be out, or one of you can bend over while the other crawls up on his back. I can get you warm in about 10 minutes."

They looked dumbfounded, then considered to their options. Some understanding passed between them. Doc Sam looked up and said, "Get the dang ladder."

As I drove off to get the ladder I tried to be angry, but really, Congress wasn't doing much better.

A Peacock's Tale

Mr. Suttle found a peacock
His neighbor, Spoak, wanted one too.
The bird traveled from yard to yard,
Doing whatever peacocks do.

Mr. Suttle claimed it as his,
Putting the peacock in a pen.
Mr. Spoak thought it was unfair,
And turned the shared bird loose again.

Suttle fed it in the mornings,
Spoak did his feedings before night.
When they heard it crying for help,
The rescue turned into a fight.

The men fought from early evening
Until the next day just passed noon.
The bird, who missed both feedings thought,
"I was subtle but spoke too soon!"

Marlene Tucker

MAENADS

IT WAS AT THE WATERIN' HOLE CAFÉ
I found Sally Rae. After countless Dr Peppers and her special vinegar pie, we became lovers. We are special, in the ways that only lovers are to one another. We got married, determined to live happily ever after.

God gave me fair warning about the nature of the new day. He gave me fair warning as I sipped my first cup of hot coffee. When I gathered clothing on the floor, I tried picking up one of Sally Rae's bras. A hook caught in the rug and stretched it taut, then it released and popped me in the face. I survived with a small cut above my left eye.

My new bride piped up, "Dave, drink that coffee now and stay away from anything sharp or mechanical until the caffeine has a chance to do some good!"

Like every newly-married couple in history we were getting to know each other, and for us it was good, mostly. Sally Rae brought me a cup of fresh brewed coffee every morning, and it generally helped prevent me from hurting myself or others around me as I struggled to generate a brain wave.

Sally Rae and I are both floating on the post-honeymoon cloud. This sort of cloud is about as close to "true happiness" as a human gets for any length of time. I don't take such things for granted and neither does Sally Rae. The world seems to conspire against such happiness and we were both determined to make ours last as long as possible. This is where we both were when my new mother-in-law came for a visit.

Beth May was my new mother-in-law's name, though I slipped and almost called her "Death Ray" to her face more than once.

When a body gets married he or she is real focused on the prospective spouse, and this is one of the main reasons so many marriages still happen, despite the institution's dismal track record. If we approached with more common sense and fewer hormones, well, odds are the human race would have disappeared a long time ago.

Anyway, I wasn't the first man who was a little shaken by his new mother-in-law. Beth May was about four inches shorter than either Sally Rae or me, but this meant little since Beth May was such a forceful personality. If her size matched what she projected, well she could have taken down the Incredible Hulk. Worse, she had been a real young mother in her time, so she was only two years younger than me.

"It don't signify," Sally Rae said about the age thing.

"It don't glorify, either," I responded.

"Momma's just happy to see me safely married," Sally Rae said.

"Every one of your four sisters has been married at least twice and I think Death Ray has flat lost count. Why should you getting married make your mother feel more secure?

"Why Darlin'," Sally Rae said with a toss of her pretty head, "we're just a family of optimists."

I also wondered what had happen to all those men, but some questions are better left unasked. I had a lot of confidence in my new bride, even if her mother made me a little nervous.

Beth May was a sort of cute, tidy little woman, in her own way, but she often fixed me with a stare of such frank appraisal I wanted to hide. Also, after a couple of frosty adult beverages in the evening she would start flirting with me enough that I felt down right uncomfortable. I didn't know if she was real, or testing me to see if I would come on to any female that might be willing. She was one temptation I found easy to resist.

I came down stairs for breakfast and Sally Rae smiled her million-dollar smile and said "Mornin', Darlin'."

"Good morning, Dear."

Beth May asked, "And what are you up to today?" A mother needs to check out the soon-in-law to see if he works, is fit, is up to the job. **Her** history isn't under review.

"I'm going out, down to the church. Remember? It's work day." I replied.

"That's right," Sally Rae said, "We'll be along about noon with a covered lunch."

Our church, Cottonwood Baptist, kept everybody busy two or three Saturdays a year with maintenance chores. Here in Heartbreak, everyone was always short on cash but long on know-how. That day I was packing my carpenter and plumbing tools. Lately "potty parity" had been a hot issue so I joined a group of men in order to move a wall between the men's room and the women's so that women had a little more maneuvering room. Women seem real big on maneuvering.

I never knew I was a male dominant pig, bent on suborning women's roles in the life of our church and society in general, until Olive Green brought us all up to date. Olive was from Dallas. She married Dale Green and the whole town was kinda trying to get her settled in, all comfortable and such, but she made it hard with her outsider ways. She insisted on washing the church's cast- iron skillet with soap and water, and rumor had it that she used store-bought envelopes of corn bread mix instead of mixing it from scratch. Old Jeb Potter, 96, had died after last Sunday's meal on the grounds, with a mouthful of Olive's cornbread still in his jaws; but still, nobody said an unkind word. We wanted Olive Green to be one of ours, new blood in an old town. Besides, Jeb had been sort of "free" and "gassy" for the last decade or so. If it was an exchange, it was a good one.

Sally Rae sat before me with a group of women about her age. I was held up at the last minute, splashing chlorine on what had been men's porcelain, now converted to feminine use. I sat beside her, not grouping into men's and women's groups like most people, and I heard: "...after the bottom split I hurt like hell, little Simon was crowning, but he wanted to stay a little longer. The doctor split me and I thought it would hurt but...."

I had sat down in the middle of a serious discussion on specifics of giving birth. I tried to eat and be respectful, but I soon found I couldn't do either.

"Sally Rae, I'm gonna go eat with the boys," I said as I exited. "After that, I'm going to T. J. Wrigley's place, south of Quick Fix, and get some hay for the goats."

Beth May broke off from her own discourse about how Sally Rae's birth damn near turned her inside out, gave her hemorrhoids too, and turned to me,

"Don't linger none 'round Quick Fix, not if you're taking up with my girl."

She said it funny, but her eyes were not smiling, and none of the other women's were either. Quick Fix was a place south of town where "women were common but ladies were rare."

About then Li'l' Billy piped up, *"Influence is what you have until you get ready to use it."*

"Hush up, Li'l' Billy," I said.

I drove my old pickup down to TJ's place. TJ was a 70-something farmer, a recluse who seldom spoke. I kind of admired him for his toughness and independence, but I had few dealings with him in my past.

"Thanks for the hay, TJ. Had you heard I just got married?"

"Women. They're complex. I stay away from them."

"Really?" I said. "I can't imagine life without them."

"Poor you." TJ hoisted the last of the big round rolls on my trailer.

Old TJ wasn't much on conversation.

My tires were seriously low with all the weight, but I headed for home.

Five miles later, in Quick Fix territory, I heard a loud pop and I swerved my pickup to the side of the road. I had a flat and sure enough, my spare was flat too. I started walking toward home.

About three miles north, I was feeling sort of dry, a little sickly, and I was ready to ask at any home I came to for a telephone to call Sally Rae for a tank full of air and some water.

As I rounded a corner, three women were walking toward me.

"Hi there!," I said. "Have any of you gals got a cell phone or something to drink?"

They came toward me until the middle one was about ten feet away. Without a word, she grabbed her dress and pulled it up. She didn't have on any underwear! I mean, there the essential 'she' was and, well, I looked. I mean, what else was a man supposed to do? Of course I looked.

The other two women never broke stride until they had my arms pinned, and the front woman dropped her dress and banged me upside the head with a tire iron, something I hadn't seen coming. My lights went out, and then I wasn't looking at anything.

Sometime later I awoke. They had stripped me nekkid, except for my shoes. I did the smart thing and walked until I was near enough Heartbreak that decent people would let me use a phone.

"Darlin', I'm at the Petersons' place. Come help me, please. I got mugged out near Quick Fix and I'm nekkid and hurt. I'll explain it all when you get here."

I heard Beth May's (Death Ray's) voice in the background, "Yeah, I bet he has a real good excuse!"

I don't take happiness for granted. I am determined to keep to the truth with a naive belief it would see me through. Honeymoon happiness is a sweet gift, seldom seen, and to be cherished as long as it may last.

MISS UNDERSTOOD

Her right thigh was on the bar stool,
Her left foot planted firmly on the ground,
She thought on words for her defense,
Watching the officers gather around.

"What took you so long to get here?
It was a dangerous situation!"
And with that she began to sob,
Not hard, but like well placed punctuation.

She used her sleeve for a hanky,
Flung her hair back and adjusted her bra,
Made sure she held their attention,
Expecting the full support of the law.

"He plain assaulted my honor,
Used my name when he was trying to curse,
He yelled that I was no lady,
And so, I knocked him out cold with my purse."

Marlene Tucker

DANCES WITH SNAKES

THE MEN OF HEARTBREAK FEEL THE burden of the Alamo like it took place yesterday, and they have a real sense that God is near, and maybe not all that happy with His people. The women age before their time, but there are a lot of laugh lines in their wrinkles as they watch their children grow. Hard work is prized and children are loved, but sudden challenge is as inevitable as summer heat.

Most social services in Heartbreak are handled on an informal basis. Great Aunt Katy runs "Food on Fords" to serve meals to the elderly. Arney Shaw is our policeman. Arney has a sweet nature and he's a lot more likely to give a rowdy drunk a ride home than lock him up. BJ Elkert runs a little ranch on the edge of town and is head of the volunteer fire department. Our school team, the Heartbreak Raccoons, provides most of the entertainment; at least during those rare times that Emmitt Bennett is sober. Emmitt gives a pretty good show when he's on one of his binges.

Ben Samuels is our mayor. Mr. Samuels runs an insurance agency and a used car lot, so he doesn't have much time to go around Mayoring. That's why we keep electing him. We want most government people to be busy somewhere else. Ron Paul loves us, one and all. Anyway, this *lassie faire* system works pretty well most of the time, which is about the best score any government can get.

Dexter "Stinkbait" Harris runs our animal control. He owns a bait shop near Heartbreak Lake and he accepts all the spare animals from the city. Above his entrance is a sign that says "Happiness is a Warm Puppy." He claims 100 percent placement for all the spare kitties and pups he accepts. People marveled at his ability to place unwanted pets.

129

Stinkbait's lodging is four old trailer houses just out of town. For a very reasonable fee, you can get a cat or dog most any time you want one. His best attraction is that you can drop off a whole litter of pups and kittens for free, no questions asked. He has operated his little place for years, with nary a complaint heard.

All that changed one morning when Stinkbait went into Picket City for a little shopping. Smoke rose up out of one of his trailers. In no time, BJ had the Heartbreak Volunteer Fire Department on the way. They quickly tore open the back of his trailer and doused the flames. In the process they found something they never expected: inside, the trailer was full of large plastic boxes with tight fitting lids, but each box had holes bored on top. Fearing he might have found a drug lab, BJ asked Arney to investigate. Arney cautiously opened a lid. A ball python stuck its head out, sniffed Arney's face, and then sort of sat there, thoughtful like, as he considered his next move.

Heartbreak men have a good fundamental understanding of the Bible. They know all about Adam, Eve and the Snake. There are *no* interpretations where the Snake is the hero of the story. Four firemen all drew their personal guns and shot at the same time. The poor ball python had less chance than an honest man on Wall Street!

After that they all stood around. The trailer was a double wide and it contained shelf after shelf, row after row of pale plastic boxes. The shots must have caused a sort of trailer wide trauma; the whole trailer shivered in a sort of collective slither. BJ, Arney, and the firemen all backed out. A quick inspection showed that two more of the trailer homes were filled with the same ominous pale plastic containers.

"Happiness is a Warm Puppy" began to take on a whole new meaning.

Mayor Samuels called an emergency City Council meeting. I happened to be in town so I sat in. I could tell there was an emergency of some sort. Preacher Hollis cut his invocation unnaturally short (under 10 minutes), and everyone said the Pledge of Alliance like it was one long run-on sentence.

"We have a problem, dear citizens," Mayor Samuels started off, "There are several hundred snakes not half a mile from here. What are we going to do about them?"

"Confiscate them, throw them all in jail!" someone said.

"Throw Stinkbait in there with them," someone else said.

This idea had a lot of popular approval. It was just beginning to dawn on everyone about the exact nature of the place their spare beagles, Chihuahuas and terriers had been relocated.

The real problem came down to what, exactly, was to be done with the snakes.

Arney finally hit the answer. "Folks, remember the old jail behind our new one? Remember the old drunk tank, the one the state won't let us use anymore? It's six feet deep and it has smooth sides. Maybe we can't use it for humans, but it ought to hold these snakes!"

That seemed to satisfy most people and in no time the fire department boys had a line going into a truck where they passed plastic box after plastic box. At the far end, Arney carefully opened each lid and poured the snake into the pit.

The town secretary duly noted each new arrival. "One 12 foot albino Burmese python, the box noted as "Sally." One Bismarck ringed python, 5 feet. The box noted as "George"...."

The next morning, Heartbreak sort of overslept. For the first time in anyone's memory (probably in all of Heartbreak's history) no rooster greeted the dawn with a "cookel-do-da-du!" Actually, the town woke up to Great Aunt Katy's monkey, Chipper, screeching at the top of his voice, followed by a shotgun blast. Great Aunt Katy saved Chipper with a good shot, neatly taking off a green tree python's head, but it cost Chipper about two inches of his tail. Chipper jumped free of the coils of the deceased snake (later determined to be "Mary Magdalene") but he kept screeching for hours. Eventually Dr. Sam (Heartbreak's veterinarian, the most important man in town) slipped him a couple of Xanax with the worldly wisdom "Best not to lose your head over a little tail." Doc Sam was a pragmatist and he had treated many species, including *Homo sapiens,* which affirmed his advice.

Meanwhile, Stinkbait had returned about dawn and he had been duly arrested by Arney. Even mild-mannered Arney was irritated enough to show his anger. He took Stinkbait to the jail and informed him, rather bluntly, about his reduced social standing in Heartbreak.

"Can I just visit my snakes for a minute? I mean, they've been my only family for years," Stinkbait pleaded.

Well, for a cop, Arney **is** a softie. Everybody knows that, that's why everyone lets him stay on as the policeman. Arney said, "Ok."

Arney led Stinkbait back to the snake pit and shined his flashlight down into the hole and except for a garden hose *it was empty.*

"Why did you do that?" Stinkbait asked.

"What?" asked Arney.

"Why did you drop a ladder down into their cell?"

"I didn't put in no ladder, I just left a slow dripping hose," Arney said.

"Well, I guess you just don't know snakes. They use something like that as a ladder," Stinkbait said. The he sort of shivered and said, "Could I get transferred up to that jail in Picket City? Three of those snakes are vipers and I never could bond with them."

Well after that, the whole thing sort of went down hill.

My new adopted son, Li'l' Billy, ran out on the front porch as I had my morning coffee. He began to pee on a garden hose in my front yard, but the garden hose started to slither off. Li'l' Billy was smart enough to be afraid but I drew my .38 and went "bang, bang." He was crying from fright, but I led him back in and changed him. Then I went into my bathroom and changed myself. These experiences are unnerving, and I brag on my dexterity of the pistolship rather than the tightness of my sphincter. Li'l' Billy is very dear to me.

Similar incidents played through Heartbreak over the next few weeks. A PETA lady came to town, trying to raise public awareness for snake's rights. She left abruptly when a large albino Burmese python dropped off of a roof and sank his teeth into her thigh. He was no vegetarian!

Most citizens of Heartbreak began wearing their guns openly, on their hips in quick-draw holsters, like in cowboy days of yore. This time most of those .38's were loaded with CCI rat shot pellets, an effective snake eradicator.

Humans turned to their dogs even more than usual for companionship. As I watched Sally Rae walk up a hill, I also watched our dog, Bandit, run alongside her. I watched them in the sunlight struck by the beauty of the moment. Suddenly, Bandit began to dance. A short time later, Sally Rae began to dance, too.

"Snake, Dave, snake!" Sally Rae screamed.

I ran up and killed it, but it was just a regular ol' six-foot diamond back rattle snake. Life was returning to normal.

Arsenio Lopez makes fine boots and traps varmints, especially raccoons, all over town. He specializes in real 'coonskin caps, just like Davey Crockett's. He eventually solved the escaped snake problem by tying a Chihuahua out under a street light. One by one, the snakes came to eat what they were conditioned to see as food, and "Bam," Arsenio had them.

Arsenio had made a living for years supplying his raccoon hats to the Heartbreak Raccoon cheer team, but a collective shudder ran through the town when he set out his first pair of bright yellow ball python boots in the window of his shop.

MOMMA KILLED A SNAKE TODAY

Momma killed a snake today
Without her glasses on.
She was trying to do the laundry,
Getting started at the crack of dawn.

The night before she had sorted,
Leaving piles right where they lay.
So before her cup of coffee,
And before dressing for the day

She gathered up the first load,
Looking down for something dropped,
Then she saw the long black figure
That's when her heart near stopped.

She grabbed the mop from the bucket
Commenced beating on the floor
The racket stopped a moment
Then she went at it a little more.

Her hair was limp and sweaty
We could see just how she felt
So none of us would tell her
She'd been beating Daddy's belt.

Marlene Tucker

THE MECHANIC

Now, I'm not much of a rancher,
but there're worse than me, much worse. Ranching is hard work, lots of it, and no let up, but there are good ways of going at it and there are bad ones.

BJ Elkert was one of God's own mechanics. He had an intuitive sort or understanding of machines that made him the Man! He could marry a Massy Ferguson 380 frame to a Ford 486 engine and make it work like nobody's business. No one in Heartbreak traded off an old pickup, threw away a chain saw, or even discarded so much as an alarm clock without consulting BJ first.

"Well, Great Aunt Katy, I soaked that old alarm clock in lighter fluid for a couple of days, and now it works just fine now," was a typical sort of pronouncement from BJ.

If Old Doc Bailey had been that good, why, we would have all been immortal. Unfortunately, our machinery seemed destined to outlive us poor frail humans, and our machinery owed its longevity directly to BJ, our own town mechanic.

BJ is a sandy-haired sort of fellow, about six-foot one, weighing about 300 pounds, and he is more muscle than suet. He's the sort of manly man that doesn't push; he's never needed to, so he never got into the habit. The few times he was ever pushed into a fight, he took his opponent down like a Ford 352 engine: every part separated, efficiently disassembled and thoroughly cleaned. I think established his place in the pecking order by late childhood. His reputation as a fighter was firmly secured about the end of high school (Go, Heartbreak Raccoons!) and never had to be refreshed. I sure never saw it; all that was years before I ever came to Heartbreak.

It seems to be that to whom God gives great gifts, He also seems to give great blind spots. Thus it is so with BJ.

Most people in Heartbreak understand animals. This isn't the city sort of understanding; it's more a sort of practical dollars and cents understanding that husbandry has forced on humans since man and animal first started to live together. The chicken that has passed the time of laying makes a final offering, usually with dumplings or rice. The cow past her bearing years finally flavors the air with a scent of barbecue.

The herd dog too arthritic to do her job gets six aspirin in her final dog chow and a swift bullet in the back of her head. The owner is obliged to get teary-eyed and pick a fight in Quick Fix after too many beers. If he is accompanied by friends, they pour a little pure alcohol in his last two beers so all he has is a foggy memory and sense of regret, thus omitting the fight sequence and the need for a dentist.

Anyway, BJ understood machines, but he was just one gene short understanding animals. This caused him some problems, not all of them of the social sort.

BJ thought of himself as a mechanic, so when he bought a big cow, a great big old dumb white Charlotte named "Miss 352," he mistakenly treated her like one of his engines.

Unfortunately for BJ, his pasture backs up to his shop on Main Street. BJ wanted to put a leather bell around Miss 352's neck. Miss 352 naturally objected to human interference with her natural grazing. Like BJ, her size and strength had made her naturally exempt from most outside interference. BJ had a new block-and-tackle in his hardware shop. He cinched it off to a stout timber in his barn and began to slap Miss 352's behind with his twitch, while he took up slack on the block-and-tackle.

All these maneuvers unfortunately located BJ directly behind Miss 352 — a strategically poor position, as events would prove. At some point in the proceedings, Miss 352 sort of did a cow's version of a hula dance, lifted her right hind hoof and sent BJ through the back side of his barn, right out onto Main Street.

I had just had one of my coffee and vinegar pie interludes with my darlin' Sally Rae and I was walking down Main Street when BJ exploded through the back side of his barn onto my feet. Our eyes locked in mutual surprise.

The South has innumerable social customs. Had I been three feet further along the sidewalk, I could have played deaf. The following week when I met BJ, nothing would have occurred. Had I been three feet short of BJ's sudden exit, I might have rushed back into The Waterin' Hole Cafe to hunt for my "lost" car keys, only to find them in my hip pocket.

In none of this was I fortuitous. BJ landed flat on his back, and pinned both of my feet under his considerable bulk, stopping me cold. Like it or not, I was going to become BJ's biographer for this event and my handling of the facts would affect the relationship between his kin and mine for at least three generations. These are the rules in a small town; I didn't make them, but I respected them — just as I respect the force of gravity and the power of rattlesnake venom.

"Hi, BJ. What's up?" I asked as innocently as I could. I knew instantly and intuitively that the next few seconds would become Heartbreak legend and determine whether or not BJ and I were friends or enemies.

BJ considered, and then he replied with the sort of modest force only a real manly man can summon during crisis.

"Miss 352 just kicked me through the back side of my barn. Watch this."

BJ climbed back up to his feet. He grabbed a board and whacked Miss 352 **hard** on her rump. The point of impact sent out a little mushroom cloud of dust, its structure reminding me of a nuclear test site. She sort of jumped forward and BJ yanked the block-and-tackle slack 'til it was up and tight. He quickly slipped the bell around her neck, unhitched her and sent her off with her own story to tell all her cow pals.

"Dave, I think I'm gonna call it a day." With that, BJ limped inside his shop and disappeared for three days. Rumor has it that he couldn't even get out of bed to pee, but you didn't hear it from me.

Anyway, about six months later I was sitting at the counter in The Waterin' Hole, eating vinegar pie and talking with Sally Rae, when BJ plopped down beside me.

"Dave, I've been thinking. You know how hard it is to trim those cow hooves with the old- fashioned bite kind of shears? How about a Dremel tool bolt cutter? They make 'em cordless now. If they'll cut a bolt, why not a trim a hoof?

I looked at my friend and saw the face of disaster. He had an appointment with destiny, and I wanted to be absent when it occurred. I sincerely doubted our relationship could withstand me witnessing another disaster.

"Tell me how it comes out," I said to him. "Sally Rae, I'll see you later," I said to her, making my exit.

If cowards live longer and have more friends, I didn't mind being one.

BARBED WIRE DOES A GOOD NEIGHBOR MAKE

In the early hours of the morning
While the sky was still twilighty blue,
There came a deep sound from the pasture;
A bovine call much more than a "moo."

The bellow was long and guttural
Followed by a steamy huff and moan.
The bull had caught a scent in the air
And he was in the pasture alone.

His weight against the strength of the fence
He got loud and held his head higher.
He pressed in grand determination,
But he couldn't get passed the barbed wire.

Marlene Tucker

WILMA ELKERT

HEARTBREAK IS FULL OF STORIES, AND
I gradually sussed them out as I worked on my goat ranch.

The biggest man in town was BJ Elkert, who ran the feed store. BJ could walk out with 2 hundred pound bags of feed under each arm and fill a rancher's wagon 'til its springs squatted. BJ was a heck of a man.

BJ's father, Joe, was a little shrimp of a guy. He could make anyone laugh, but mostly, he bored folks bragging about his boy, BJ. That boy was the pride of his life.

The richest man in Heartbreak was Mean Old Man Storm. Some folks said it was on account of his having lost his son in the Army, two weeks into basic training, but most folks agreed that meanness was just his nature. He was a big man and despite his age he would fight any one around for any reason. All the men he fought got hurt some way, usually in some way that lasted.

Great Aunt Katy ran the local Food on Fords. Her little organization fed the old people and the truly hopeless all though Heartbreak. I sometimes wondered who those "old people" might be. I knew she was somewhat north of 90 and many of her workers looked older than her. Anyway, Heartbreak had a way that it sort of took care of itself.

A number of old crones and a few old men took part in this social welfare system. Great Aunt Katy was the heart, head and soul of the entire thing. I just took the rest of the old codgers for granted. They all stood together each Sunday in the Cottonwood Baptist Church and sang "The Old Rugged Cross," "Nearer My God to Thee," and at funerals, "In the Garden." Some things and some people, you just sort of took for granted, no matter how much of the bedrock of your life they might compose.

Anyway, I showed up with a few pounds of black-eyed peas from our garden for the Food on Fords group. I could seldom tithe but I gave the Widow's Mite on a regular basis. People in Heartbreak do what they can.

About the time I arrived, there was some sort of fire out at Great Aunt Katy's outdoor cooking pit. Parker House and Ginger Punch grabbed buckets of water and ran toward the smoke. Curley Endive took Olive Green by the elbow and walked her that direction. Curley was 80 if he was a day and Olive was barely 20. She had just married into Heartbreak from Dallas, so she had a lot to prove. The group moved to the back with buckets in hand.

One old lady I only knew as "Mrs. Elkert," sat still except for her shucking husks off the black-eyed peas. I doubt her calloused hands had slowed much since Truman was president. She fixed her bright green eyes on me and said," Don't you want the excitement? Why aren't you out there with the rest of them?"

Mrs. Elkert was one of those old crones a man best be careful of. She could do real damage if she disliked you. I quickly ran through my short list of facts about her. She was Joe's wife and BJ's mother. She was one of Heartbreak's few Catholics, an active member of Christ's Sacred Bleeding Heart Catholic Church, and a member of some devotional group named, "Little Daughters of Perpetual Guilt and Shame."

"I think they got it under control without me," I said, and dropping about 15 pounds of peas at her feet. "Think these might feed someone?" I asked.

Without a word she picked up the bag and carried it inside without as much as a "thank you." When Mrs. Elkert sat back down she did so very slowly. She raised her hand to her jaw, and for the first time she looked straight at me with her bright piecing green eyes. A look of concern settled on her face. Then she massaged her jaw.

She coughed once and leaned forward, then leaned back and clutched her chest.

"Oh no," she said.

"What?" I asked.

"My time, my time has come!" she said. She reached out her old claw and captured my hand.

"Stay here. Promise!"

"I will," I said, flummoxed by her sudden change.

"My final moments are come, I have told no one my sin, No One!" She sort of choked, but when she looked back up into my face I saw such distress that I cradled her frail old body in my arms. I know little about dying and such, but I acted instinctively.

"Hear my final confession, I'm going fast."

I was just struck dumb by a situation I had never seen before. All I could do was nod "Yes," numbly.

"You can't see it now, but once I was a pretty young thing. Royce Storm took me down to Heartbreak Lake. He was drafted for the Army. Royce was a big young man, pretty in a way. I let him, well, I let him take liberties with me no girl should risk. The next day he rode off on the bus, just smiling like he owned the world. Two weeks later, a tank ran over him while he was sleeping in a tent. I guess that's why Old Man Storm is so mean, you know, losing his only boy. A month later, I was sure. I quick up and married Joe Elkert. All my life is a lie. I only tell you now so BJ can inherit Old Man Storm's land. I always meant to set it right, but I ran out of time…."

Her bright green eyes set and she exhaled for the last time. Gently as I could, I set her head down. There was nothing I could do but close her eyes; she was gone.

After the usual drama of such a passing, all us Christians stood at the edge of the open grave. It was a sweet service, one full of a life well-lived and a reward well-earned.

BJ was happy where he was, running the feed store. Mean Old Man Storm looked like a thunder cloud that would never give rain, just thunder.

Sally Rae stood at my shoulder as we all threw a bit of sod over Wilma Elkert's grave.

"Did she say anything to you at the end?" Sally Rae whispered.

I looked over at old Joe Elkert. That day he had lost half his life. He held onto his boy like a drowning man held a life jacket.

"No, not a word," I answered. "She died in peace."

No Justice for All

Mr. Justice Smith was a traveler,
A horse shoer and trainer by trade.
He was known best as a lady's man,
And so his reputation was made.

Good old Justice died a wealthy man.
The county looked for potential heirs.
One young man thought how all that money,
Could take away his financial cares.

He carried to the law his pleadings
And the court listened to what he said.
He claimed the man Smith was his daddy,
That his mother neglected to wed.

The judge replied, "I knew your Momma,
To this court it is perfectly clear,
You look like the man that she married.
You can't claim any Justice in here!"

Marlene Tucker

Bio-illogical Warfare

PRESBYTERIANS HAVE AS A PART OF their essential theology a belief in Man's Perversity. This is an original character defect that goes back to Adam. Personally, I don't know if it's all true, but I'll allow that the Presbyterians have more in the way of objective proof on this point than most theologies.

Take Hank Whitter, for example. The other day he and his brother, Jim Bob, got in an argument. Actually, the argument has been going on about 40 years. When their paw, Hiram, died, he divided the ranch between them, 80 acres each. Sounds fair, don't it?

Well, that's just enough land to hang on, but never to prosper. To make it worse, they have houses right next to each other. Over the years they have chosen to compete with the hard-bitten anger only siblings can bring to the table. They bought two tractors when one would do, two cultivators, installed separate well systems, and mostly waited for the other to die with the unfounded confidence that the deceased brother would will the survivor the soil and thereby "restore" the family land.

No one is exactly sure when things went bad between them, but at some point things went *really* bad.

One day Hank's dog, Rouser, mysteriously gained an extra three feet on his chain, and he successfully managed to fulfill his life's ambition. He took a hunk of leg off Gus, our postman. Consequences followed.

A short time later, Hank went coon hunting. This trip was no big deal in itself, but Jim Bob soon had juvenile raccoons living under his house, and in his attic. They also showed up in his barn. Most suspiciously, a number of Girl Scout cookie wrappers came to light in the vicinity of the damage that followed. I never met a raccoon yet that could turn down a Peanut Butter Pattie.

Adolescent 'coons are among the most destructive animals known to man. Hank was sitting around The Waterin' Hole Café, speaking, no, really bragging, about all the troubles the 'coons had caused his brother's house.

"They tore open his feed sacks, they ate his wiring, and when that burned their greedy little mouths, they chewed into his plumbing."

Hank seemed really up-to-date on Jim Bob's misfortunes for a fella not welcome in his brother's house for four decades. Somewhat brazenly, Hank wore a set of binoculars around his neck.

The Waterin' Hole Café became suddenly quiet when Jim Bob walked in. Poor Ol' Jim Bob was covered head to foot with, well, something like mud, but it stunk worse. "Give me an iced tea," is all he said, and he sat there sort of nursing his wounds.

The iced tea came, and in the general way of folks, Hank began to speak again, "And then the 'coons found the plumbing and the well system. That's when the real problem started...."

Hank talked on and on. All Jim Bob did was suck down his iced tea. It seemed to me almost as if he was trying to get Hank to drag it out.

After an hour or more, Hank finished his discourse and walked back out to his truck, a new Ford F150, the pride of his life.

Without a word, Jim Bob sort of snuck quietly out through the back door of Sally Rae's kitchen.

Seconds later, Hank burst through the front door, holding a terrified yellow cat by its tail. "Who put this spraying male cat in my truck? Where is that no-good brother of mine? How am I ever going to get that stink out of my truck?"

Jim Bob was nowhere to be seen — though I'm fairly sure I heard a guffaw as Sally Rae's kitchen door swung shut. Nor was there any answer to how to remove a tom cat's stink from new leather upholstery after an hour's simmering in the sun.

Cat spray can compete with skunk spray in intensity, but it can long outlast the odor of a skunk. Hank's truck was about a month old, so I figured that when it hit 200,000 miles the smell would have dissipated enough not to hurt its resale value.

People in Heartbreak don't need TV or Internet, except for business. We entertain each other right well.

Less than a week later Perlene, Jim Bob's favorite sow, came to a tragic end – and not in a frying pan. Jim Bob raised that sow from a piglet and he was almost unreasonably fond of her. More than once her had been heard to say, "If she had just been born a human, I'd probably have married her. She sprang good shoats every spring, she never complained, and she always bred regular."

I'll have to agree, that's a pretty high standard for marriage — though personally I think I value conversation and emotional intimacy more than Jim Bob might. Oh, well. It's not for me to judge....

Perlene, though, had some urgent need for human ordure and when the lid to his septic tank was inexplicably left open, she drowned in her greed. We all have our faults, so most of us grieved with Jim Bob's loss.

Whenever Jim Bob drove his pickup to The Waterin' Hole Café, people sort of drifted in for a piece of pie and the latest gossip. The same held true if they smelled Hank's new pickup wheeling into Heartbreak.

Well, after that, one disaster after another seemed to befall those two brothers. A stray mongrel managed to climb Hank's fence, even though it was 12-feet high and electrified. By morning, he had bred every one of Hank's purebred Catahoula bitches.

Jim Bob vomited when he was brushing his teeth from the taste of the water. It seems a large rat crawled into his main well intake in order to find his final resting place.

One of Hank's pigs, a notorious glutton known as "Caligula" got into his garden. Caligula, like his namesake, not so much ate Hank's garden as ravished it. Hank lost an entire spring planting of raw vegetables before he awoke.

The postman almost refused to deliver any more to Jim Bob after he found a nest of live scorpions in Jim's mail box. The poor postman DID refuse to deliver to either of them when he open Hank's box and faced a live and understandably unsociable skunk.

"I work for the United States Government, and this is interfering with official business," Gus declared. For the first time in his 20 plus years as a mail carrier, he invoked federal code .004654854, subsection C, twice in one day. He kicked them both off his route.

Meanwhile, things got worse. Hank's bees started dying. Jim Bob delivered some 30 gallons of fresh milk, only to have everyone complain that it tasted wrong. The sourness was finally traced to china berries in the cow feed. I tasted some. It wasn't that bad, but it could keep a man *profoundly* regular if he took more than a sip or two. A whole glass would cause a general purge, as several hapless Heartbreak citizens discovered.

Hank came into Heartbreak and began to complain about how he had pulled a viper to his chest; it sounded rather Old Testament and it didn't make much sense. Jim Bob pulled up outside, but he declined to come in. After a short pause next to Hank's truck he drove on.

Half an hour later; Hank walked out to his truck and it was covered with grackle splatter. Someone had thrown birdseed into the truck bed.

It finally got so bad that Arney, our town policeman, had to intervene. He had little time for family squabbles, but this was getting bad. Half the town was in an outhouse and the other half was in a hurry for the earlier arrivers to finish off. The escalating warfare was a matter of public safety.

"Both you old buzzards come out here!" Arney announced. He used his best no-nonsense voice and underscored it with a whoop from his siren. "Get out here now! I mean it."

He got them both lined up on the curb and scolded, "I expect both of you old geezers to show up at Cottonwood Baptist tomorrow morning, no excuses. I'll make it plenty hot for either one of you if you don't show!"

The next morning, Pastor Hollis preached on the joys and freedom of forgiveness. Then he did the whole Communion routine.

"If you have something against your brother, go out to him and forgive." Rev. Horace laid it on as stern as I ever heard. Then came the serving of the Bread and the Wine.

Publicly shamed, Hank got out of his pew and walked over to Jim Bob. "Will you forgive me? Can we start over?"

Jim Bob said "I will."

In public, at church, they made their peace.

Hank started up toward the sacraments.

Jim Bob started toward the door.

Hank turned, "Won't you partake of the sacraments with me?" he asked.

"Sure I will," Jim Bob said, as he walked out of the church down the center aisle. "But first, though, let me just get that rattler out of your pickup...."

OWNING UP

I watched my neighbor, it was no mistake,
He stole my shovel, and also my rake.
Peace among neighbors was about to break,
If he wasn't stopped what else would he take?

He stole my shovel and he made me mad!
My wife cautioned how my memory was bad,
"You borrowed his tools!" her voice was so sad.
I thought it over, and indeed I had.

Marlene Tucker

CITY SLICKER

HEARTBREAK HAS 27 CHURCHES AND at least three times that many beer joints. Outside of town a single graveyard marks the place where all denominations cease; in fact the graveyard hill is the final stopping place for all disagreements, petty or righteous. It's peaceful and serene, a record of eight generations of people who found Heartbreak a full life, deep in the richness and complexity only humans can generate.

Back on Main Street, life was humming and strumming. It was auction day, so more than the usual numbers of Heartbreak's denizens were present. Sally Rae poured weak, over-boiled coffee into her patron's cups. The lingering ranchers noted that as the morning wore on, the coffee got weaker and more over-boiled. Refills were free, new coffee grounds were not.

I was hanging around waiting for the mid-morning lull. Sally Rae and I are "dating" — a darn peculiar word for people our age.

"Sally Rae," I said, "if this coffee gets any weaker, I might just as well pour it on the petunias outside."

"Go ahead. In about 10 minutes I'm going to empty the rest of the urn directly on them myself. Huh, I wonder who THAT could be?" she said, motioning toward a late model Altima that pulled up outside.

A man walked in and before he opened his mouth every person there had the same thought: *city slicker.* He was too lean and too tan to be local. His blue jeans were too blue and too creased his shirt too western, his hat too shiny white, like his teeth. His mustache looked like he'd invested several hours of labor in it.

"Hi, everybody, I'm Jeff Hatburn, and I'm new here," he announced. Several of us nodded politely. "I came here on auction day because I wanted to meet you good folks; I'm bringing opportunity with me in my briefcase. I'm going to remake this little burg and you're going to love it!"

A century ago, someone would probably have shot him right then, but the idea of community service has taken a beating in recent years. Mr. Hatburn took the ensuing silence as encouragement. "This here's a town with lots and lots of land, but no money. I want to show every one of you how to clean things up and make a mint off it." He was sure off to a sorry start.

At first, when I was just a tenderfoot in Heartbreak, I was a little put off by all the junkyness of the place. Everybody seemed to have their houses surrounded by junk. Like most newcomers, I was looking at the wrong thing.

First, look at the "junk." If it's spread in neat rows at 15-foot intervals around the house, has new paint on 'em, then these old washer and dryers just might work and they're for sale. If it's new and painted green, it's something you pull behind a plow, then it belongs to the town supplier. If it's worn, and there's a whole lot of other junky looking machinery with it, it belongs to the richest man in town. If it's new, evenly placed, and ready to go, he is a sushi bar salesman from Houston and nobody will talk to him, except to be exceedingly polite.

My tools are all old, bent, need paint, and I just bought a welder to fix them. People are starting to talk nicer about me. There's even a suspicion I might be "serious" but I've just been here two years; I'm still got at least another decade to go to be considered "real folk."

Appliances two deep on the front porch doesn't prove anything. Neither do cast-iron bathtubs growing tulips or obsolete horse drawn McCullagh plowing machinery. Shingles and worn out saw blades painted with bluebonnets landscapes are a sure sign of a tourist trap. By the time someone hauls a load of scrap iron to the next city, you can bet its past redemption for all other uses.

People in Heartbreak aren't exactly hostile to new things, but with national laws, state regulations and unreasonable taxes, we all lived in a sort of perpetual readiness to defend our land from the latest threat. Miss Scarlett Hawkins' boy, Jimmy, does real well with electrical things, and electronic, too. That why he does all the computer and speaker work at the auction. Anyway, Hatburn showed up and made his same spiel again to the ranchers there. Of course, he parked his fancy new car right in an area clearly marked "No Parking."

Now, I don't know how much of what happened next was pure chance, Divine Intervention, or just Jimmy Hawkins having a good time, but when Hatburn ran outside to answer his cell phone everybody in Heartbreak Auction Barn heard his conversation over the loud speakers.

"Yea Sammy, this is Jeff. Listen, it's just like I thought, this bunch of hicks couldn't sort apples from horse apples. This town's ready and ripe for picking. Tell the chemical company not to worry about a thing...." He rattled on, describing how in five years no one could even recognize this pitiful little patch of fly-blown manure.

When the auction ended at 3 p.m., Hatburn tried to cage every rancher there. By silent agreement they each gave him 10 or 15 minutes, but no one signed the contracts he kept shoving under their noses.

Most of the cattle trailers in Heartbreak were made in the 1950's and '60's out of heavy welded iron. They were meant to last, and none of them got gentle treatment. That day bad driving seemed to be "in." Most every truck that hauled out that day managed to use its trailer to sideswipe Hatburn's Altima. About 4, Jimmy cleaned out the barn with a front end loader and managed to load another 500 pounds or so of fresh manure onto Hatburn's wreck.

Finally, Hatburn released the last rancher from his sales pitch and walked out to where he had parked his shiny new car. For the first time that day he didn't have much to say. The people of Heartbreak had voted to go green.

STUCK IN THE COUNTRY

The country folks saw him coming,
They referred to him as "Slick".
The city man's plans were to sell
His product to every hick.

Slick showed the men at the station,
His sharpest, best selling knives,
And informed them how they should all,
Invest in some for their wives.

He then handed out some samples,
Bragged they were sharp and forged in fire.
They laughed as they all walked away,
At the sample stuck in his tire.

Marlene Tucker

Job Evans

JOB EVANS LIVED RIGHT ACROSS FROM me. He was a nice enough sort, but rather short on luck. In fact, his luck seemed like it had been chosen by a jury of ex-wives. He taught me some important lessons, though, especially about standing up to adversity.

"Dave, forgive your enemies," he told me. "It saves you the hardship of having to hate them, and it will 'most always confuse them."

You see, when some people get knocked down by life's events, they run to the Lord all crying and wanting restitution. The Lord is mighty generous, but I've see hardly any restitution in my life. Far more often we get substitution. That means we have to accept something different than what we had. Often it's a lot better, but it takes a bit of grace and faith to know how to recognize those new found riches.

Most of us just try to live one day at a time, scratch where it itches and keep on trying. Job wasn't like that. He always seemed to be engaged; a sort of mud wrestling contest with life. He lost more than he won, but I always got the idea he didn't keep score, he just wrestled.

Our pastor, the Rev. Horace Hollis, was the best man in Heartbreak. He had been here for forty-three years; Heartbreak got him when he was young and he had stayed here for all his life. When Job came to him with his new religious convictions, Rev. Horace encouraged him.

154

One day Job and I fenced a broken down border between our properties. We met at sunrise and by sunset it was done. The big difference was that while I worked it, he fought it. By the end of the day, Job looked like he'd been beaten like a tied goat. Blood oozed from a dozen nicks and a few real gashes. Still, Job seemed oblivious to life's little shortcuts.

"Job, let's just fence around that stump," I'd say.

"That'd be cheating," he'd say, and start chopping.

Anyway, when Job got knocked down, he went running to the Lord like any of us, but the whole time he was looking over his shoulder, flipping off the devil. Job had as much room for anger as any man, but he also knew how to look around. He knew how to forgive, but that's pretty much an empty gesture 'til you considered that he knew how to condemn, too.

When his wife of a quarter century got drunk for about six months and then ran off with another man, he went out and got a satellite dish and a talking parrot. "At my age, I figure I just about got my bases covered," he said.

"Pardon me, Job, but these replacements seem like mighty thin substitutes," I said.

He looked at me sharply. "What's the matter? You don't like parrots?"

Back in Houston I had a Jewish friend that gave me an old proverb: "When a goy hears someone is a Jew, he thinks he knows something about him. When a Jew hears someone is a Jew, he knows he doesn't know anything about him."

Baptists are a lot like that. Trying to herd Baptists is like chasing a gaggle of ducks. They'll just scatter, then slowly regroup. We Baptists have sort of a group mentality like a herd, but little in the way of a common directionality. It's easy enough to pack a couple of hundred into a church Sunday morning, but try getting them quiet for worship? Once they're talking, they think they're already worshiping.

All this is compounded by all the different brand names out there. There are the Southern Baptists (of course), but there are also the Primitive Baptists, the Cooperative Baptists, the Free Will Baptists, and so forth. In Heartbreak we were most called Bathodists (kind of like Methodists, but without any Bishops to order us around). Others called us "Free Wheeling Baptists," except for the ones who didn't really like us. They called us "Loose Wheel Baptists." Confusing? If you ever figure it out, please let me know.

The Rev. Horace wasn't perfect, but he was about as close to it as you could get. He had christened all the children at their births, married them when they were ready, and said nice things about them when they died. He lived every day like he was preaching a sermon. If he ever told a lie, it was at a funeral, and it was always in the favor of the deceased.

Job, on the other hand, looked the part of a prophet from the wilderness. His beard was never trimmed and like other prophets, one could see bits of locusts caught in it. His preaching was several cuts above the norm, not half bad for a self-educated, home-grown prophet. He was six- foot-four, had a resounding voice and his sermons led me and Janey closer to grace than I ever imagined when I first moved to Heartbreak. There were many contestants in Heartbreak, but he was the emerging home grown wonder.

I felt pretty good that Sunday. Sally Rae sat on my right hand (fingers clasped with mine) and Janey sat on my left. I had a protective arm around her. Communion was set on the altar and I thought that my worst sins were venal. It would be easy to take communion that day.

Communion is a special time. It has rules. You must be in peace and in communion with everyone around you. The whole purpose is to get right, get level, about your fears and anger for what has happened in the last month.

Emmitt Bennett hadn't kept his cows out of my property. We had spoken bad words back and forth, but at the end we had agreed he'd pay range fees and get his fence fixed.

My daughter Janey was praying hard. I didn't really want to know what she was praying about; I knew that she had come in at 2, though.

This was a special Sunday; Rev. Horace was letting Job serve the communion. This act was beyond encouragement. It was Rev. Horace's endorsement to allow Job to follow the ministry.

We all prayed silently, eyes closed, until there was a *thump* up on the altar.

As we all sat there, wanting the cup and the bread, waiting God's individual forgiveness for our special sins, Job collapsed on the altar rail. He lay without moving, across the steps. Old Doc Bailey sprung up and felt Job's neck.

"He's dead." Old Doc announced.

Great Aunt Katy was the first. She walked up to the communion rail and tore off a little bread. She dipped it in the wine, ate it, and walked out the back door. In time all 184 of us did the same. As we walked out of the church, we were silent. We were empty: we were empty of our angers, we were empty of our fears, and we were all sure in the knowledge of God's redemptive Grace. God had taken Job back home to his reward.

STANDING ON THE PROMISES

There was a cute little 5-year- old,
Whose mother dropped him off for service,
He distracted the congregation,
By spinning like a whirling dervish.

The pianist of the Rockfaith Church,
Greeted everyone with a smile.
She stopped and spoke with the little boy,
Before continuing down the aisle.

Through the sermon the boy sat so still,
Hardly even turning his head.
There was no jumping or thrashing,
He was quiet and peaceful instead.

He stood for the invitation,
And kept standing for the last song.
He stood still for the closing prayer,
That seemed almost two Sundays long.

After Church someone asked the child,
"What stopped you from wiggling like you do?"
He explained the pianist promised,
To tell his mom and help spank him too.

Marlene Tucker

Sam Bass' Treasure

In this life there are gamblers, suicidal risk takers — and ranchers. A rancher depends on his animals being fecund, his daughter being sterile, and enough rain to feed the animals and water the garden. He needs a favorable market, a generous banker, and even then, if God has a hiccup, it's the rancher that goes under. A rancher doesn't expect life to be fair, but he prays for tolerable.

Every since the world divided into peasants and noblemen, people like me have had to work hard, but we also know we have to live by our wits. Hard work alone is not enough.

This is how my thoughts were running one spring morning as I sat looking at my tractor, Daisy. Maybe I should say, my former tractor. For much of the previous week I had been cranking it, changing its oil, blowing out its air filter, even playing Beethoven to it at night. Daisy was not going to start.

Meanwhile time was ticking. Some things won't wait. I had 40 acres in the north that had to get plowed, and plowed real soon. The hay had to go in now or in three months I would go broke. I already missed one good rain this spring, and that was one more than I could afford to miss.

I've had more than my necessary share of book learning earlier in life. It seemed to profit me little in my need to turn the soil. Like many a farmer before me, I wished I could look over my shoulder when I was plowing and turn up some treasure. The thought of it…

159

wait! If desperate times can lead to desperate measures, it can also bring up some creative solutions to the problem.

In a different life long ago, I used to teach History, and I also knew a bit of calligraphy. My thoughts began to churn. I was up late that night, and I only left the house the next day to feed the goats.

Wednesday noon is the main day at The Waterin' Hole Café. I went in at 11 and I asked BJ to grind a new edge on my old rusty plow.

"Sorry to bring you such a muddy old piece of equipment," I said.

"No problem, Dave, I've worked on worse."

BJ got right to work. First he hit the side with a hammer to knock the dried mud loose. A big clump fell on the floor, then another.

"Why, what's this?" BJ said in wonder.

Stuck in the trough between the plow blade and the bolts that held it on was a Liberty Head Double Eagle, minted in 1882. It was a little bent, but still shiny and bright as the day it was minted.

"Well, I guess I'm buying us lunch over at The Waterin' Hole," I said.

When we got there it was already crowded. People talked from table to table in the way folks will who have spent a lifetime together.

"Guess what, Sam?" BJ called across to another table. "I found a gold double eagle stuck in Dave's old plow share. Purtyist thing I've seen in a while."

"I haven't been here long, but didn't someone tell me that Sam Bass buried some of his loot around here just before they shot him?" I asked.

Bill Smith answered, "Somewhere. I don't rightly know it was your place, though. It could have been the next county over, just as easy."

"After lunch I'm going to go over to the Museum and look around a little," I said.

Sally Rae gave me a strange look, sort of hard, when she put our food down, but she didn't say anything.

After lunch I knocked on Millie's door and got her to unlock our little museum.

"I never took you to be all that historically inclined, Dave," Millie said.

"Well, I got a little mystery needs clearing up," I said.

160

After half an hour of digging through old dusty files and coughing a bunch, I brought a ragged little paper back to the office where Millie sat, gossiping on the phone. Lordy, sometimes I wondered how the Heartbreak Herald stayed in business, the way Millie passed other people's business around.

Finally, Millie condescended to pause long enough to say, "What do you need?"

"Would you please copy this for me?" I asked.

She picked up her phone and swung around on her swivel chair long enough to reach the copier. A moment later I had the copy back in my hand.

"Do you want me to put the paper back in the files?" I asked.

"No, you'll just get it in the wrong spot," she said crossly.

I took my plow back out to my ranch and waited anxiously.

About two hours later, our doorbell rang.

It was the Bennetts, from next door. "Could we, uh, dig some worms off in your north 40?" they asked.

"No worms on your place?" I asked.

"Not this year."

The Carter clan was next. After that it was the Mendez tribe. Soon I just walked outside and started pouring tea as my neighbors showed up. Jesse Kellum showed up on his little Farm-All Tractor.

Well, there are 90-day wonders and 90-minute wonders. Mine lasted about two days. By then, the north 40 was churned up from one end to the other.

By the third day, people were tired of digging and they disappeared as quickly as they had shown up.

As Sally Rae put dinner on the table she gave me "The Look" again.

"Just how'd you manage to find Sam Bass' treasure map over at the museum," she asked sternly.

"I didn't find it. I made it at home and asked Millie to copy it for me, that's all," I said innocently enough. "By the way, here's your Double Eagle back. When I sell the goats at Fall auction, I'll replace the band so you can wear it as a necklace again. You might want to hold off for a while, though, just for diplomacy's sake."

"Don't you feel bad about tricking all your neighbors?" she asked.

"It's hard to con an honest man. Anyway, finish up, Li'l' Billy; you and Sally Rae are going to throw out seed from the back of the pickup truck. We got to get that north 40 planted before the rain hits."

The next morning I sat brooding over my morning coffee.

"What's got you thinking so hard, Dave?" Sally Rae asked.

"It's that 20 acres in the south. I was just wondering if I should risk sending the FBI a tip about Jimmy Hoffa?"

ROCKING OUT

My garden was covered with rocks.
They got stuck in the 'tiler tines.
The rocks seemed to double each spring.
I was glad they didn't grow vines.

One spring a local school teacher,
Asked if she could bring out her class,
To see garden preparation.
It was a chance I couldn't pass.

Rocks turned up as I was plowing.
Kids asked "Hey Mister, what are these?"
"They're 'Leaverites'", I assured them,
"Y'all take as many as you please."

I put a rock in my pocket.
The group then filled their pockets full.
The students were soon on the bus,
So they could return back to school.

Before leaving the teacher asked,
The rock's name that grew in the spring.
I told her they were Leaverites
(Leaverite there, they aren't worth a thing.)

Marlene Tucker

GUS AND MAE

HEARTBREAK TEXAS IS *50* OR *500*
miles west of Houston's sushi bars. It's a place where Texas isn't like
it ever was, but most Texans remember it as being. It's a place full of
real men and real women, real goodness, and real badness, too. The
same cactus that can pierce a foot so unforgivingly can also have the
thorns burned off and give a starving herd a last month of graze until
the forgiving Fall showers. It can deliver unexpected love, beauty,
and (of course) heartbreak.

I moved my daughter, Janey, there from Houston after a painful
divorce. Janey is just 16 and she could give Barbie a run for her
money on beauty, if not brains. Don't think me harsh; Janey has been
through a lot and done pretty well, and she's just 16. She's a girl-child
with an attitude and a plan, even if the plan changes daily.

Hi, I'm Dave. I sort of found Heartbreak by accident. I mean,
when I fled all the nastiness of Houston (only part of it from the
divorce) I was heading toward a place where my father took us briefly
when I was so young I could hardly remember any of it. By luck or
chance I found my way to the right place.

Men in Heartbreak consider hard work a right, and most of
them die right away after they can't work any more. Women
raise lots of children and most of them turn out right, whether
they follow the dying profession of being a cowboy, or end up
in the New York Philharmonic as first fiddle. Heartbreak parents
are PROUD of their children, even when they're in the knuckle-

headed phase. For the boys this often lasts into their 30's. Of course, most of the girls grow up quicker. Biology never gives a fool a break, especially females.

Anyway, there is this one particular couple, Gus and Mae Hempstead, I have to tell you about. They were neighbors of mine and some evenings (well, several actually) Gus and I would share two fingers of Jack Daniels at the creek that divided our property. Gus and Mae grew up together, got time out for kissing in grade school, lead the make-out crew during hay rides at Cottonwood Baptist Youth night, and got married right after graduation from Heartbreak High. Mae was starting to show a little during her valedictorian speech, but most folks gave them points for making it all the way through school. Gus, of course, was the football team captain on a winning year. Most folks felt pretty good about them, figured that they'd be some of the Next Generation in Heartbreak, but then Gus joined the Army right after 9-11 and ended up in Afghanistan before Mae had their first baby.

The next two years were the longest two years of Gus' or Mae's life. Little Bobby was born, or course, and the town waited for every one of Gus's letters almost as much as Mae did. Finally, one day, word came that Gus was coming home. The whole town set up a parade. The VFW was there, the local politicos, and most everyone else. When the Greyhound bus pulled in Gus stepped off in full uniform, including two purple hearts and a Bronze Star. Mae kissed Gus like a returning hero deserves, and the whole town marched him down Main Street to the front of the Civil War Memorial. A couple of windbags made their speeches (mercifully short, for once) and then the Mayor turned to Gus.

"Got anything to say, Gus?" Mayor Ben Samuels asked.

Gus turned, a full military 180 by all accounts, and marched to the base of the Civil War Memorial, and pissed all over it. Zipping up, he turned to Mae and gently took her hand.

"We're going home now," he said.

That was the first hint that something might not be right.

Of course, I didn't know any of this when I moved to Heartbreak. Gus and I were neighbors. We met at the fence line and he handed the first sip of Jack Black over to me. The next day I handed my

Johnny Walker back. Being a good neighbor has a strict etiquette, and over time we became friends. Mostly we talked about breeding stock: cows, goats, wives and daughters. You think I'm crude or denigrating toward women? It's my unapologetic opinion that most people nowadays are a lot more worried about how their poodles breed than their daughters. That's my opinion, and if you don't like it, quit reading.

I love my goats and I care about careful breeding. I love my daughter a whole lot more. The best principle I have always tried to instill in Janey was to be right cautious who she made children with, and when. All those who disagree with this are invited to stand at least 200 yards away from me and my family. After 200 yards my rifle tends to veer to the left a little, so you might get lucky.

Gee, I just got on a soap box; darn near lost my train of thought. Anyhow, Gus and Mae had about six more kids, but the real story isn't their fertility, but their discomfort with each other. Well, Gus had about two real benders a year and every other bender Mae had a new baby.

One day I was driving to town. First I saw some underwear, then some blue jeans, and then I saw a favorite blue-checked shirt of Gus' flapping in the breeze. When I rounded the hill I saw Mae throwing out more blue jeans. Darn, that was some kind of unhappy woman.

"What's happening, Mae?" I asked as I pulled up beside her.

"Gus ran off with some bar room slut after a two-week drinking binge!" she replied. "Everybody in Quick Fix knows it, so I figured I'd spread the news to Heartbreak!"

"Now, slow down, Mae," I shouted just before we went into town. "Has this ever happened before?"

"Yea, five times before this time. You got to draw the line somewhere," she replied.

"Well, how about at seven? It could save your marriage."

At that point she pulled over, and I did too. I got out to hear her, but Mae just ran over and grabbed me and began crying.

About that time Gus pulled up, ran over, and knocked me on my jaw so solid I didn't remember anything clearly for at least about a day.

Four months passed. I saw Gus in the next pasture and he waved. I walked over and he handed a bottle of Jack Black over to me. I'm not too small a man to recognize an apology when I see one.

"Did you hear? Mae and I are expecting number eight in the spring."

Human weakness is too often a public spectacle, and true love is too often ignored.

LOVE IS IN THE YEARS

"Your momma is a good woman",
Dad told me when I was a kid.
I wondered how he could say that,
When I saw the things she did.

She washed up Daddy's favorite grill,
With vinegar and kerosene.
Nothing cooked up good after that,
But dog gone, that thing was clean!

Most every meal she cooked was burnt,
She didn't like to clean the house,
She wouldn't often wash the clothes,
She just wanted to be a spouse.

Dad lived a long and happy life.
When I was grown I heard him say,
"Sometimes in marriage you must learn
Love's in the years not the day."

Marlene Tucker

Holidays

July 4ᵀᴴ

THE FOURTH OF JULY PICNIC WAS SET at Heartbreak Lake that year. Well, last year, too, and the one before, if I'm not mistaken.

Heartbreak's a place out of old Texas, but still a live place where decency and foolishness sprout anew every day, like a rose bush flowering from the foundations of a decaying church, or toad stools from cow plop. Take your choice, they're both there. Remember, though, before you choose, both the roses and the toad stools are native and natural. It's your choice, not their presence that defines you.

Anyway, it was the Fourth of July and the whole town was out at the lake for a picnic and fireworks. People tempered themselves like iron: first they baked red hot in the sun, then they quenched that fire by diving into the cool waters of Heartbreak Lake. Platters of fried chicken and tubs of fresh-made potato salad were scattered on bright colored quilts. Huge quantities of iced tea were served up in mason jars, and dozens of coolers held a variety of, well, other sources of hydration. A carnival atmosphere wafted among the scents of suntan oil and barbecue. Leroy Heichenbacher and the Strumming Fools played both kinds of music for the citizenry. That is, they played Country *and* Western.

A lot of people wear their patriotism on their shirt sleeves, literally. I figure the veterans earned it. I'm not a vet, but I still love my country. On days like this, and voting days, I feel that sense especially strong. I looked at my fellow Heartbreakers— white, black and brown— and I felt a huge surge of pride. We were all displaced a few generations back, but we are the country that decided a person's worth was more important than his genealogy. I don't deny we have our problems, but we are the country that looked those problems in the eye and have tried to do something about it over time.

Janey was off with a bunch of her teenage friends, moving through the crowd like a pack of, well, hungry teenagers. About a dozen of them went from family to family, devastating their stores of chicken and watermelon along the way. Anytime their little bladders got too full, they all piled into the lakes for a "swim." I guess that sort of thing kinda knocks the edge off of the catfish enjoying the Fourth, but oh well. Love of your country always means some sort of sacrifice, even if you're a catfish.

Some people like to bunch up in one group or family and spend all day telling old stories or swapping lies, but I'm sort of a drifter. Actually, I'm more of an eavesdropper. Nothing malicious about it; it's awful entertaining is all. What good's gossip if you can't pass it on?

My first visit was in the shaded pavilion, where the three old men were holding court. Old Sam and Old Joe had already pre-cussed, cussed and discussed every president from Franklin D. to Barak H. Their general opinion was that all of them, maybe excepting Truman, was a Communist, or worse. They were pretty sure it was worse, but they were sorta stumped on what *could* be worse.

Old Red was a different story. He was lank and tall, in sharp contrast to Old Sam and Old Joe who grew more spherical and toad-like every decade. Old Red (who was now entirely bald) was a WWII vet. This was his day. He wore his VFW vest and cap, and his khaki pants had a military crease in them.

"…So that lieutenant told us to go up on the ridge and lob a couple of grenades over in the machine gun nest. He said it'd be easy. I told him that every ship could be a mine sweeper, once. He scowled at us and said, 'That's an order, soldier.' Well, we knowed not all of us were going to make it, but, there it was, so we slipped off into the dark…."

A half dozen young men sat around, drinking something clear that smelled like lighter fluid. Home-made moonshine it was — clear as creek water, smooth on palate as rainwater. These kids wanted their own war so bad it showed on their eager faces. I pitied them; odds were their wish would come true, but it would be a miracle if all of them made it back, too.

The next group was some middle-aged cowboys. They'd already had enough beer in them that they were arguing over who had screwed up the worst, and the most often. Each claimed pre-eminence for himself.

"Why, I jest got three fingers and a stub of a thumb on this hand here, but I roped that old mossy back out of the briars and mesquite even after he tore my hand half off," Louie said.

"Well, when Juno threw me and broke my leg. I lassoed him, crawled back up, and rode him four miles for help. Every step of the way, my dang leg bones grated back and forth in time with his trot," Samboy followed up.

About then Miss Scarlet walked through the group, shooing them out of her way like pesky chickens. "If you boys were half as good at roping and branding as you tell it, you wouldn't be getting hurt all the time."

Miss Scarlett weighed about 250 pounds, but it was hard fat. She hardly jiggled as she walked. A widow, she had raised four boys and 200 Herefords. What she lacked in aesthetics she made up for in efficiency.

The cowboys shut up respectfully, at least until she was out of ear shot.

Louie hated getting disdained; even if it was by a woman who could probably beat him at arm wrestling. "A man can't help getting hurt if he takes his work seriously. But you listen to any of those women. Women are always having babies. Don't tell me women don't know how to avoid *that*."

I ambled on. I had a feeling that in no time, Louie was going to find himself in his own little Alamo and I was in no mood to be one of his doomed volunteers.

About that time Sally Rae walked up. She smelled like lilacs and woman, and she smiled at me like I'd just invented happiness. Others can say what they want, but the best and the worst I ever felt in my life was because of a woman. Sally Rae had eyes the color of love. We were at the happy part of the courtship dance, and if there was one thing I had learned, it was to make such times last as long as possible.

"Hey, Sally Rae," I said smiling.

"Hey, handsome."

I knew it was a lie. I'm short, bespectacled, overweight and balding. When the phone rang I knew it wasn't going to be Gentleman's Quarterly callin' me up for a new modeling job. But Sally Rae's greeting put a skip back in my step, and made me want to whistle. I pulled her behind some bushes and kissed her instead.

"Kinda frisky, aren't you?" she asked after a time.

I shut her up the kindest way a man can. A while later I said, "Just feeling patriotic, I guess."

She laughed. When Sally Rae laughed, it sounded like song birds. "Don't get too patriotic on me. I got to live in this little town, don't forget."

We walked down one of the paths around the lake. About then I heard a sound like a bull makes the moment he realizes he's now a steer. Sally Rae trotted forward and found Miss Scarlet, just bawling her eyes out. The second she saw Sally Rae, she seized onto her faster than a possum on a ripe tomato.

"Men, they're so mean. They want what a woman gives, then turn you out to pasture like a used-up guard donkey. I know I'm huge, but I was naturally big boned before I had four boys. Now my cousin Velma is down from Chicago. She weighs 200 pounds if she weighs an ounce, but she's always dropping all sorts of hints about Weight Watchers and such. How come she has to travel half way across the country just to find someone bigger than her?"

I sensed there was more to come, so I discretely back-peddled around the tree at the corner of the trail.

"It wouldn't be half so bad if Bill hadn't died."

By now I could tell that Miss Scarlet had enjoyed a little of the clear liquid the Old Men were passing out. She was at the "crying confession" stage. I didn't want to leave Sally Rae, but I wasn't anxious to hear things that would leave everyone embarrassed for a year or two.

"I never meant to have four kids, you know. I was a skinny little cheerleader when Bill got me pregnant, and the next kid happened when we were just crazy kids in love. I thought that'd be enough, but then we had this Fourth of July picnic and bingo, by October I was competing with the pumpkins."

"Lord, Miss Scarlet, I never knew..." Sally Rae said, trying to break the tearful flow of words .

"The fourth one I don't even remember. I think I was just passed out tired asleep when Bill came in one night...and then he died, right in the middle of trying for number five! Oh, boohoo...." She sobbed.

About then I *did* tippy-toe away. I figured Sally Rae would eventually forgive me leaving, but if Miss Scarlet saw me forgiveness would never come.

Great Aunt Katy sat in a shaded little glen that had been there as long as the lake. She and most of the lunch crew were doing what they did best, serving weenies and fried chicken to any passerby.

"Hi Dave, come sit a spell, take a weight off your feet." I walked over. I always figured that if angels showed their age they'd look about like Great Aunt Katy. The sun reflected off the lake behind her, giving her white hair a halo she'd earned many times over.

"Great Aunt Katy," I said, using her full formal title, "Tell me about Heartbreak Lake."

"Dave, it's like this. Heartbreak Lake is the first place people around here built after basic feeding and housing got done. I remember the valley that was here, and the creek that ran through it. The whole area was full of rattle snakes and hoot owls."

"Then, like now, most marriage proposals happened out in these woods, though many of those proposals started as just ordinary old propositions. There been more citizens started out here than you can imagine. Why, for years if a girl got in trouble we womenfolk called it 'gone swimming at Heartbreak Lake'," she laughed.

"Preachers come through talking about our sinful ways, but most of us see the pure joy and beauty of living, not the evil of it. I've watched this place so long it almost seems a hundred years. I've see lots of goodness, a little ignorance in action, but precious little real evil."

Great Aunt Katy could talk about most anything and it came out a sermon on human goodness. When I have to make my excuses to God Himself, face to face, I hope I can get Great Aunt Katy to do my talking for me.

A little further on I heard some women talking women stuff.

"That traveling salesman wanted to sell me clothes dryer. I said this here area's dry enough without importing more. He asked me if I hung out my wash because it was greener. I said 'Heck no! If bleach and blueing won't do it, why would I pour in something green?'"

Country really does speak a different language than the city.

I turned a corner and ran into the four Most Notable gents in the city. Old Doc Bailey was arguing with Doc Sam, the veterinarian. These were easily the two most important men in town and their jobs had a significant overlap. Doc Sam had delivered a number of babies, human kind, in a pinch. Old Doc Bailey had pulled a number of new born calves in his time, and had once given CPR to a litter of four new Catahoula pups. Three made it, but most agreed they were all a little hard to train. Brain damage is hard to overcome, human or pups.

I walked on.

"Sam, you just got to quit worming my patients! You ain't any kind of a medical doctor. Emmitt Bennett couldn't do a day of work for almost a week after you dosed him."

"Ivamax is Ivamax, whether it's humans or donkeys. With Emmitt, who's to say what the difference is, anyway? The pin worms sure don't care. As to missing a day of work, it's easier to scare Emmitt out of a day's work than it is to kick a frog into that dang lake there! Besides, he ain't seen a doctor in 50 years"

Arney Shaw, our lone policeman, just hated discord. "Fellas, ain't no one dead. Why don't you just let it hang?" Everyone agreed Arney was the best man in Heartbreak to be a peace officer. More than once he'd talked down an armed drunk. The idea of his shooting someone was about as foreign to him as it was to Mother Teresa. Besides, if there needed to be shooting, Heartbreak had no shortage of volunteers.

Ben Samuels felt a need to assert himself. Samuels was the town mayor, mostly because he looked the part. He owned Samuels Insurance Agency and he saw being Mayor as a natural outgrowth of his position. I got nothing too strong against insurance men; I just don't have too much use for them, either.

Samuels drove one of those big, red Dodge Rams with duellies and mud tires, but no one had ever seen it leave the pavement. Above all else, Samuels loved to give speeches. He was a natural-born court-holder, the kind of man that had rather talk about a good dinner than eat one.

"Gentlemen, gentlemen, let not this fine day of celebrating our country's proud heritage be besmirched with discord! You both sow, you both reap! The community prospers, who can lose, one might well ask?"

Mr. Samuels loved to sound Old Testament. Sometimes he even slipped into "thee and ye (you and me). Most people at Heartbreak understood Mr. Samuels' unique story: an orphaned Jew brought up by Baptist parents to respect his heritage. Heartbreak doesn't often use the word "conflicted" but we did have Samuels.

I crept off. I'd rather hear the women's birthing stories than that old wind bag.

I got to looking for Sally Rae and Janey. Last thing I wanted was my daughter to get to feeling a little too patriotic and be "gone swimming at Heartbreak Lake," as Great Aunt Katy put it. As for Sally Rae, I didn't need a reason. I thought I better watch myself; at 60 I was running around like a 16-year-old struck love-dumb. At the same time I was more than a little worried about my own 16-year-old, Janey, who was as susceptible to hormone mismanagement any other healthy young lady.

John Briarsworth stepped in front of me. He had a way of just sort of appearing. John was a Vietnam vet who still lived in fatigues and camouflage paint; a man on permanent patrol. A little while back he saved me when my cousin and I got tried for murder.

"Hi, Dave."

"Hi there, John. Say, I never got a chance to thank you for saving me back at that trial...."

"All I did was tell the truth. No thanks needed."

"John, sure as young girls grow up too fast and goats are born to die, you told the truth. Others might not. I don't ever take truth for granted. Anyhow, I haven't seen you around lately. What you been up to?"

Heartbreak, Texas

Soon as I said it I felt foolish. Nobody saw John unless he wanted them to. He was just always a little out the corner of your eye, watching. It was the duty of a man on permanent patrol and he had chosen it as his calling.

"I got a new bivouac and a new mission."

"What's that?" I asked.

"Your Mayor, Ben Samuels, decided I must know all about explosives. Of course, I do. He had me make up the pyrotechnics this year. He said he didn't mind helping a vet and saving Heartbreak some money."

"Great. How's it going to look?"

"Real," John said. With that, he disappeared back into the woods.

I knew a warning when I heard one. I started looking for Janey and Sally Rae in earnest.

By luck I finally did locate them, both together and talking all private like. Dusk was starting to settle and the formal part of the ceremony was about to begin.

Hizzoner stood on the city's floating dock but today it was detached and moved out to the center of Lake Heartbreak. The official start was when Leroy Heichenbacher and the Strumming Fools played the Star Spangled Banner. We all rose up and saluted the song (well, more the idea of the song than the mangled mess the Strumming Fools delivered).

Samuels stood up and with all the superannuated specious dignity only a small town blowhard can manage, he bloviated until the fireflies came out about the role Heartbreak had in United States history. I was kinda impressed. This guy really *could* make bricks without straw. Of course, he was the only one on the stage.

Finally, just before he killed the spirit of the event, Mayor Samuels finished up with: "This year we have a special treat. John Briarsworth, our very own Vietnam Vet, has arranged a special fireworks event for us. He promised that it won't be just sparklers and Black Cat firecrackers. He said it would be like the real thing!"

No sooner were the words out of his mouth than a star shell flare burst over the lake. One of Mean Old Man Storm's pastures backs up to the lake. A series of strong explosions "walked" across the field, getting ever closer. I mean, these were BIG, not like anything I ever heard in civilian life.

176

The next explosion was under the City Dock and it threw Mayor Samuels 20 feet toward the shore. Samuels surfaced swimming like a muskrat chased by a hungry Cajun! Everyone applauded. Then the City Dock blew to pieces and something like white phosphorus lit the whole park from the center of the lake. Samuels' pretty red Ram truck blew up and spiraled to about where the dock had been. Next, the power pole that fed the dock blew straight into the air, exploded again with a slow charge, and landed head down in the lake, near where the truck sank. Its splintered top sat like grave marker for Mayor Samuels' truck.

John, the vet on permanent patrol, took his work seriously.

I hunkered down behind a boulder with one arm around Janey and another around Sally Rae. The whole town sat awed to silence when John's voice thundered over a loud speaker. "Are you going to just sit there and take this? Return Fire!"

In no time firecrackers and bottle rockets arched from all around the lake as the citizens responded. Homemade "can" bombs pelted the water's surface and a whole variety of Chinese-made rockets celebrated freedom. Potato cannon powered by hair spray supplied the heavy artillery. It went on until midnight.

The next day citizens were out on their own, picking up litter. The only casualty was Samboy, the cowboy, who had finally caught up with Louie. Samboy proudly held up a mangled hand swathed in bandages.

"I lost a finger and a thumb when my firecracker bag went off. Now let Louie get ahead of that!"

As I helped with the litter, John stepped out from behind a tree.

"You know Samuels has sworn out a warrant with Arney for your arrest, don't you?" I asked. "He is some sort of upset on account his unscheduled swim and his pretty red truck."

"Yeah, Arney told me that about 10 minutes ago. I ain't too worried. Samuels owns the insurance agency, so I figure he'll probably just make money off the deal. Lots of places need to be patrolled. Take care, I'll be back through."

With that, John, the Vet on permanent patrol, stepped back into the woods and disappeared.

CELEBRATE AMERICA

Pour the coffee, America,
In our great land of liberty,
Watching the orange-pink sunrise,
Over our home where we live free.

Take a moment, America,
To reflect on our history,
Remembering our first patriots,
The battles and the victory.

Stand strong and proud, America,
United is how we should be.
Let songs still sing of brotherhood,
From sea to shining sea.

Please celebrate, America,
Like they did when the war was done,
And they saw the flag still waving,
And realized that they had won!

Pour the coffee, America,
Wave as the parade passes by.
Be proud to be American
Have a happy Fourth of July.

Marlene Tucker

OF GHOSTS AND RESTLESS SPIRITS

THERE ISN'T MUCH NEW AROUND Heartbreak, but some old things can kind of change without you noticing at first. For example, Halloween has been getting a little bigger every year. The old men sitting around the wood stove in at The Waterin' Hole Café noted these changes—and all others—with uniform pessimism.

"Kids nowadays are just plain rotten," Old Sam threw out as a beginning proposition. This one was sure to get agreement, but it was so used up no one could get much inspiration.

"Ain't nothin' been right since Emma Bennett disappeared," Old Joe tried. Emma was Emmitt Bennett's twin. He was the town plumber and drunk; she was the town mystery. Twenty-six years ago, her boyfriend's car broke down. It was raining, so she stayed while he walked a mile up the road for help. When he returned, she was missing, and never was heard of again.

"Ain't nothing' been right since Roosevelt, that communist, ruined it all," Old Red said. He spat to prove his point, and the others agreed. Every President since Hoover came into disrespectful review. The old men were off for another glorious round, about as happy as they could get without a rabies or an anthrax outbreak to exercise their jawbones.

I sympathized with their plight, if not their analysis. They were old and broken in a place where most of us worked our tails off for uncertain rewards. "Sally Rae, I better get my check, day light's a wasting."

179

Sally Rae rewarded me with a brilliant smile. "Sure, Dave, come on back any time." Ever since I got caught skinny dipping at Heartbreak Lake, my personal stock had seemed to increase around town, at least with the ladyfolk. Go figure. "What's Janey going to come as tonight?" she asked.

"Some sort of princess, I imagine. She does adore Halloween." One of the things I liked best about Heartbreak was how the kids could get out and move around without much to fear.

On my way home, I stopped at Great Aunt Katy's for some fresh eggs. She was no direct relation, but Great Aunt Katy sort of mothered the whole little town. She was the real thing, old and shrunken as a leather glove left in the rain, but she was also spry and naturally kind as a body could get.

"How're your peacocks doing?" I asked as I pulled up. She kept all sorts of animals; donkeys, rabbits, and even an aged monkey named Chipper.

"Most are fine, but I'm worried about Chipper. He don't get round too well anymore." Sure enough, Chipper stood by her side, holding her hand. Chipper's face was pulled down in a set of wrinkles that gave him a permanent downcast expression. Texas doesn't let anyone off cheap.

"Now don't forget these eggs, like the last ones you did." She cautioned.

"I promise," I said. The last batch stayed under my pick up seat, forgotten like an unpopular scripture, until I happened to throw a wrench under my seat. On a calm day I could still smell them.

About dark thirty Janey and I headed back to town. "Nice princess get-up you got on today, darlin'." As a single dad, I acutely felt my inability to do the little things a gal expected from her mother, like sewing costumes.

"I just threw a few things together, guess it worked," Janey said. "I told some of my friends I might go with them for a little while. Is that alright?"

"Sure darlin'," I said. At 16, she was on the cusp — part kid, part woman, and all princess.

When we arrived back in Heartbreak, there were goblins and ghosts most everywhere. A rare but dense fog added to the atmosphere. Emmitt Bennett, dressed as a preacher, herded his tribe along one side of the street. I had to admire his sense of irony. BJ Elkert and Johnny Ruth walked their kids down the other side. Widow Johnson helped her grandkids along, from dim streetlight to door side. In a moment, Janey was whisked away by a band of marauding teens. Great Aunt Katy walked by, holding Chipper's hand.

"With this feller I don't even need a costume," she said brightly. I agreed. Still, they were better paired than a lot of other couples I knew.

"Hi, Dave," said a familiar voice beneath a witches' hat.

"Why, hi there, Sally Rae," I said. Latent ideas of romance stirred somewhere in the back of my shrunken libido. We walked down the darkening street together, not quite touching. I wanted to take her hand, but didn't quite dare. I wondered again if I could ever get over the awkwardness of adolescence. Just before I reached for her, though, a bag lady stumbled around the corner. She was pale as a ghost, prematurely aged, and mumbling to herself.

"Heck, you startled me. Who are you?" Sally Rae asked in some alarm.

"I'm Emma Bennett, help me, I'm so lost," the poor thing said. There, under the streetlight, I could see it. She was a dead ringer for Emmitt, only female. She even wore the little gold cross she had worn the night of her disappearance all those years ago.

Sally Rae gasped, and then caught herself. "You sure are. Come on, Emma, we're going to get you some help."

Her hand was dry as an autumn leaf and her skin was freakishly pale. Something about her just wasn't *right*.

We shuffled her down another block to the police station. It was empty. Our one cop, Arney, was extra busy that night.

"Just sit here, Emma. We'll be right back." Sally Rae dragged me out the door. "Dave, go on that side of the street and check for Emmitt. I saw him just a little while ago."

We split and searched. In no time it seems we found the Bennetts. Amid general excitement we ran back to the police station.

"Emmitt, come on, she's just inside," Sally Rae said as we all ran in.

The place was empty. There, on the counter, was a little gold cross. Emma had disappeared again.

A WHISPER IN THE WOODS

Beautiful autumn enticed the boy,
To make his way through the woods that day.
It was a quicker route home for him,
Though his mother told him not to stray.

The fall wind picked up and was blowing,
Through the tree limbs that shielded the light.
What seemed like a lovely afternoon,
Was beginning to take on the night.

The thicket no longer seemed friendly,
On the path leaves were tumbled and tossed.
A sudden chill ran down the boy's spine,
When he heard someone sighing "I'm lost."

At the woods edge stood the boy's mother.
He told of the sad, whispering moan.
She called it the wind but he wondered,
Might there be someone lost and alone?

Marlene Tucker

FALSE COLORS

RATHER LATE ONE FALL NIGHT I DROVE
up to The Waterin' Hole Café from our little ranch. It was raining
fiercely and a cold north wind made even the warmest-clad person
shiver and wish for a fire. Sally Rae's car was broken down again and
I was her ride home.

Inside The Waterin' Hole, things were downright poorly. One
couple ate and squabbled at a side table. I assumed the red Mini-
Cooper parked outside had to be theirs.

Sally Rae signaled me to a private spot in her kitchen. "Dave, I'm
glad you're here tonight. Something just ain't right with these folks.
Keep your eyes open, will you?"

The couple continued to argue with varying degrees of heat. I sat
quietly with my slice of vinegar pie as they finished eating and Sally
Rae cleaned up in her kitchen.

The man was tall and lanky, he had a pencil mustache and he had
fancy clothes that would have stood out even in a big city. His collar
did not quite cover a multicolored tattoo. He flashed a diamond-
studded Rolex on his left wrist.

She wore a gold-framed broach. These were their badges of wealth
and they didn't want anyone to miss it. The woman had honey-blonde
hair and blood-red lips. She had a figure that some plastic surgeon
had surely enhanced, or maybe she was Barbie come to life. It was
obvious that they thought themselves "fancy."

183

In a few minutes they finished up eating. The man walked over to my table. He tried to put on a friendly face, but I could tell it was an act for us yokels.

"Hey, stranger, how does a man get to the next town from here?" he asked.

"Just keep heading sort of north on the main street. There will be some twists and turns, but always stay on the largest road and you will hit the highway in about eight or 10 miles. Take a left and you'll find Culver City in about 20 more miles," I said.

He nodded, dropped a dime on Sally Rae's table, and walked off. I don't know if it was a deliberate insult or just ignorance, but Sally Rae and I both felt better when they were gone.

The word *glamour* has a peculiar history. Today it refers to the glitz and drama that Hollywood stars clothe themselves in; but in olden times *glamour* referred to sinister beings that shape shifted by misdirection into something hidden, always for the purpose of gaining an edge over their prey.

What happened next ultimately took months to piece together and it finally involved police in three different states.

Jedadiah Hull was a truck farmer who lived about seven miles down the road toward the turn. He lived by himself. Now, in Heartbreak, where most people consider it to be a privilege written into the Constitution to be a little strange, Jedadiah stood out as downright peculiar. The word "rube" springs to mind whenever I think of him.

Jedadiah was strong and bent before his time from his constant work in his gardens. His hygiene, his barbering, his whole affect seemed to hale from a century or so before now. He seldom spoke. He considered electricity a frivolous and unnecessary imposition. He heated by wood and illuminated by kerosene lamp. His sole concession to marketing was a hand-scrawled sign on his vegetable stand that said "Honk!"

We learned much later that as Jedadiah sat in the near dark of his home, staring at his fireplace, a knock came on his door.

"Yup?" he said.

"Mister, can you let us in? We have car trouble and we're sort of stuck."

Jedadiah was struck dumb for a long moment, and then he replied, "Yup."

As the wet couple came in, he made what was for him a great social concession; he lit a lamp.

The couple crowded on each side of Jedadiah in front of the fireplace. Soon steam began to fill the room as they dried. Outside the storm raged on. The fancy man exhibited a new found (but passionate) interest in growing tomatoes and cabbage. The woman crowded closer to Jedadiah than absolutely necessary, rubbing up against him in a way that could distract a saint from his good conduct.

"So, is there any money to be made in this truck farming?" the fancy man asked for the second or third time.

"Yup. More than most would imagine." Jedadiah nodded sagely toward a row of carefully stacked coffee cans in his simple, open kitchen.

The air thickened as the couple leaned closer, anxious to learn even the smallest bits of tomato and cabbage lore.

"I only grow Beefsteak Tomatoes; they're the sweetest of them all. Now cabbages are different. If you don't follow the moon charts, nothing will come up right. Celery, well celery is the real deal...." Jedadiah talked more than he had in years. People with a real interest in growing truck crops were rare, especially on cold, stormy nights.

As the fancy woman sank even closer to Jedadiah, the man with the thin mustache reached his hand into his coat.

With some apparent reluctance, Jedadiah at last remembered his social duties. "Can I get you folks something hot to drink?"

He stood up abruptly, and walked over to his stove.

The fancy couple sank back into their chairs. They never saw him lift his shotgun as he blasted them both from behind.

The next morning, Jedadiah hooked his tractor to the Mini-Cooper and drug it over to the ditch behind his place, the same ditch that held a half-dozen other cars of unfortunate travelers who had honked at the wrong place.

It's likely no one would have ever known anything about the whole incident if Jedadiah had not made the mistake of trying to pawn the diamond-encrusted Rolex over at Culver City. It had serial numbers relating to a theft in Colorado. The broach was also distinctive and listed as part of the haul in an armed robbery in Oklahoma.

Heartbreak, Texas

Jedadiah turned out to have his own interesting history, but most of you have already read those gory details in the newspapers.

For a time, it seemed that Heartbreak was about to become famous. But the people of Heartbreak don't do fame and generally find glamor of any sort to be a foreign concept. After a time things, quieted back down.

THE FOLLOWING NOTICE

Walking from the library,
On a chilly autumn night,
I found a discarded note,
At the base of a dimmed street light.

It read:
"Thank you for taking the time,
To read these words that I share.
Spending your precious moments,
Shows off your curious flair.

My words have special purpose,
Please pause to think them through,
Which will give me time enough
To slip right up behind you."

Marlene Tucker, 2014

A Wet Dog Needs Petting the Worst

ABOUT THREE YEARS AGO I FLED TO Heartbreak Texas, 50 or 500 miles west of Houston's sushi bars. I fled a painful divorce and pulled into a little town too small to be on any map I have ever carried, and with almost my last bit of energy I helped my daughter, Janey, into The Waterin' Hole Café for some relief. There, I got a piece of vinegar pie and a full breakfast for Janey. I couldn't have been lower. Sally Rae showed me kindness; I showed appreciation right back.

By the end of the week, I owned an old run-down goat ranch outside of the town too small to matter much to the rest of the world, and a dog. After two years (and many servings of vinegar pie) Sally Rae and I were married.

A man in the country has to have a dog, no matter how good his wife is. My dog believes in me absolutely. Whenever I start to doubt myself, I look into the brown eyes of my dog, and I get absolute acceptance. No questions. My dog thought more of me than I did myself and he was also a darn good goat dog. Well, I had the goat ranch, the goat dog and now I needed goats! Ah, goats.

At one of the first goat auctions I went to, I got a big Rodeo Red, a great old sweet-natured billy, and 18 females of uncertain breeding, but all looking real fecund. In my 45-mile run home, I ran my underpowered pickup truck to its best, but cold rains showered us all. I was in the cab, Janey was in school, Sally Rae was at The

Waterin' Hole Café, but I had a load of goats getting pelted with a combination of sleet and spring rain.

Anyway, I made it to my main barn and I unloaded all my goats. They ran inside to get out of the rain. Horses, sheep and cattle have a sort of oil on their skin that can give them protection from cold and rain. Goats don't. The first thing I did was light a fire in a little Ben Franklin stove. Next, I dosed them all with a molasses mix to give them a little immediate sugar. Then, I settled near to the Ben Franklin stove to rest a bit myself.

Suddenly, I had 19 goats pressing me away from the fire. The ones too close to the fire dried out quick, caught fire, and suddenly I'm stomping out flaming goats! The last thing I needed was a flaming kid running through my hay filled barn! It's funny how much more baby goats fear compression over combustion, but there you go. Don't get me trying to explain the contents of a goat's mind. It's like explaining the contents of a perfect vacuum. After stomping out each kid two or three times each, I got my idea across. And I managed to access only about three goats across the fire at a time. Later on, I cut some fencing panels around the stove to create "baby flaming goat preventers".

Meanwhile, Big Billy Red managed to get himself in position by leaning over my shoulder to gradually dry off.

A wet, fully testosterone-empowered billy is about the worst smelling thing on earth, except maybe one that's drying out. Big Red had manners; he appreciated me rotating him in and out like all the females, so he showed his gratitude by biting my ear, rubbing up against me, Oh Lord, the smell...! But the smell brought me to my senses. I needed help, hired help.

After taking Janey to school the next day, I stopped by The Waterin' Hole Café and I asked Sally Rae where I could find some labor. She said to check with Arney at the jail, and there I met John Briarsworth for the first time, a veteran of the Vietnam War. He is a man with a thousand yard stare, a man who had never come home from some distant patrol noone else remembers, in a land most Americans work hard to forget.

Arney said, "It's raining really hard and this guy comes in and asks to come into the jail, so I let him."

John Briarsworth was sort of a shaggy, grey-haired guy of medium height, with a professionally neutral look on his face. From all I could tell, he could be anything from a serial killer to an idiot. That day, I took a chance.

"Arney, parole him to me. If I don't certify him in 24 hours, you can go after him."

Me and John looked each other in the eyes, and we had an understanding.

I took him home and the first thing I asked was, "Are you hungry?"

"Yeah, I haven't eaten in a while."

I took him to my kitchen and fed him four eggs, three biscuits, a half pound of bacon, and as much jam as he needed. He was sort of like a silent eating machine; I fed him until he stopped eating.

"Are you full?" I asked.

"Yeah, let's get to work," John said.

That day John and I worked about 95 goats. I said, "Wait here," and I went to fix supper for my family; when I came out to invite him to join us, he was gone.

He has been back several times in my life, when his being back has been real important. It's a sort of a knack he has, showing up like Lone Ranger, and then disappearing off into the bush again.

John is a patchy sort of guy; he comes and he goes on his own sort of system. Sometimes he sort of loves me and sometimes he seems sort of angry at me. If I see him at Thanksgiving, I sort of try to get him in. Sometimes he comes, some Thanksgivings he isn't here. Sometimes he skips a year and sometimes he hovers around my ranch for a month.

To me, our veterans are a special sort of lot. These are the really good boys who went out there, fought and died, or got really injured. Some came home, some didn't and some sort of did. Many of the worst injuries leave no visible scars at all.

I am 63 now; I only tell the truth, because with my medical condition it is the only thing I have left. At 21, I became a conscientious objector. I refused to join the Army for a war I saw as already lost. I had many relatives off in the war. Forty years later, I stand by my position, but I stand by the positions of all my cousins, friends, brothers-in-law and other Americans who saw their moral choices differently.

John is about my age. Over time, John has gradually become a friend. Sometimes I sit on my back porch and I see him walk through my back pasture. I think one of his camping spots is back there. Sometimes I really wish that John would come in and have dinner with us. More, though, I hope John can find the missing parts of his soul on one of his patrols.

At the end of the day, I often stare into my mirror and think. I see unquestioning loyalty in my dog's eyes. I see love and devotion in Sally Rae's eyes. I see something much higher in John's eyes. I stare into my own eyes, and I pray to God that I have made the right choices.

SOLITUDE OF SERVICE

Ever silent are those who watch,
Protecting us with purpose clear.
The war is ugly and it's loud,
It's something we at home don't hear.

In hushed thoughts they travel quiet,
Forever changed by what they've seen.
Some come home dead and some alive,
Some suffer somewhere in between.

Returning home they make no sound,
Let them find thanks in how we cheer!
For every veteran's sacrifice,
Gave us the freedom we have here.

Marlene Tucker

THANKSGIVING SOUP

TWO YEARS AGO I MOVED TO
Heartbreak Texas with my daughter Janey. Heartbreak is a place where all the men expect meat for dinner, all the women want love but get children, and all the cows chew with philosophic stoicism as they smell barbecue and wonder about their missing cousins.

BJ Elkert and his brothers held Heartbreak together, though most people didn't much recognize it. Elkert's Auto Repair is Heartbreak's technology center. BJ could hardly write a comprehensible English sentence, but what he did with machinery was pure poetry. A typical Ford pickup was 30 percent Chevy and 20 percent John Deere by the time it hit 300,000 miles, the usual life span of a truck in Heartbreak. His understanding of machinery was more philosophical than mechanical.

I don't understand much more about mechanics than how to break something. That's why I sat and watched him as he repaired the city's fire truck before I went out to buy my Thanksgiving fixings.

"If I rout this little do-jigger this way, and turn it back there, I bet I can get another 30 percent more head pressure at the spout," BJ muttered. He was fixing Heartbreak's ancient fire truck pump.

"How'd you learn all this mechanical stuff?" I asked.

"Well, I was just too dumb to do well in school, so I did what I could," BJ answered.

It hurt to hear BJ call himself dumb. It was like hearing Michelangelo say that he drifted into painting because Latin was too hard. Changing the subject I asked, "Are you and Johnny Ruth doing anything special for Thanksgiving?"

"Nothing much. Just my four kids, their husbands and wives, grandkids, and a brother or three. I hope you and Janey can make it. Not much over about 17 of us, I reckon. I just wish Johnny Ruth didn't get so wadded up about fixing lunch."

Housewives in Heartbreak approached Thanksgiving dinner like Eisenhower approached D-Day. It wasn't a meal, it was a campaign. Johnny Ruth had started three days earlier, cooking copious batches of cornbread for the dressing. I'd give BJ an 'A' in mechanics any day or the week, but his understanding of women was as poor as his grammar.

When I drove up to the ranch, Janey and the neighbor boy, Jube, were sitting on my front porch. I didn't dislike Jube, exactly, but experience had taught me to be wary.

"I brought y'all somethin' special for Thanksgiving," Jube said.

He was grinning like a raccoon in breeding season. My anxiety level climbed.

"What now?" I asked cautiously. His last present was a baby skunk with adult size stink capacity.

"It's around here, in your tub."

My worry meter continued to rise. One of the few citified luxuries I brought with me from Houston was my hot tub. I didn't brag it about and I think most people thought it was some sort of hi-tech watering trough.

"Just wait 'till you see this," Jube continued.

Janey shook with barely stifled giggles. I didn't know what was coming, but I tried to remember if I had any Xanax left in my medicine cabinet.

Jube proudly pulled back my hot tub lid and there floating belly up was the biggest catfish I've ever met face to face. Jube's proud smile faded.

"He was just fine when I put him in here!" Jube exclaimed.

"I expect the chlorine killed him," I explained.

Jube's expression was one of Bambi-like innocence. "Chlorine, what's chlorine?"

Before I could explain, Jube pulled the big whiskered monster out and shook it a few times. "No problem, Mr. Dave. He's still limber."

Thanksgiving morning I saw BJ outside his house with the fire truck.

"Got a problem there, BJ?

"Naw. I need to test this rig and the old house is sort of dirty. I figured Johnny Ruth would like me to clean it off before everyone arrives." With that, BJ shoved down a lever and the hose came alive in his hands. He began a long sweep of his house. The new system worked fine, too fine, really. BJ must not have seen the windows collapse inward as the hose sprayed its jet of water.

I started toward him but Johnny Ruth ran out the door just as the stream hit her in the face, propelling her back inside. It would have been funny, if you didn't know Johnny Ruth. BJ finally figured out there was some sort of problem. He aimed the hose away and reached for the "off" lever; the errant stream knocked off about a third of his shingles before he could stop it.

Johnny Ruth recovered right fast. She was in BJ's face like a nose canker, madder than, well, a wet hen. "BJ, you numbskull!" she screamed, "The whole insides of our house is ruined. Dishes got blown off the wall, the refrigerator is knocked over, and the turkey went plumb into the dish water." Then Johnny Ruth proceeded to give poor BJ a broad-based cussin' that pealed paint off the ancient fire truck. I sort of tippy-toed off. I've never been much of a fan of public executions.

Back home, Janey helped me carry in the groceries for our family feast.

"Daddy, I thought we were going over to BJ and Johnny Ruth's place for Thanksgiving. Why are we cooking?"

"There's been a change of plans, honey. It appears BJ isn't so thankful after all and Johnny Ruth's just having Turkey soup. This year we're going to start a new tradition. I hope you like grilled catfish and dressing."

A Thankful Place

The homeless man sat by the railroad tracks,
Watching the upper class house down the hill.
It was the festive day of Thanksgiving,
Where folks were gathering to share a meal.

The cars drove up one after another,
Until they used all the space in the drive.
It gave the appearance of happiness,
Suggesting thankfulness might be alive.

The aroma of food wafted upward,
Serving the watcher a sweet memory,
He recalled when he was a happy boy,
And didn't know hunger or poverty.

A sudden scene at the house erupted.
Some angry people drove their cars away.
The man then gave thanks for Spam and crackers,
And his solitude on Thanksgiving Day.

Marlene Tucker

NANNIES, GIRLS, AND WOMEN:
A CHRISTMAS SURPRISE

I'M PART CHEROKEE. WE WERE THE
"civilized" tribe, which is Indian code for being easy to sneak up on.
It's no wonder that I was plumb slow at finally understanding a few
of the underlying parts of Heartbreak's social order. "Redneck" was
another word for "neighbor", "smart" was usually a contraction for
"smart aleck", and "city fella" was code for "damn fool."

The sweetest women around began the most devastating social
critiques with "Bless her heart, she's doing the best she can." The
phrase was often applied to Sally Rae, my girlfriend and favorite
waitress at The Waterin' Hole Café, who had a child out of wed lock
about 20 years before I arrived in Heartbreak.

Most agreed it wasn't her fault that her fiancée died in a wreck a
just before her wedding. Her son, Jerry, had been a "little rounder,"
probably because of the shock Sally Rae got when Arney, the local
law, drove up and told her that her wedding had been replaced by a
funeral. She fainted outright. Poor Sally Rae knew she had been a
little "previous," and now she was in Dutch.

Small towns can be awfully judgmental, but they can also be
surprisingly tolerant. She was given the usual baby showers, and she
received the usual amount of help young mothers get, plus (she told
me, giggling) about 20 Bibles. After all, Poor Sally Rae, bless her
heart, was doing the best she could.

Heartbreak, Texas

Nature decreed that baby goats mostly were born in the worst weather in mid-winter. This Christmas was proving no exception. I didn't forget Janey's presents, but we mostly didn't have time for decorating the mesquite bushes around the barn with tinsel and mini-lights. Even if we had, the goats would have eaten them, tinsel and all.

Janey adapted to country life with surprisingly little complaint. She loved our goats better than I did and she had a better sense of animals than I ever would. She could milk out a swollen udder with kindness and dexterity I could only wish I had. Many nights, I held a kerosene lantern and read aloud from my goat book with its accumulated wisdom while my daughter assisted in a difficult birth, her arm buried up to the elbow inside a desperately unhappy nanny, bless her heart.

Birthing times got pretty lively around the goat ranch. A strict rule of momma goats was that no kid could be nursed by anyone except the mother. Frequently if a nanny has twins she will be so distracted licking and fussing over the first one that she won't even notice the second one. She has to be convinced the new one is hers, too.

It was not unusual for 30 goats to all birth on the same day, almost the same hour. Birthing always left the mothers a little dazed; kids are born dumber than a bag of hammers. Imagine 30 perplexed mothers sorting for their own among 40 or 50 new kids, everyone running around in frenzy. The technical term for this is "udder confusion."

It was after just such a day that Janey, with all the energy of youth, ran down to the creek and gigged a half dozen bull frogs. She ran back up and cleaned and sautéed them in garlic butter.

"I got something special for you tonight, Daddy," she said as I sat, exhausted, at the table. Suddenly a pair of legs (sans body) jumped clean out of the skillet. "Oops, guess I forgot to pull the nerves on that one." Without hesitation, she washed the legs and pulled the offending nerve cords.

Something was bothering me. During the Christmas ham'n'yams dinner at the Cottonwood Baptist Church the previous week, I had picked up on a snatch of gossip about Janey and me from the women's table.

"I'm sure Dave does the best he can, but, bless his heart.... (something, something)...poor Janey."

198

I finally realized maybe I was short changing Janey on how to grow up and be a woman. I definitely had higher hopes for her than raising a big crop of kids in Heartbreak with some sweaty redneck. But I also didn't feel right closing the door into the "women's world" without her having a full set of options.

"Darlin', there's nothing better than a plate of your smothered frog legs," I said, but my mind was elsewhere.

Next day at The Waterin' Hole, I lingered over my pie and coffee until I got a quiet moment without other customers. I asked, "Sally Rae, could you do me a big favor?"

"Not unless we're married first; for one thing I couldn't store all the new Bibles."

We both laughed. Sally Rae was quick.

"Naw, naw, nothing like that. I'm just a little worried about Janey. She's growing up a little short on femininity in her life. Most days she can out tomboy half the boys her own age. That suits me just fine, but I'm worried I may be short changing her on women stuff."

What came next shouldn't have surprised me. Sally Rae and I had been dating a little, but we had hardly gotten past holding hands and a little kissing. My divorce in Houston had left me pretty much burned down to the stump.

All of a sudden as I sat there, Sally Rae walked up close, real close. So close in fact, my side vision was cut off by two of the finest examples of womanhood to be found in Heartbreak; and the Valley of Opportunity and Indecision opened before my nose. I felt dazed as a new-born kid, and felt tempted by the same set of options. As I inhaled the scent of a woman, my knees went so weak I was glad I was already seated. Had Christmas come early this year?

Sally Rae looked down at me, no humor in her voice this time. "Were you wanting part-time lessons for Janey, or full-time?"

I took a deep breath of lilacs and woman. Udder confusion wasn't just for new born kids.

Perky Business

Buxom Betty was a new employee,
At the salon where she did pedicures.
Around town she handed out some coupons,
Hoping they would work as customer lures.

Mr. Perklow was a grumpy old man,
Who owned the small town's only hardware store.
He never smiled at anyone he saw,
And he complained about his feet being sore.

He went in with a coupon for service.
Betty sat low on a stool at his feet.
He smiled at the professional attention,
And thought the view was especially sweet.

No longer is Mr. Perklow frowning.
He's seen grinning at all who happen by.
He and Betty are soon getting married.
He's so happy and now you know why.

Marlene Tucker

The Chip on My Shoulder

ABOUT 50 OR 500 MILES WEST OF Houston's sushi bars is a little town called Heartbreak, Texas. I fled there four years ago after a painful divorce with purt near nothing but my broken-down pickup truck and my daughter Janey. My wife, Beverly, had left me for another man, with all my worldly possessions but my broken-down pickup truck, and my beautiful teenage daughter, Janey.

We arrived at sunup and ate breakfast at the town's only restaurant, The Waterin' Hole Café. Our waitress, Sally Rae, married me on a stormy day two years later. A whole lot happened in between, but this is about the chip on my shoulder.

I spent two years in my own personal Hell, being angry about my divorce, angry about how much work it took to keep my little ranch together; why, a man never catches up. I wanted to replace a mile and a half of bad fence but all I could do was patch it. I wanted to plow a fire ring around my place when fires surrounded me in the summer drought, but all I could afford to do was patch my old hoses and hope for rain. I wanted to buy Janey a fine dress for her senior prom, but I just managed to get the material that Sally Rae sewed up for Janey the night before the big event.

Anyway, Sally Rae and I got to be better friends over times.

For way too long, I was angry about what Janey's momma had done to me: taking up with another man, cheating on me, leaving us. I was angry, *angry,* **angry.**

201

Heartbreak, Texas

Anger takes a whole lot of energy. Laughter and beauty feeds the soul, but anger saps it. It's a good thing people aren't logical. I mean, Aristotle did a great thing for humans—inventing logic, writing the first encyclopedia, and all his other fine theories. Western cultures benefited enormously, but Aristotle had little insight into the human soul *(psyche)*.

I was angry, but I found relief in religion. I found the most relief in the beliefs of my fathers, at Cottonwood Baptist, but I also found relief in one of the few personal treasures I had carried out with me when I fled Houston: I had my (mostly) unread textbooks from college.

For a time I re-read (or first read) my old text books. One told me about how the Arapaho live in beauty, walk in beauty, and have healing ceremonies after conflict so they can dwell in beauty again. I read it one day as I sat watching my goats. A feral dog was stalking them and I was stalking him or I wouldn't have had the time. A walk in beauty in Heartbreak is a relative sort of thing.

It sounded a lot like living in grace, a Baptist sort of concept. I worked and I pondered. Also, time did its work. Never underestimate the power of time for healing.

About this time I piled up a bunch of brush. Saturday night in the country has its own pleasures. Trees fall; limbs and trunks go into firewood and make a modest amount of money. The tops I pile up and a few times a year we have friends over for a bonfire. We called it watching "Medieval TV." It's a country pleasure.

To start it I poured gasoline over the brush (as I had many times in the past) and threw a torch at it. But the wind unexpectedly reversed, and I was suddenly engulfed in a ball of blue flame.

I only had time to blink. My eyes were protected but my hands were much closer to the fire. I heard "foof!" and I walked away, stunned, but I had been toasted! Long sleeves saved my arms, but my hands suddenly began giving up water to the surface; I knew I was burned. My eyebrows were suddenly crusty and my eye lashes felt brittle. Yep, I was toast.

Among my friends, Sal turned and poured ice water on my hands. Then God began to take me on His walk in beauty. A rain came, ice cold. It showered my hands. I was really burned, but none of my friends knew it. The rain continued to shower my hands. After about

20 minutes, the bonfire fire went out and we all went inside. By then my hands felt almost normal. The next day I just had a couple of small blisters and shed skin in some others, but my old rancher's hands have been through a lot. I healed. It took more time than I wish it did, but I healed.

The shock of the burn and the fear it inspired as I reflected on the closeness of my own near destruction worked together to make me appreciate what I had, rather than what I had lost. It changed my channel.

One evening shortly before Christmas, Sally Rae was sitting around sewing a dress for Janey's church program when a big car pulled up. It was Janey's mother, Beverly, and her parents, Josh and Wendy.

I was first on the porch, with a light in their eyes. "Who're you?" I asked?

Janey busted past me into her mother's arms. I knew who they were. We all stood there for a moment or two, and then I said, "This here is Sally Rae, my wife. Come one in, if you dare."

I felt like a hen that had just laid a square egg.

My ex-father-in-law looked like a donkey passing fresh peach pits.

We looked at each other. Then I remembered how I had always liked him.

"Josh, can I get you something," and we all started talking at once.

We had a fine time that night. I even enjoyed catching up with my ex on her news. I always liked her family.

I have my limits. Her lover had caught a "sudden cold" on news that Janey's family intended to stop by my place. Funny how things are. A year ago I would probably have shot him dead on the spot, but now, well, now was different. He wasn't welcome, but I was developing a new found relief that I had Sally Rae and Janey. I felt a moment of communion with my ex, Beverly, and somehow, I saw my path into beauty. We talked until very late.

We had a few awkward moments, but we all ended up in the Living Room. Janey was half crazy for want of her mother and Beverly was the same. They hugged and kissed, and kissed and hugged. For a moment the rest of us just sat here, uncomfortable. About then Li'l'

Billy walked in, all sleepy-eyed and rubbing his face.

"Everybody, this is Li'l' Billy, our new foster son." I announced.

There's nothing like a little child to thaw the atmosphere.

"Of what vain effort do we all conceive when we first conceive?" Li'l' Billy announced, but Wendy, my ex-mother-in-law, just said,

"Sit in my lap."

"If Men did not know of honey, they would think of figs sweeter than they do." With that he snuggled down between her grandmotherly bosoms and went immediately back to sleep.

After that we all talked for about two or three hours. As time passed even my ex and I spoke civilly to each other. I don't remember what we said, but afterward we felt relief.

I finally learned the essential truth of forgiveness: by lightening the other person's load a little, I had lightened my own burden a lot. Forgiveness is about personal healing, not surrender.

I can still wake up and feel a chip on my shoulder about my divorce. More and more it weighs like a fallen leaf. I can shrug, and it continues its journey without weighing me down.

In a lot of important ways, this was the best Christmas I ever had.

Pining Away

"It made it one more year!" Mom said,
As out came the old silver tree.
I had hoped it'd turned to ashes,
We had owned it since '63.

In minutes Mom had it in place,
A small sheet wrapped around the stand,
A wheel of rotating colors,
Worked to make the silver look grand.

Oh, how I wanted a pine tree,
That was green, full and eight feet tall,
With a scent that smelled like Christmas.
That would be the best part of all!

Mom hugged me up close to her cheek
Sweetly speaking without a clue,
"Someday, dear when you are grown-up,
I'll give the little tree to you."

Marlene Tucker, 2014

205

Heartbreak High

The Waterin' Hole for Democracy

Heartbreak often presents itself as a time-frozen place a hundred years ago, a convenient mask for the sorts of complexities that enrich and bedevil every human village on the planet.

Take Heartbreak High school, for example. I've always thought our schools are a perfect mirror of our world; they make up the best and the worst of our society. The teachers are lazy and dedicated, enlightened and backward. Sometimes one person might fall in several categories at once. It's all a little messy, just like democracy.

Those were my thoughts as I tried to drive Janey to school one morning. It was a raw, cold day where ice crystals boldly marched down the road ahead of my truck. I have a theory on schools and bad weather. If the school closes in a timely manner for a blue norther, don't worry too much. If the school stays open in the face of an icy prediction, hunker down! This day was a hunker down day if I ever saw one. My heater and wipers couldn't keep up with the freezing rain and the roads were turning bad real fast.

Three large deer bounded across the road in front of me.

"Did you see that?" I asked Janey.

"What, the rabbit?"

"No, two does and a beautiful buck just jumped the fence in front of us," I replied.

Silence, then finally, "I saw a rabbit. That's my story and I'm sticking to it," Janey replied, a little petulantly.

I thought about kids, Gestalt psychology and bad music. I understand why kids shouldn't drink. They are herded around all day, given countless tasks they can't control, and the whole time their minds are a simmering swamp of mercurial emotion. I looked again at Janey. Yep, she had a hormone hangover if I ever saw one.

Back in Houston, I had been a teacher myself for 15 years. I'm not about to say I've seen it all—no one has—but I've seen enough to be glad my daily due was dealing with goat kids, not human ones. I remembered the stories one accumulates; once a boy shyly gave me a note from his mother before class that read, "Pleas watch Johnny today. His father died last nite and he may be sad." I did watch Johnny, and prayed for him, too.

Another day, blustery and cold as today, the principal delivered two feral girls to my class. They spoke no English and both were dressed in shorts and t-shirts. Their heads were full of lice. Were their parents bad parents? Probably not. I imagine they arrived late the night before from Mexico, tired and hungry. Their parents would not have heat, food, or warm clothes at home, so they delivered their precious daughters to class, my class. They were doing the best they could, bless their hearts. Like more than one teacher before me, I worked a private, emergency deal through the school. At least those girls went home with jackets that day.

I finally putty-putted my old truck into the school yard about 15 minutes late, proud to have made it and worried about the return trip.

"I'll walk you in, Janey," I said. I knew how sticky school has to be about tardy arrivals and I didn't want Janey getting in trouble.

The first person I met was Assistant Principal Dwight Johnson. He was ticking students off as they arrived.

"Do I need to sign any papers?" I asked.

"No, anyone who makes it today is a hero, or they just can't stand their kids. Hold on, Dave, I have a favor to ask. Several of our teachers are snowed in and we're really short-handed today. You are a teacher, aren't you?"

Well, being a teacher is sort of like being a convict; once you get your papers you have to die before clemency is granted. "Yeah, before I raised goats."

"Can you stay today? Stay and teach? I don't know about pay and such, but I do know I got a situation on my hands. Frankly, I'm a little worried."

I looked through a window at the road disappearing behind me. I knew Dwight Johnson from church and town and such. He is good sort; started as a coach but grew a brain and a heart along the way.

"Sure, where do you want me?"

In no time I was in an English class in front of 20 young minds straining for new knowledge. Actually, they laughed and giggled and wanted to watch snow, not read books. I forced aside the first sense of panic that always comes with a new class and started reciting Chaucer's *Prologue to Canterbury Tales*, all in Middle English. If you are going to do a job, act like you know what you're doing; don't ever show fear or uncertainty.

For about three minutes I had them; I was almost finished and was ready to go to a discussion of Middle English humor when Jerry Lawson interrupted me.

"This is English, teach, are you crazy or foreign?" Jerry's voice made it clear that either was equally unacceptable.

Conner Kincaid, sitting next to him chimed up, "He's stupid as you are, Jerry. That's his problem."

Jerry knew he couldn't win on eloquence, so he popped Conner on his jaw. Two seconds later, they were out of their desks exchanging blows like prize fighters. I walked between them. Neither hit me; I was counting on it. The idea was not to fight, but to disrupt class.

Soon as I got them separated I said, "Out in the hall. NOW, both of you!"

For the next three minutes I berated each of them with the meanest teacher talk I had, but darn it, I was rusty. There is a long list of things a teacher **can't** say, including profanity. The problem is I knew their parents, and it usually took a 10 minute cussing just to get them out of bed. Nothing I was allowed to say would even reach their hearing level, much less change behavior.

Don't be a teacher if you can't think on your feet. I knew I had about 30 more seconds before I lost the whole class, so I herded both boys back in.

Heartbreak High is an old, old school, reflecting the community's distrust of new ideas and new land taxes. In the back of a class was a long coat closet with a door at each end. I set a desk at each entrance with the boys firmly seated, facing the class.

During the next 40 minutes I actually did get a little real teaching done as Jerry and Conner glared at each other. Finally, at the last of the class I heard loud smacks and a fight going on in the back of the closet. Those boys were the same size. All their lives they had counted on adults separating them before any real damage was done. I tried something different. I got selectively deaf and kept on teaching.

"...and so, I think we can all see that Geoffrey Chaucer lived in the time of Black Plague, faced problems not too different than ours, and matched life with a sort of humorous valor not too different than our own." The bell rang and everyone walked out, nice as lambs. The closet had gotten noticeably quieter.

Jerry walked out first, rather subdued. He had a split lip and a beautiful shiner underway. Conner followed with a bad limp and a little seepage of blood from his right ear. He was not a happy camper.

Assistant Principal Johnson stood outside in the hall. "I heard a little disturbance as I walked by," he began. "Want to tell me about it?"

"Why, that was just Jerry and Conner learning how to be responsible for their own actions," I offered.

A twinkle crossed his eyes and was gone so fast I almost missed it. "Dave, if the goat thing doesn't work out, come see me. I can always use a teacher with experience."

Snow in the Night

White and fluffy free-falling flakes,
Floating softly to the ground,
Covering the earth in a blanket,
Without ever making a sound.

Blowing and piling snow crystals,
Accumulating inches deep,
A sparkling surprise for morning,
Made in the night while we're asleep.

Marlene Tucker

WERT THE QUIRT

PART I

CLAUDIUS D. WERT WAS THE PUBLIC face of education in Heartbreak, and scarcely anybody can remember when that wasn't true. He had stayed on decades after most educators of his years would have retired. In some cases, he has taught the great-grandchildren of his original pupils.

He has been known—for as long as anyone can remember—as "Wert the Quirt" because of his penchant for enforcing school discipline with his old riding crop.

Recently, Wert was steadily whacking away on Josh Kaeineke, a big-boned junior from Quick Fix. Josh and another knucklehead from Quick Fix were in a contest to see who could get the most licks before mid-term. Back in the day, a swat from Wert's quirt would sting for half an hour. The years were catching up with the sainted authoritarian, though. He just didn't have the zing of his younger days of whuppings.

"Twenty, 21, 22 . . . *arggghhhh!*" Old Wert said.

Josh turned around, and to his amazement found the elderly Superintendent-for-life collapsed on the floor and a puddle of urine trickling off beside him.

Josh ran into the hallway. "Come quick," he called out. "Mr. Wert is sick, real bad!"

A cluster of teachers huddled around him.

The way Old Wert was holding his chest, it was obvious that he was having a heart attack. Ellie Jones, the English teacher, called for an ambulance. Mildred Lockhart, the school nurse, gave him 5 baby aspirin and propped a blanket behind his head. Wert hung on, with the expression of bull-turned-steer, sort of amazed at his own looming mortality.

Josh Kaeineke interrupted the solemn gathering with the request, "Uh, could someone give me another three licks? I need to get back to class."

"We're going to let you off the hook this time; punishment is canceled," Junie Hathouse said.

"Well, you see," Josh explained, politely as he could, "Johnny Salinger has 142 licks for the year. Right now I'm stuck at 140. I mean, there's this sort of bet going on…."

Mrs. Jones glared at him with her best Teacher Death Gaze. Josh wilted and shuffled off, all unfulfilled.

In short, an era came to an end. For more than 60 years, Mr. Wert had terrorized students and teachers alike. He was the only man in Heartbreak's history to wear the double crown of Superintendent *and* Principal of Heartbreak High School.

Over the years, he had originated Raccoons as the school mascot and he had introduced photography classes in the 1960's. At the end of each school year, every one of his teachers was required to meticulously record each student's grades in nib pen ink and hand-deliver said report to Mr. Wert.

Then Mr. Wert would deliver *his* nib pen-written evaluation of each teacher. The teacher was allowed to read it one time, sign it and hand it back. With great ceremony, Mr. Wert would seal all the documents in multiple layers of cellophane and masking tape. At the close of school, Old Wert would shoulder the giant package and walk it up the stairs to the school attic. J. Edgar Hoover was no more proud of his files than Claudius D. Wert was of his package. Neither shared, neither talked, but each lived with access to immense personal data that made them feared and loathed.

Heartbreak ISD had a real problem. Wert had run things for decades. He paid the lawn boy, the kitchen staff and ran most everything. His sudden loss created a vacuum, and, as Aristotle noted, nature abhors a vacuum.

A lively young man of 60, Dr. Norman Adam, was brought in. His title was as imposing as it was long: Acting Superintendent/Principal Dr. Norman Adam. Most people liked him; still, he was an Outsider.

It soon becomes obvious that, much like his health, Wert had let a few too many things slide in recent years. The school was cluttered with trophy-filled cases fairly groaning with football glory. These displays lined both sides of the hallway, and in recent years had begun to ooze into classroom space. Classes were dangerously over crowded already. Two chemistry rooms, in fact, were permanently sealed because of the random, unspecified sorts of compounds stored within. Most of the ancient brass fire extinguishers were old enough to seek tenure. The attic was filled to the point of imminent collapse with annual records, as well as broken and obsolete furnishings.

Dr. Adam called an emergency board meeting to get rid of the trophies.

"We don't have a school so much as a museum of all the things the team has won over six decades," he complained. "If we had a fire inspection tomorrow they would shut the entire school down. We need more space, and I mean right now!" he declared.

He might have gotten his way without further ado except that he finished his thought. "After all, what is our school? An institution of learning or a monument to the history of football?"

He meant this as a rhetorical question, but Dr. Adam had seriously underestimated the true temperament of Heartbreak. Football was the real, actual soul of Heartbreak, if not its true religion. Old timers often sat around arguing about who had *really* fumbled the ball in games where most of the players had long ago joined Knute Rockne on that great gridiron in the sky. Love of the Game had held the community together through war, fire and even drought. Few of the old ranchers on the school board had used quadratic equations or the pluperfect tense to maintain their property, but all of them had relied on the old boy network of football's true believers at one crisis or another.

Not realizing his error, Dr. Adam compounded it by announcing, too avidly, "Those dusty old trophy cabinets just have to go!"

In no time, this caused Heartbreak to split into two competing factions: Pro-trophy and Anti-trophy.

The Pro-trophy Party anxiously awaited the return of Wert, the past and future king. They adopted the slogan, "Wert It Not For Our Past..."

The Anti-trophy Party used the slogan, "Our School Is Sick; Better Call the Doctor."

Like only small town politics is capable of, the air soon was poisoned with extremist and inflexible positions. "I Wert NEVER change!" :Wert it all for naught?" Discussions quickly turned bitter, as only inter-family problems can.

For a while it seemed that the Pro-Wert faction would triumph. Scarcely a man or woman in Heartbreak had grown up without a walloping from Wert the Quirt. Many feared for the future of their children if a generation were spared the "board of education."

To invite change was to inspire real slander; the Anti-trophy group was rumored to be closet *liberals*. One must understand, the word "Liberal" was pronounced like a swear word, like a surrogate for "Communist," as in *'That Comm'nist, Roosevelt'*."

Finally, word reached the state — probably through that snarky food inspector, Rufus Toby. He was Heartbreak's mainline to the state's authority, and as such he was despised by all freedom-loving folk. A state official showed up on the steps of Heartbreak High one day. He emerged somewhat ashen-faced a few minutes later and gave citizens 10 days to get the halls cleared in their venerable old fire trap.

Put against the wall, the school board entertained a suggestion from Dr. Adam: The attic would be cleared of all but the last 10 years of records. Spare furnishings and old supplies would be sold. The newly-found attic space could temporarily be filled with trophies and cases so that classes could continue.

The records would be returned to former students. Democracies don't like sealed files, no matter what they contain. It was a compromise that all but the most extreme partisans could agree to.

It sounded so simple, straight forward, and even democratic. No one (except possibly Wert the Quirt) could imagine the vexation and town-wide crisis this would cause.

HIDDEN ANIMOSITY
(Part 1, Suza)

Suza had eighteen broken clocks,
And twenty thousand rubber bands.
She kept ten pounds of fishing weights,
Under her bed in coffee cans.

Her magazines and news papers,
Stood in stacks at least six feet high,
Next to boxes of broken tile,
With just a path for walking by.

Her dull kitchen looked abandoned,
Heaped up with things covered in rust.
A display of dolls and tea pots,
Sat on old boxes holding dust.

Suza knew she was a hoarder.
People often asked her "Why?"
"Collecting is how I spend my life"
Says she, "I'll stop it when I die."

Marlene Tucker

215

THE GREAT HOUSE CLEANING

PART 2

HEARTBREAK IS 50 OR 500 MILES WEST of Houston's sushi bars. Heartbreak is the best and the worst of where our grandparents grew up. It holds on to Reconstruction grimness and Depression Era values like an old maid loves her sense of propriety. Still, folks here can be gentle and kind as any I ever met.

Three years after I came to Heartbreak Texas I was married to Sally Rae, waitress at The Waterin' Hole Café, and we had a four-year old foster son, Li'l' Billy, a devilishly smart sort of a lad that learned to read too early and never missed a chance to quote something. My beautiful daughter, Janey, was off at college.

Wert the Quirt was a great disciplinarian. He had run Heartbreak's education system for about 60 years when a sudden heart attack sent him to a rest home. Wert got his nick name from his generous use of a riding crop on malcontent students. Still, some called him Wert the Quirk for some of his strange ways.

For one thing, he always had new cameras (at the school expense), but for some reason or another, some looming crisis always prevented him from being able to teach the photography class he occasionally spoke about. For another, he kept the attic of Heartbreak Highs School crammed with years and years of sealed records.

Our new chief educator, Acting Superintendent/Principal Dr. Norman Adam, almost got himself fired at the git-go by trying to get rid of the trophies and dusty old paperwork. It's likely he would have lost his job for messing with "the holy of holies," football, but the mighty State of Texas stepped in, in the form of a fire inspector from Austin. This inspector had more respect for child safety than the sacred institution of football. Go figure. He probably moved to Texas from one of those northern, subversively liberal states, like Oklahoma or Kansas.

"Either get rid of the trophies or get rid of the students. This is profoundly unsafe," he said, after seeing how narrow the hallways had become after being lined on both sides with display cases. The plan finally agreed upon was to distribute all the personal records Wert had kept over the years, to give them directly to the people involved, and move at least some trophies upstairs.

The day before this action was put into place, Mr. Wert left Shady Rest Home for parts unknown. Upon hearing this most folks were puzzled, and Sister Alva said she'd hold his name up for special prayer next Sunday at Cottonwood Baptist. Several people around her said, "Amen," and then moved quietly away from her. Such open piety did not generally characterize folks around here.

On the day of the Great House Cleaning, most of Heartbreak's assorted generations gathered together on a big lawn beneath the shade trees near the school. Raccoon Band Boosters were selling cookies to the gathering crowd. First, they auctioned off the furniture. Some question was raised about all the fine, late model photography equipment; no one could exactly remember the last year Wert had offered a photography class.

Finally, five lines formed at five tables, 1960 through 2006, and people started getting their permanently sealed records. Due to Dr. Adam's careful organization, passing out all those documents did not take long at all.

Sudden as a Texas cloud burst, a great change came over the entire crowd. Like any person long denied a look at personal information, each recipient tore open their personal, sealed records, right then and there. All at once, a general muttering started. Some people laughed, others cried. Outrage to the point of homicidal anger characterized many. A few began making barking noises like dogs. It sounded a little like the fabled old time tent revivals, but the cause was far different.

I sat right next to Sally Rae as she opened hers. In her senior year file was a photograph. I recognized her — that is, all of her. There was my beautiful bride, walking out of the girl's shower, nekkid as a hard truth! The photograph was obviously taken deep from within the sacrosanct confines of the Girls' side of the gym complex. I mean, it was sort of full-frontal and way too informative.

Sally Rae sat down, sort of stunned, on the back of my old pickup truck. Sure enough, right next to her grades was an 8X10 black and white photo of Sally Rae at 18, dressed exactly as God had designed her. Say what you will about Old Wert; he knew how to get a fine focus from a camera.

So dismayed was she that she did not hear Li'l' Billy creeping up, all curious like, in the pickup bed.

Behind us, in his clear, high voice, Li'l' Billy started in,

Your breasts are like two fawns,
like twin fawns of a gazelle
that browse among the lilies.
Until the day breaks
and the shadows flee,
I will go to the mountain of myrrh
and to the hill of incense.

Sally Rae slapped the file shut and in one of those decisive moves a mother instinctively knows how to make, she turned and boxed Li'l' Billy's ears.

"Daddy, did I get it wrong? It's right there in the Bible. That's what it says in Song of Solomon!

"No, son, you got it right. One day you'll learn that getting it right will get you in a lot more trouble than getting it wrong," I said. "Did you think Christ got crucified for *lying* about people?

There was also, apparently a yearly photo essay on each of the female teachers as well. Wert the Quirt was speedily re-dubbed Wert the Perv.

By then, most of the people had turned varying shades of red, and many of them could see red.

Junie Hathouse, who had taught gym and High School Literature in the '70's and 80's, said, "So that's how that conniving old snake caught me at just four months! I thought I could serve out the rest of the semester if I just kept wearing baggy clothes."

"Why that old pervert done just shit all over my whole high school experience," yelled Sara Gene, wife of one of the Quick Fix Cedar Choppers.

Ellie Jones, the English teacher, corrected her automatically, "Why, that old pervert shat all over my high school experience." Then she caught herself and blushed even deeper. "And say 'poop' in public, if at all possible."

The spirit of general dismay continued to grow. Boisterous discontent grew exponentially. Of course, the formerly Pro-Werts were the loudest faction, like any new set of converts.

Great Aunt Katy, who had taught English for some years at Heartbreak High, finally walked up to the microphone and tapped it a few times to get everyone's attention. She was our spiritual heart and soul, even more than football, and we sure needed her wisdom now.

"None of us have been shown around publicly except to that randy old coot, Wert. Odds are *he* can't remember much, anyhow, that senile old goat. We could prosecute, but why? You have the pictures back in your own hands. Do with them what you like."

Then Great Aunt Katy held her own photograph up to her nose for close inspection.

"Darn, you know, I forgot what it was like to have a waist line. I'd almost forgotten what it was like to have Lucy and Ethel both standing at attention." Laughter rippled around the crowd and soon people started to lighten up.

About then Mrs. Brigadier General Ashford Miller Forest stood up. "As for all the trophies, well, we have some unexpected space at Le Beaux Art Metropolitan Museum. We could store them there, uh, I don't know, until a new high school gets built."

Sally Rae and I both looked over at her former nemesis with more indulgence than we had ever felt before. We had weathered this crisis; Heartbreak had started to move on.

HIDDEN ANIMOSITY
(Part 2, Milton)

Now, Milton was Suza's husband,
He couldn't live within her hoard.
Often he couldn't find his wife,
And soon found himself quite bored.

He took a job as a waiter,
At the town's local bar and grill.
He seemed like a careful worker,
Except for the drinks he would spill.

He only spilt near the women,
Always cleaning the best he could,
Letting his mind and hands wander,
A little closer than they should.

One mad husband looked for vengeance.
Milton ran in fear for his life.
He hid in the fullness of his house,
But was found with the help of his wife.

Marlene Tucker

CRIMSON AND CLOVER

SALLY RAE AND I ARE SORT OF DATING.
I'm 60 and she's about 45. She is the waitress at The Waterin' Hole Café; I'm her most loyal patron. Sally Rae has eyes the color of love: they're green on the outside and blue toward the middle. I could just fall into those eyes over my daily Dr Pepper if she let me.

Sally Rae has had a hard life. Her fiancée got killed just before her wedding and a few months later she had his son. Most folks forgave her (and judged her), but her son never quite fit in. He had a little "sugar in his shorts" as we say in the South; Heartbreak could forgive that too, but he couldn't. He fled when he was 18.

All this happened years before I came to Heartbreak. I came with my own luggage. Janey was a handful, and so were my goats. I bought the old Miller place. It was really run down. Soon after I moved there, I was overwhelmed with cutting mesquite trees, fixing fences, birthing kids, fixing the water system, fixing my broken truck, fixing the water mill, chasing escaped goats, and smelling like sweat 20 hours a day. Also I hurt and I was tired. My Dr Peppers under the cool ceiling fans of The Waterin' Hole Café were my reward for working 'til I was tuckered. Sally Rae came as a surprise and a bonus.

Like any woman in Heartbreak over age 25, Sally Rae was a little shop-worn and prematurely aged. Don't get me wrong. Sixty years in Houston, many of it teaching, had left me with a pot belly, wrinkles, and an attitude I tried hard to fight. My wife had left me for some handsome young buck with the morality of one of my billy

221

goats....damn; I'm still fighting that attitude. Any way, Sally Rae soon became a cooler drink to my eyes than the mid-day Dr Pepper was to my throat.

Meanwhile, Janey grew Up, and Out and Around. If you have goats you have flies. If you have a pretty daughter you have boys sticking around like flies. I had both. Janey finally helped engineer a breakthrough with Sally Rae. All of a sudden, Janey and I were both dating! I moved to Heartbreak to get Simple, and all of a sudden it turned Complex.

"You treat her with respect. Get her home by 10:30. Don't do anything I can't be in the room for!" That was my daughter parroting me about how I needed to treat Sally Rae. That's what I mean by complex.

So anyway, one afternoon I was in The Waterin' Hole and Sally Rae came up to me and said, all tentative like, "A high school reunion is coming up in a couple of weeks. Would you like to go? I mean, you know, I didn't really graduate because of my boy and all, but it would be nice to see a lot of my old friends. I just don't want to go alone."

"Sure thing, Sally Rae. I'd be proud to have you on my arm." I meant it, too.

Sally Rae beamed at me strong as a Texas sunset. If her smile could have tanned me, I would have been sun burnt.

I knew this much from small town experience: being invited to a high school reunion in a small town was big medicine, as the old chief said. Now days most kids go to really big schools. Colleges are even bigger, so kids use all kinds of fraternities and clubs and such to sort the number downward. People naturally choose like kinds, so in a way a sorority or fraternity is a little inbred, compared to a country high school. Every one in a particular senior class was in it together, no votes taken. They learned language in kindergarten, threw spitballs in Mrs. Monroe's fifth-grade math class, gave each other black eyes in the seventh grade and broke each other's hearts in the twelfth grade. Aside from the usual dangers, getting physical in a small town carried its own set of risks. This other person in a backseat now might go on to be your choir leader, your brother's spouse, your sister's boss.... Anyway, small towns have more intersections than a root ball on a septic line. I was being asked by Sally Rae to be with her while she navigated this tangle of old emotions and relationships.

The Heartbreak Raccoons Reunion tool place, of course, at the Veterans of Foreign Wars hall. Most public and private events that weren't strictly religious met there. The SPJSC hall was further up the road by 21 miles. Raccoons weren't that pretentious, anyhow. However, they were dressed up; that is, only new blue jeans and black felt cowboy hats dominated. Deceased members were recorded on posters with pictures around the walls, along with "before and after" pictures of the alumni and their current wives or husbands. "Real" Heartbreak Raccoons had drawn dark rings around their eyes. It took a little getting used to. I knew a few of them: BJ Elkert, looking like 300 pounds of solid muscle even then, but others were a surprise. I saw Miss Scarlet's photo. Miss Scarlet used to be a cheerleader, and one hundred pounds lighter.

The football players were drawn to the beer keg. After more than a quarter of a century of worship there, they were starting to look like the keg, art imitating life. Great Aunt Katy surprised me by giving a speech. Turns out she was the 12th grade English teacher at HBH. Sam Clancey had to get in his two cents by reciting Chaucer's Prologue to Canterbury Tales in Middle English.

"Whan that Aprille with the shores sota, the draught of March has pierced to the rote..." all the way to "for him hath hopen them that were sake."

The Texas Kow Boys, a local band, started up right after that. Raccoons and Raccoonettes clasped each other desperately, and they all began to roam around the cedar shavings floor. It was part magic and part parody. They would be easy to make fun of as a group, but I felt sort of left out of something important: Raccoonism.

Beer and drinks flowed as the dancers flowed around the VFW hall. About midnight the Texas Kow Boys struck up "Crimson and Clover." This had been the main parking and make out song for about three years back at Heartbreak High.

Psychologists talk about conditioned response, but I saw something different. The couples melted even closer together. For a moment Miss Scarlett developed a grace that overcame her bulk. BJ Elkert had a lift in his steps unseen since he had danced the football over the goal line decades ago. My Sally Rae's face felt softer than a morning breeze against my cheek. That special magic of being 18, of being fresh and having the entire world ahead of you had returned. I felt honored to be an honorary Raccoon for the night.

What happen next shouldn't have surprised anyone. Fully a third of this group had made important discoveries and reshaped their view of life with Crimson and Clover playing in the background all those years ago. Tonight couples, not necessarily the married to each other, began disappearing off the dance floor. It seems there was still some unfinished business.

We all began those soft moments we did in our childhood, *Crimson and Clover over and over.....*

We were all pushing middle age, but we were all 18 again.

THE CLASS OF '74

The reunion had just gotten started,
Darla was looking for an open door,
She was anxious to see her old classmates,
But there was something she wanted more.

She snuck from the lively gymnasium,
While all the others were starting to dance,
She had to go to locker fifty-three,
And didn't want to pass up her chance.

Down the hall of the old preserved high school,
In the dim light along the walls of green,
She turned down past the auditorium,
And crossed her fingers she hadn't been seen.

She ran quickly to the rows of lockers,
Her new high heels clicked lightly on the tile,
The thin doors in rows were standing open,
Darla took a breath and began to smile.

Her fingers felt along the inner edge,
To a slight bend in the old metal frame,
She tugged on a piece of folded paper,
Pulling out an old note with her name.

It was a promise to her from Johnny,
That still read "I owe one kiss to you,"
Now, at her 40 year class reunion,
She planned to claim what was long overdue.

Marlene Tucker

Daily Horrors

Fishing

HEARTBREAK TEXAS IS ABOUT *50* OR 500 miles west of Houston's Sushi bars. It's a place where most of the women fret on whose gonna have a baby next, most of the men are more stressed about which cows are going to birth next, and the cows mostly chew grass, disregarding the constant smell of barbecue. None aspire to immortality, but all expect their individual end at its own right time. God should be so kind to all of us.

It was August, hot and dry; Janey was off to a cheerleading camp, Sally Rae was off to visit her son in Memphis, and I was FREE. I paid Jube the neighbor boy $20 to feed my animals and went fishing.

Real freedom is a wonderful and scary thing to have. I took a lesser course. I could have gone to Houston and tried to pick up women in bars (or Dallas, or Waco) but after my divorce I had gradually picked up enough self-respect that I just wanted to go fishing.

I brought all the fine reels, grubs, and minnows and a cooler full of beer. By now I knew the local lakes. Around here we had dammed seven in a row. The State of Texas had stocked them all with bass. I went to number seven, the bottom most on the row that a shallow ravine lined up like a string of worms. By 7 a.m. I was parked on the banks of Lake Doggie, the bottom-most of seven little lakes.

As I pitched my tent, large clouds gathered. Thunder and lightning crossed my ranch, several miles to the north. I felt good, at one with the land. Take note: *Whether you are a New Yorker or a Texan, feeling safe is the first precursor to sudden destruction.*

I went to sleep on my hammock. Sometime later, I awoke to raindrops the size of Republican tears hitting all over my body. The rain hurt, and it just got harder. I ran down to my boat, fearing it could be swept away. By the time I found it, it had floated free. All I could grab was a life preserver from the stern.

One big wave after another came in on me. I looked at the shore. It was 50-feet away, then 100; then I was too busy paddling to worry. For about 20 or 30 minutes I got swept downward. Scary? Trees and cows went right past me. I had always read that more people drowned in the desert than ever died of dehydration, but before tonight I never believed it. Now I believed, but I doubted my chances of ever making another convert.

A big white dog swam up to me. I recognized the breed immediately; he was a Great Pyrenees, bred for battle. This dog just had desperation in his eyes; he was as alarmed by this turn of events as I was. I grabbed his paw and put him on my little life preserver. We were both in big trouble.

About then I heard the sound of falling water. We both swam to the side. The U.S. Army Corps of Engineers had built a giant waterfall. I knew that going over that low water dam was going to be curtains. The dog and I swam for the bank as best we could. I was so cold now that all I could grip was his tail. He pulled me up the side to ground. Then he turned around and licked my hand. I crawled up the bank little further, rolled over, and looked at the sky.

Texas weather is its own thing; stars were breaking out and a cool wind blew over us. I closed my eyes and said a short but very sincere prayer to God for just being alive.

The next day I hitchhiked home with my new dog. I named him Bandit. He has dark rings around his eyes and a perpetual guilty look. That fits — he's usually guilty, but guilty of dog-type crimes: guilty of running away when called, guilty of barking all night, guilty of smelling like a stray skunk. Over all, I'd have to say he's dumber than a sack of hammers, but none of that changes the fact he let me grab his tail and haul me out of about the worst fix of my life.

City people ask, "What is this thing about people and their dogs?" Well, I know, and Bandit ain't telling. Some things people just have to figure out on their own.

A NOTE OF NUISANCE

After working hard I needed a break,
So I took my john boat down to the lake.
The lake was smooth and the blue sky was clear,
But I heard a thumping that caught my ear.

I threw in my line to get my bait wet,
For a day of fishing I was all set.
I had some snacks and my drinks were on ice,
As I reeled my line I heard the thump twice.

When I hummed a tune the thump kept a beat.
The sound seemed to come from under my feet.
I wondered if there might be a lake ghost,
But after can six I was braver than most.

Somehow I managed to fall from the boat,
That was floating on top of a bottle with note.
The note inside gave much more than a clue,
It read:
"This once bothered me now it bothered you."

Marlene Tucker

An Adventure

THE NATURALISTS WERE AN EARLY Nineteenth Century Literary movement that believed nature was a benign sort of teacher; that the forest and sky, birds and gentle animals were a special gift from God to teach us humans how to be better. One of the early Transcendentalist authors said, "An hour in nature can teach more than a day of study."

God mostly protected these folks by keeping them in Connecticut, where they belonged.

Personally, I think it's mostly all bull-pucky, except for the part about the learning curve. You better be quick on your feet or you're gonna die, usually sooner than later. You can't live around a ranch very long and keep up your belief in a benign universe. There are only two things "peaceful" about a country place: pictures of it on the wall, and the ignorant perception of city folk when they gaze upon some misbegotten hillside the goats haven't quite picked as clean as my billfold.

I'd been sitting on that hillside for about three hours when Janey came up. I definitely wasn't being very quick on my feet and I was worried.

It was Saturday morning and Janey wanted to go to town. She asked, "Daddy, are you going to sit there all day?"

"I may."

"Oh, you're just aggravating me! Come on, now, get up and let's go." She was getting bossy now. Sometimes, it wasn't just her

230

looks that reminded me of her mother.

"It's not that simple," I said.

"Well, why not? You've been moping here for hours. I've seen you from the window."

"Well, I mean it's complicated…" I started.

"The only thing complicated about this whole day is getting you in the truck and headed toward the city…." she started.

Calling Heartbreak a city was a bigger lie than even a campaigning politician would tell, but I let it pass.

"What's complicated is my leg. I'm stuck."

"What do you mean, Daddy?" Janey said, suspicious as a wise man hunting for a virgin birth.

"My foot went in a gopher hole. Last year, I stuffed some barbed wire in the hole so none of the livestock would cut themselves on it. Earlier this year, the day it rained, the hole washed open. Right now my leg feels broken, my boot is trapped in bob wire, and about half an hour a go I'm pretty sure a rattle snake crawled in my boot to keep warm. Oh yes, my leg went to sleep, too. THAT'S what I mean by complicated." I felt better. Real men shouldn't complain, but there are limits.

Janey stood there silently with her thinking frown in place. I knew she hadn't given up on town. Goodness, she was pretty in the way only 16-year-olds can get; which is to say what on earth was God thinking about when he issued all that adult equipment to teenagers. There's just something wrong when a person looks like Barbie and wants to play with Barbie dolls at the same time.

I brought my mind back to focus. Clearly I was avoiding thinking about the snake and barbed wire wrapped and trapped foot that had gone to sleep. I guessed this is what psychologists call displacement. I called it a predicament with overtones of a pending trip to the emergency room.

"I could pour gasoline in your boot," Janey suggested.

"Darlin', I don't know that'd improve matters all that much. One thing I don't want is a flaming rattle snake in my boot."

"Oh, I don't mean to light it, just chase the snake out."

"I don't want any desperately unhappy snakes in my boot, either. Besides, I think he's asleep. Lean close and listen. I think he's snoring."

"Oh Dad, DO something. Don't just sit there waitin' for that ole snake to just die of old age," Janey cried. "Saturday's a-wastin'! I want to go to town." Empathy never has been a strong point with children and the trick thing about teenagers is that they're still children, appearances not withstanding.

"Darlin', I'm not so much wastin' my time as biding it. This is definitely one of those situations where I better choose my moment so as to lend an advantage. I'm kinda hoping this snake would wake up hungry and go chase a mouse, like honest snakes ought to."

Janey piped right back, "What if he's sleeping off a big ole rat right now and might not get hungry for several days? I heard it's going to be 103 degrees tomorrow. Are you just gonna sit here and turn to jerky?"

About then several goats ran by. Next I heard a pig squeal. "Javelinas, Janey!" I've had my share of adrenaline rushes before. Usually it adds speed and strength, but today it was a lubricant. Before I knew it I had slipped my foot out of my boot. I left the poor rattler in it, but I felt a little guilty. After all, we'd been mighty close for a little while, even though it turned out to be a passing sort of relationship. If the javelinas found him I knew they'd eat him, and maybe my boot, too. Those pigs are plenty mean and they don't fool around.

Anyway, we ended up in the pickup. Janey was going to get a new dress and I needed a new boot. I know it's wasteful since I still had one good boot on, but I figured I was probably going to have to break down and buy a new pair.

Happy as milk fed pup now that she was getting her way, Janey said, "Drive fast Daddy. I feel like I'm going to have an adventure today!"

LOOK BEFORE YOU SMILE

In the spring the fields and medians
Are filled with a purplish hue
As millions of Texas bluebonnets
Are grown by God for us to view.

We find these places so picturesque
With flowers growing thick and wild
Nature provides the perfect backdrop
Where we can photograph our child

The bluebonnets are so beautiful
But there are other things God makes
When you stop to photograph your child
Remember to look out for snakes!

Marlene Tucker

"No greater love has any man..."

HEARTBREAK IS A PLACE WHERE
Nature hasn't been defeated by Progress. Men don't have to consult
their Political Correctness charts when something needs setting
straight, a place where women think of a big family as a Big Blessing,
not a Big Mistake, and the children grown up in such a way snakes
tend to run from them, not the other way around. The cattle have the
best deal of all. Most are cared for with generations of expertise from
their humans, right up to the day the humans marinate them. Don't
wince; in Heartbreak it's just the circle of life.

Most things in the country smell sweeter than in the city. Quality
of life is measured in bluebonnets per pasture rather than square feet
of enclosed space. Please note; I said most things. Some things smell
a lot worse than the city, and with good reason.

Anyone who lives in the country knows that about the worst thing
about being there is plumbing. Most of us have wells, and that means
pressure systems, and then it all goes to a septic tank. These tanks
can last for years, but when they go, oh man, it's a nightmare. Some
people claim its better to just burn the house and be done with it.

Arney Shaw is our local policeman. He got hired for that job
mostly because he couldn't do anything else. He's generally too nice
to shoot anyone and too nice to get shot at, even considering that
Heartbreak has never run short on guns or people willing to use them.
One thing's for sure, Arney is a natural born klutz. Giving him a
hammer is almost as imprudent as giving him a hand grenade.

234

Arney had been after me to help him with his bad septic system for about 3 months. It became obvious no other sucker was going to get pulled in, so I went out to help him. He had one of those old fashioned kinds that were meant to last 20 years, but it had been put in 30 years ago. It was about the size, shape and depth of a grave, but graves generally smell better.

After about 3 dozen buckets I told Arney I had to go breath, and maybe throw up a few times, but I'd be right back.

"Sure," Arney said. What else could he say, "You're fired"?

As I left I yelled, "Don't fall in, I ain't diving for you!"

After emptying my stomach and washing my face, I sat down. I'm not a shirker, but this job wasn't going to get finished by rushing. After about 10 minutes I reluctantly walked back, and there, right on top of the bubbly brown cake sat Arney's police hat. I looked all around, but no Arney was to be seen. My worst fears were being realized. I took the shove and poked down in that awful goo, at the same time my anxiety grew. Before long, I drug up a boot, and I was almost sure it was Arney's!

Hoping against hope he might still be alive, I threw my keys and wallet to one side and, well, I stepped in. I'll try to spare you the details, but anything your imagination can reach, my experience can top. A brief moment of horror passed me as I thought of giving him mouth-to-mouth respiration. I felt all around, waded from end to end, and about that time Arney walked around the end of his hay baler.

"Gone swimming, Dave?" He drawled.

"Why was your hat floating out here?" I asked, getting madder and madder.

"It blew off my head. It's awful nice of you to get it for me, but I gave up on it as soon as I heard it go 'plop' in, well, all that plop."

Right that second I realized how murders happen. It was a good thing I had a shovel in my hand and not a rifle. 'Bout then I realized that Arney wasn't getting any closer than about 30 feet; if I wanted out I better engineer it myself. I put my shovel handle across one corner and tried to pull myself up—and the handle broke! When I resurfaced everything was—oh hell, you figure it out. Worse, I was cut and had several splinters in my hands from the shovel handle.

I eventually crawled out. It's not as hard as you might think to crawl out of a septic pit if you got nothing left to lose.

"Arney, get me to a doctor." I could only imagine gazillions of microbes crawling through my various scrapes and punctures.

"Not in my car!" He said, squealing like a teenager.

"I'll ride in the back of my truck, now get driving!"

So that's how I came to riding into Heartbreak looking like a chocolate dipped version of the tar baby. Even on the highway I could hear him laughing. He must have had one of those belt radios; otherwise I don't know how half the town could have been out cheering me as we went by. Doc's of course, was at the far end of town. Old Doc Bailey is a kindly enough sort, but he made me hose off for half an hour before he would see me. While I was getting jabbed by a tetanus needle in the hip, various splinters removed and raw spots scrubbed with pure alcohol, Sally Rae showed up with some new store bought duds for me.

Eventually, like all dirty deals, it passed. I went driving home. Janey met me at the door, just wailing. She had been home all day babysitting Alice Mendez, a cute little 18-month-old.

"Daddy, I know little Alice is the sweetest little thing on earth, but you know what she did in her diaper? Three times?"

I always tried to be a good daddy, understand her problems, but today I just looked at her.

CHIPPING IN FOR A DATE

Jethro went to Lucy's house,
To ask her for a date.
Her father said she could not go,
But he could stay 'til late.
If he'd help Lucy with her chores,
He could even stay to eat.
He gladly agreed to stay and help,
Because Lucy was so sweet.

Lucy's chore was to gather fuel,
To put in the stove to burn.
The west Texas Plains had no wood,
For Lucy it was no concern.
Dried cow manure was gathered,
The dried patties proved to burn great.
Lucy thought it nice to have help.
(It wasn't Jethro's idea of a date.)

He noted how the smell grew stronger,
As they gathered dried chips from the sand.
It took away all his desire,
To hold or kiss her hand.
The supper cooked on the iron stove,
Look good but he declined.
He had lost his desire for supper,
After picking up poop of bovine.

Marlene Tucker

THE BAR FIGHT

PART 1 OF 3

I'M DAVE, A 60 YEAR OLD CITY dweller that got fed up with the whole urban crowding thing and left after a painful divorce to do something cleaner with my life, and, I hope, Janey's too.

I raise goats. Now goats are rangy, stinky, shameless animals that would breed on my porch and birth in my kitchen, if I let 'em. I don't, but those goats can catch your fancy in some odd ways. I'll never forget the morning that T2, my favorite nanny, gave birth to twins on a cold, snowy morning in January. She grinned at me with sheer pleasure, happy as any new mother I've ever seen.

Another favorite was Swimsuit. Most goats would stomp a stray kid to death before they would share milk with one that wasn't their own kid, but Swimsuit was that rarity who always was willing to give a sip to a hungry stray kid. We called her Swimsuit because she had good teats. I'm not talking dirty or nothing, that's just what ranch life is about.

A goat herd is 30 or 50 mommas (some good, some selfish), a billy, and hopefully, a passel of kids sporting all around the grass and hills. Goats breed like jack rabbits, die like flies, and enjoy life in between. That makes 'em a whole lot like me and my neighbors, I suppose, except they don't waste as much time arguing about religion and politics.

When I moved to Heartbreak I tried to get away, to separate myself as far as possible from everyone I knew. I had some heartbreak of my own going on and I wanted to think things through. I didn't want friends or relatives messin' any of that up. I soon learned that it's easier to out run your friends than your DNA. About 18 months after I bought the old Miller place, a distant cousin of mine, Barry, showed up on my door step with a couple of six packs and a real yen to talk.

Barry was a real likable sort of guy, even if he did squat in my kitchen and drink his beers while I cooked an extra dinner for him. He was obviously lonely. Barry was a runt of a man, red haired, freckled, and the wiry kind of strong. He didn't naturally attract people. I could tell 'cause he never shut up when he got someone to talk to. To make his nonstop talking worse, about every ten minutes he slipped in something important.

"You'll never convince me that pasteurized milk isn't the ruin of my stomach and the downfall of the nation! Why, look at the records, the Democrats and the Republicans BOTH voted for it! If that ain't collusion, what is? By the way, your billy has a black spot tick on his left nut. Better fix it, or you'll have no kids next spring. It's like most things the government tries to do, run up the prices on home products and ruin your health while they charge extra for it."

He was right about the tick and my billy, but you see what I mean? Once in a while you could mine a nugget out of the all the swill, but it took wearing full-time wader boots not to get something all over your feet.

About his forth beer I nodded at Janey and said, "Time to do your homework?

Janey winked back and went right upstairs to her bedroom. There were some things I didn't want her to hear, and there were some things she didn't want to hear either.

Barry and I ended up on the porch. We sipped a few more cold ones and Barry went on and on about a new knife and gun club that had opened up in Quick Fix. Quick Fix isn't so much a town as an area south of Heartbreak where men go on Friday to do things for which they repent on Sunday. It is a place of sin, cheap whiskey, rentable women, trash, and all the other things a good Baptist community like Heartbreak needs to both condemn and endure. Think about two sides to a coin. North of Heartbreak, we have Baptist summer camps, retreat centers for weekenders from Houston and Dallas that want "Real Texas," (weekends only, at exorbitant prices) and West of Heartbreak we have wedding chapels. East of Heartbreak there wasn't much 'cept those hell holes of sin and perdition, like Houston.

Anyhow, Barry was going on and on about a place called "Dancers Anonymous."

"Down at Dancers Anonymous there're *women*, good looking ones, too. It's a fine place. Sure, it's got a few bullet holes, but nothing new. Old cuz, you're working too hard. Come go down there with me this weekend and I promise I'll show you a good time. I'll pick you up Friday at 6."

This is what temptation looks like. I was tired of birthing goats, burying goats, and smelling goats. Janey was off to a Baptist camp for the weekend; Sally Rae went along as an adult volunteer. At 16, Janey was hard bitten by deep Baptist morality. With no real professional sinners around, she had been sharpening her moral talons on me. Living with her had gotten like a moral review conducted by a jury of ex-wives.

"See you at six on Friday." I said.

It was three days to Friday and I sweated in the merciless Texas sun, fixin' fences and castratin' kids. Horseflies bit me and I let myself get dehydrated. I had an outbreak of pink eye with the herd. Swimsuit got mastitis and before I could milk her clean two more kids died. It was a hard week. Anyway, I dropped off Janey at our church.

Lord help me; I bought a six-pack headin back to my ranch. Now I was in deep temptation. Most any well-seasoned sinner can tell you that this was the last stop before wadding off into deep do-do in low quarter shoes.

When Barry showed up I jumped into his pickup and off we went to Quick Fix.

Barry had a cooler that sat between us.

"The trick is," Barry told me, "you nurse the $3 beers in the saloon and slip outside to my cooler when you're thirsty."

I was a novice at this sort of thing, so I just said "Yep" like I already knew, and we went on truckin'.

"Watch my moves, it's easy." Barry provided me with more information as we bounced along.

David Mosley

We arrived at Dancers Anonymous and finished our beers before going inside. I don't know how different life would be if Barry had not been a faster drinker than me. We finished on the way and Barry led the way inside.

A giant of a man stood up and knocked Barry under his chin with a fist the size of a mule shoe. Poor Barry flew back and landed in my arms like a late delivery UPS package. Barry went limper than an anxious man that mistook a muscle relaxer when he reached for Viagra. I grabbed him and started to pull him back but the giant grabbed his legs and pulled him forward.

"Don't be afraid. I mean you no harm," the giant rumbled as he dragged Barry to a table and sat him in a chair.

I followed, not wanting to leave Barry there, but to be honest, I was ready to bolt.

After a few minutes the giant came over to our table with two beers. Barry had begun to move a little.

The giant looked down at us, laughed, and said, "Nothing personal, I just bet my friend that I could knock out the next man that walked through the door. I'm Jed Alderson from the Top Forty Ranch." With that Jed walked back over to his own table and started drinking with his friends like nothing had happened.

Barry gradually woke up. We sat in silence and sipped our free beers. Barry spent a lot of time rubbing his chin.

About every five minutes I asked, "Barry, are you OK?" He never said anything. He wrinkled up his face like he was doing a moral inventory. I could tell he was thinking, and that it hurt. Heck, thinking hurt for Barry when he *hadn't* been cold cocked.

"Barry, are you OK?"

Barry stood up and walked out. I followed. I guessed the night was over. Barry began rummaging under his seat.

"Where is my .38 when I need it?" he complained. His voice wasn't steady yet, but he settled for a large ball peen hammer and ran back in.

"Stop, Barry. He'll kill you!" I whispered.

Barry was walking up to Jed.

Jed Anderson, in all his arrogance, asked "You want some more, son?"

241

That moment little Barry pulled the ball peen hammer out of his back pocket and swung at Jed's head. Jed was quick. Barry only hit his shoulder.

"Damn, you broke my left collar bone!" the giant swore.

"Sorry, I was aiming at your head. I meant to kill you." Southerners never seem able to outrun their politeness. Barry calmly swung again and broke two or three ribs on the giant.

The giant began running around the table. The bald headed man next to him suddenly developed an abiding interest in the tattoos on his forearm. Barry was fast. He caught the giant in the back once or twice. About the second round Jed busted open the doors and ran outside. The rest of the bar folk followed, including me.

Barry chased the bully around the car about three times. Every time Barry couldn't hit Jed he put a large dent in his car. Finally Jed showed enough good sense to dive through an open window and drive away.

Barry threw his hammer through the back window of Jed's pick up truck.

"Git in!" Barry said. He and I left out before the Laws arrived. As we drove off, I could hear the crowd at Dancers Anonymous clapping.

Plain Spoken

The bar was open six days a week,
It smelled like beer and sin.
It was on this particular night,
That Mr. Plain walked in.

He was tending to his own business,
Just ordering a beer,
When an intoxicated patron,
Stood purposely too near.

Mr. Plain said "I dated your mom."
The drunkard lost his grin.
"I'd've dated your mother's sister too,
But she was way too thin".

The pie-eyed man pulled Plain off the stool,
From there the fight was on.
Mr. Plain was tall and slender built,
The drunk was bulk and brawn.

Mr. Plain asked quickly, "How's your sis?
Still ugly to the core?"
The drunk, overcome from drink and rage,
Then passed out on the floor

Marlene Tucker

THE DINNER INVITATION

PART 2 OF 3

WE ARE A TOLERANT LOT IN Heartbreak. Mostly we talk across the fence or at The Waterin' Hole Café. The waitress there is Sally Rae, a pretty woman with eyes the color of love. She and I had become "special" friends over time and most days my high point was sipping a Dr Pepper with her before Janey got out of school.

"Dave, have you see that drifter yet?" Sally Rae asked.

"You mean the feller with the camo face paint who's always moving off the left, out of sight?

"Yea, I wonder what it is with him."

"I think he's another one of those 'professional vets'. You know, the kind of guy that never got over Vietnam, or whatever war messed him up," I said. "He's real shy. I used to see a lot more men like him back in Houston. Lately he's been camped toward the back of my place."

"Doesn't he bother you? I mean, it'd make me nervous to have someone like that hanging around," Sally said.

"Naw, I doubt he's any real trouble. Poor fella went out on some patrol one night and something happened. His body made it back but his soul is still out on permanent patrol. I tried to meet him once, carried him out some food, but I never saw him. I left the food and next day it was gone. Wish I could do more for him, but, naw, he doesn't make me too fearful. The world is full of broken souls."

Shifting subjects, Sally Rae said, "You know, Judge Bother is going to be back in town next week."

My blood pressure went up a little. "At least he makes a happy day for the town when he leaves."

Percy Bother was an embarrassment to the legal system. When you think about how much it takes to embarrass a lawyer, you can see what I mean.

Percy Bother (or Judge Blather, as most folks here called him) was a native Heartbreak boy who had "made good." As a child, nobody liked him much, except, maybe, his mother. On second thought, maybe she saw something in him early on that no one else had yet. Why else would you name a Texas boy "Percy"?

Judge Blather was in every way an unremarkable child, except for his studies and his natural born meanness. Even Great Aunt Katy didn't much care for him when she taught him, and that really says something. Great Aunt Katy had been known to nurse rattle snakes back to health. She loved God and almost all His creations, Judge Blather excepted.

Early on Blather had moved to Pringo, the county seat. There he politicked endlessly, a Democrat when the winds blew one way, a Republican when the winds blew another. He must have piled up some political favors somewhere because when Judge Morris died, the Governor appointed Blather fill the vacant seat. As an incumbent he just kept getting re-elected.

Once every few months, Judge Blather had to come back to Heartbreak to judge the felonies a few of our upstanding citizens manage to get caught at. Blather was one of the last circuit judges in Texas, a pretty good indicator that his standing wasn't too high back at Pringo. His nickname in legal circles was "Maximum Bother" because he always gave the maximum sentence to any redneck convicted in his court. All in all, Bother was one of the worst things I could say about our democracy, despite all the competition.

Why am I so down on Judge Bother? I have a few rent houses to help subsidize my goat-raising addiction. One is in Pringo. I rented it to some college girls for a year. After two months they hadn't paid rent and I had to evict them. I almost cried when I saw the place. It had trash two feet deep with little paint trails in between. The walls were covered with marker drawings. Most windows were broken. All in all, it cost me $10,000 to repair it. I sued them for the difference on the deposit and it was in Blather's court back when he was a JP.

Justice is supposed to be blind, but that old goat couldn't tear his eyes away from the defendants' chests. Every time my lawyer objected he said "Over ruled!" and every time their lawyer objected Blather said "Sustained." My lawyer told me to drop my case but I knew I was in the right. The girls, of course, counter-sued. In the end it cost me another $8,000. That was the day I learned that, far from being blind, Justice was a randy old coot that was willing to ruin me for a few blonde smiles and a deep chest look from the other side. After that, I adopted the attitude of "keep skunks and judges at a distance."

Sally Rae said, "Have you heard any more about that Anderson murder?"

"Naw, what's that?"

"Some ranch hand named Anderson got killed last Friday night. There was a bar fight of some sort and they found Anderson about five miles down the road with his head all beat in."

It was slow at first, but all my alarm bells went off. My cousin Barry had dragged me (well, drove me) to a little knife and gun club called "Dancers Anonymous." A big bear of a guy named Anderson cold-cocked Barry the moment he walked in; a few minutes later Barry came back with a ball peen hammer and got a little justice. The last I saw of Anderson, he was peeling out of the parking lot and Barry threw his hammer through the guy's back windshield. Right after that, Barry and I left.

"Oh, heck, tell me all you know," I said.

"Nothing much, just the state police are looking for the guys that beat him up," Sally Rae said.

I looked at my watch. "Time for me to get Janey. I better scoot." I had some thinking to do. I knew Barry and I hadn't killed Anderson, but it's kind of scary to think about the state police asking for me.

About the time I got Janey home and started dinner Barry showed up with a six pack, of course. He had an infallible, though toxic, sense of timing.

"Hey Cuz, how's it going?" he asked.

"Glad you showed when you did, Barry. I'll set another plate for dinner."

Janey made a face and went upstairs to her room.

About 10 minutes later I heard another car pull up. Barry and walked outside. I had a spatula in my hand and, of course, Barry had a beer. It was only Arney, the town policeman.

"Hi Arney, what up?" I asked.

Suddenly three state cruisers whipped around the corner. Six of the biggest men I ever saw piled out right fast. Every one of them had a gun in hand and they were pointing at me and Barry.

Do you know what a .357 revolver is? The slug is just over a third of an inch wide and I knew that the highway patrolmen always carried 158 grain bullets. That .357 is designed to break an engine block. If you ever have the misfortune to be looking down the wrong end of one the bore looks big enough to crawl into.

I know Barry was upset, he dropped his beer. I don't think he ever did that before in all his fifty-some odd years. I raised my spatula over my head.

When you're really stressed there ain't no telling what you might say. I looked them in the eye and with all my best Southern hospitality I asked, "So, how many of y'all are staying for dinner?"

Bombastic on the Fly

The congratulations were over,
The new D.A. hadn't had enough.
He was feeling the fame and power.
He wanted the town to know he was tough.

He stood on the steps of the courthouse,
And waited for a gathering crowd.
Then he flexed his vocabulary.
He was full arrogant and he was loud.

People stood smiling as they listened,
Some people snickered until it hurt.
The irony was in appearance.
His open fly and two inches of shirt.

Marlene Tucker

THE TRIAL

PART 3 OF 3

WELL, JANEY AND I HAD LIVED IN Heartbreak almost two years when my cousin Barry and I got brought up to trial for killing Jed Anderson.

Anyway, Barry and I had gone to a little knife and gun club down in Quick Fix. I just wanted a night out; Barry wanted some other sort of relief from his private devils. Barry walked into the saloon and a big, beefy ranch hand, Jed Anderson, stood up and cold-cocked Barry back into my arms.

After Barry woke up he grabbed a ball peen hammer from his truck and extracted a little justice from Mr. Anderson's hide. Actually, for a little guy, Barry got a *lot* of justice from Mr. Anderson. Barry beat him from top to bottom, hit his car a few times, and sent ole Jed down the road in a terrible hurry.

As a parting gesture, Barry had thrown his hammer through Jed's back window. The bar crew had walked outside by then, and they clapped. Texans enjoy a good show, and, after all, Barry weighed at least 100 pounds less than Jed. The crowd at Dancers Anonymous broke up quickly after that. Many of them had their own personal reasons to not want to hit the attention of the local constabulary. Other ran away just out of habit.

Less than five miles down the road, Jed Anderson was found inverted in his car, deader than John Brown's body, and the back of his head was bashed in. Less than a week, later Barry got arrested for murder and I got arrested as an accessory after the fact. Janey was remanded to some Baptist Youth Home and I had to rely on the good intentions of Sally Rae to feed my goats in addition to feeding and watering much of the citizenry of Heartbreak.

It was time to call in the big guns. I called "Super Jew." Lew Koring had been my family's lawyer for 50 years. He had fought civil rights cases back when he had to get out of town before the jury recessed, just to avoid getting lynched. Now Lew was almost as old as God, and he looked about as distinguished.

The whole trial went a lot faster than I had ever imagined. The State put on witnesses that saw Barry get punched, respond in his own spectacular manner, and saw old Jed peel out. Of particular disadvantage to us was the bald, tattooed man, named Bill Summers that said that Barry was "killin' mad." The prosecution loved this witness, and let Summers repeat himself several times. Then the prosecution rested. It seemed this guy wanted to get us both. I fantasized about another good use for duct tape as I watched him flap his jaws. My tie seemed to be choking me, until I realized I wasn't wearing one. Nobody, of course, wants a State of Texas necktie.

To make something bad even worse, Judge Percy Bother made it clear from the first that he was dead set against us. Poor Lew couldn't get "objection" out of his mouth without being drowned out by Judge Bother's, "Over ruled!"

Lew told me before the trial that Bother was one of those judges that got terminal constipation if he couldn't sentence someone to death at least once a month. Bother looked to be three months overdue. I swear, he was a skinny little toad of an excuse for a human. I always figured that if I could slip him a couple of Ex-Lax he might disappear altogether.

We broke for lunch. For once food didn't tempt me. Even Barry seemed subdued. All of us were eating at The Waterin' Hole Café. Poor Sally Rae was so busy serving the big crowd that she barely had time to give me a worried little smile. Lew had a faraway look in his eyes that I wasn't going to disturb. All in all, I had the uncertain feeling you get when you're way out on the prairie and all of a sudden the sky is dark grey, roiling around with thunder, and the only cover you see is a lightning-blasted mesquite tree.

Everyone was there at The Waterin' Hole. A murder trial was better than anything on the Dish, the Internet, or even Quick Fix had to offer. 'Bout that time John, the Vietnam vet on permanent patrol who had been living out at the back of my place came in. All secretative-like, he pushed over to speak into Lew's ear. They walked outside, deep in private conversation.

Back in court, Judge Bother was obliged to let the defense present its case, though he did his best to imply it was a waste of time. By then, I was starting to believe Barry and I really had done the dirty deed, even though I knew we hadn't. I avoided trying to meet the eyes of any of my neighbors. I didn't want them looking away and then having to feel bad about it later.

Lew surprised us all by recalling Bill Summers, the tattooed loudmouth that was trying even harder than Judge Bother to get me convicted.

"Now Mr. Summers, tell me about your impressions of the defendants on the night in question."

This gave Summers the chance to paint Barry as an aggressor, and me as his henchman. Truth is, I never hit anyone the whole night, but according to Summers I was in it up to my neck. Lew encouraged him to go on and on, and friends, Summers did. He was right comfortable in trashing Barry and I.

At just the right moment, when he paused to draw another breath, Lew asked, "And how much money did you owe the deceased?" Lew was looking at a set of papers, not the witness, making it clear he knew the answer already.

Summers stopped, "Uh, a few thousand, I reckon."

Lew looked over his glasses like a school marm catching a cheat. In his hands he held an old fashioned tally book, grey with red corners. "Try again, Mr. Summers."

"Well, maybe more like $130,000, give or take. But you have to remember, Jed was a really nice guy. Gentle and kind, you might say."

"So this gentle, kind man, Jed Anderson, he didn't knock out a man he'd never seen before, a stranger, to prove what would happen to you if you continued to hold out on him?"

"Well, uh, you might say, uh..." Summers stuttered.

"Question withdrawn. I'm finished with this witness," Lew said. I looked inside the tally book. It was blank, never written on. We didn't call Lew "Super Jew" for nothing.

"My next witness is John Briarsworth." The doors of the court opened and the old Vietnam vet, ragged fatigues, grease paint and all walked in and got sworn.

"What do you do, Mr. Briarsworth?"

"I prefer 'sergeant'. I'm on permanent patrol," he said.

"How long, now, sergeant?" Lew asked, gently.

"Every day, since I arrive stateside in June of 1969," he replied.

"And what have you seen on these patrols?" Lew asked.

"All sorts of things. I've seen strangers afraid of me for no good reason, decent men, like Dave over there, set out food and not bother me when I'm billeted. I've see Judge Bother stop along the highway and throw out pornography when he thought no one was looking. One night outside Quick Fix I saw a car weaving down a road and get pulled over by a friend."

"Go on," Lew urged.

"It had to be that Anderson fellow that got murdered. I know 'cause the man that pulled him over was that Summers fella. I saw his tattoos in the headlights. He picked up the hammer and beat Anderson to death. I remember thinking, 'Justice done'."

Lew turned to the bailiff.

"Recall Summers to the stand." There was a moment or two of milling around, and then the bailiff said, "It seems Mr. Summers has found urgent business elsewhere. He sped outta here about three minutes ago like his hair was on fire."

The Attorney Got Her Goat

Dave was on trial for stealing a goat.
He affirmed that he didn't do it.
It was a cash buy from a stranger,
With no receipt for him to prove it

A greedy neighbor claimed the prized buck,
Said Friday Dave took it through the fence.
Her story was very convincing.
Dave was left without much for defense.

Dave's lawyer said, "Judge, I must tell you,
She surely saw someone at the wire
Because she had a terrific view
From where she set the roadside on fire.

"I didn't do that!" yelled the neighbor,
"I spent all Friday in town with friends!"
"There was no fire" smirked the defense.
Silence brought Dave's trial to an end.

Marlene Tucker

The Great Heartbreak Bank Robbery

BJ Elkert was a regular fixture on Main Street. He weighed in at 300 pounds, all muscle. Johnny Ruth was his wife. She weighed at least 220. Not given to fat, she was all blonde hair and pink skin. She had a figure that would make a Holstein milk cow moo with envy. Even the slightest off color joke made her collapse in giggles and turn even pinker. With enough hard giggles, parts of her generous body would start to vibrate and gyrate in different rhythms. She could keep an entire table laughing (and somewhat transfixed) for minutes at a time.

BJ Elkert and his wife, Johnny Ruth, run the Heartbreak Bank, Pawn and Knife Co. in our little town. BJ and Johnny Ruth bought out the last bank for mostly the decayed brick front work. They set up a notions and pawn store next to BJ's feed and repair shop.

The "Bank" was mostly left over from when Heartbreak still had a bank sometime back in the 50's. Now, it was mostly a curio shop specializing in BJ's custom made knives. When BJ tired of fixing all the cars and trucks, tractors, chainsaws, weed eaters, and everything else that needed working parts in Heartbreak, he practiced his real love of forging beautiful blades.

A flashy Cadillac with thee-spoke chrome wheels slowly cruised through Heartbreak at noon one Friday. It was driven by a cheap looking sort of young woman who had never mastered the art of bleaching her hair. Nor did she know when to stop applying makeup, especially eye liner. That day it saved her life. Still, she would have been sort of pretty if she hadn't tried so hard, bless her heart.

The two men in the back seat both wore cheap suits. Both had tattoos sort of creeping above their collars and out their cuffs, skin art curling from their clothes like untrimmed nose hair. They both wore some kind of strong after shave, the stench of which could permeate a room faster than their bad attitudes.

After cruising through Heartbreak very slowly three times, the Cadillac pulled up out front of The Waterin' Hole Café. One of the men jumped out with a big automatic weapon and ran across the street to Heartbreak Bank, Pawn, and Knife Co, his weapon at the ready.

The other gunny jumped out on the curb and kicked opens the door of The Waterin' Hole. This was an unnecessary rudeness, since it was about to fall off its hinges, anyway.

The first bandit kicked the door of Johnny Ruth's Bank, Pawn and Knife Co, but BJ had just rebuilt the doors out of aged oak, so all he got was a loud "klunk" and a sore foot. Frustrated, he turned and let out a burst of fire from his weapon that ruined hours of BJ's hard work, but it **did** open the door. It also put all of Heartbreak on notice that something big was going down.

Johnny Ruth, being BJ's dutiful wife, sank to the floor under a three-inch steel plate, just like BJ told her to do if ever there was an "incident." By now poor Johnny Ruth was quivering and jiggling in earnest. She immediately pulled out the 9mm Glock BJ had given her for her birthday, and while laying on the floor she reached her arm over the counter top and began a random spray of bullets throughout the store.

The lead bank robber had made an unfortunate choice of buying a knockoff AK-47. It jammed almost immediately. Also, one of Johnny Ruth's bullets had neatly sheared off his left ear lobe. Even a person of his limited intelligence could imagine another outcome.

"Gunny 1," as he was later designated in Arney Shaw's police report, made the equally unfortunate decision of running out of the bank and into the street. He then made the near tragic error of grabbing the first gate to the right. This is the gate that goes right into BJ's blacksmithing yard.

BJ was working on a new sort of knife at the forge with his four pound sledge when Gunny 1 stepped in to clear his chamber. BJ swung his four pound sledge and it was lights out for Gunny 1 for about 3 weeks.

Gunny 2 backed across the street into The Waterin' Hole Café. He announced "Holdup! Raise your hands with your wallet in one hand and your keys in the other!"

Gunny 2 had had little experience with small Texas towns.

Ten of the diners raised a gun instead of raising their hands. He suddenly found himself staring down more dark tubes than a plumber shopping for pipe.

For a few moments it was a stand off. Then he commenced to shaking like a donkey passing peach pits. This was NOT part of his plan.

About then Sally Rae walked out of the kitchen. She had tried a new dish that day, steaming hot beef fajitas in a medium sized cast iron skillet with grilled peppers and onions.

Gunny 2 tried to regain control of the situation. He abruptly raised his automatic rifle and knocked her skillet up in the air.

Sally Rae had decades of experience with unruly customers. She brought the hot skillet back down, hard, on the would-be bandit's head. He dropped, insensible.

To her everlasting credit, Sally Rae then walked over to Sam Clancy and served his meal.

"Sorry about the burned hair on the bottom of the skillet, but the food's still hot," she said. Sam wasn't about to disagree with her. In her café, Sally Rae was Queen.

The blonde in the Cadillac impatiently honked her horn 3 times. This is considered very rude in Heartbreak.

About this time we got our only casualty: Sven Halburtson, the oldest man in Heartbreak, started running down the main road. He had a six-shooter in one hand and an ax in the other. At some point he nicked his throat while swing his ax back and forth. He was a 106 years old and he often talked about how he wished he'd had died in action. I guess he figured it was his last chance. If all your favorite ancestors are berserkers and cowboys, it sort of limits your options.

Arney, the town policeman, sped up in his car, skidded sideways, and opened his door.

Totally flustered, the overly made-up blonde opened her door and jumped out into the middle of the street. For some reason known only to her and God, she had chosen a big old .44 magnum as her gun. It was way too big for her slender wrists to control, but it **did** sound impressive. BJ walked to the door of Heartbreak Bank, Pawn and Knife Co, and she made her only half-way accurate shot, splintering the new oak door (yet again) with one of her slugs.

Several men (but not all) in The Waterin' Hole Café choose the gunfight over Sally Rae's fajitas. They lined up inside the Café and began shooting near the poor blonde's feet.

Meanwhile she screamed and cried. Tears ran down her face, smearing her eyeliner until she looked like a genuine Heartbreak Raccoon. A common emotion gripped all the dozen or so men watching her cry and spin around, shooting wildly in the air. Most had had daughters graduating from Heartbreak High School. They had sent them off to countless football games with the signatory Raccoon black eyes. Anyone could have picked her off, but instead they fired close to her feet, distracting her somewhat questionable aim.

At some length she pirouetted close enough that Arney could reach out with his night stick. With a sort of professional courtesy and experienced ease he tapped her on the back of her head and she went down.

Sven Halbertson, the blood of his Viking ancestors boiling, finally got to the scene of the crime. "Where is they, where is they, the robbin' murderin' scum?!" he shouted.

"It's all over," Arney said. "Put up your gun and for goodness sakes, put down that ax before you cut yourself again."

Only then did Old Sven look down at himself. His shirt was covered in blood. His large beard had been saved him from a far worse cut; still, it was his first shaving cut in about 50 years.

"Dadblameit, I been wanting to tangle with desperadoes for over a century. You mean I'm too late?"

Arney, like all good small town policemen, was something of a diplomat.

"Come on, Sven, you can help me disarm them."

Happy again, Old Sven started collecting the shooting' irons.

In all, about 200 shots were fired. All three of the hapless bandits had concussions. Gunny 1, a guy named Michael, was hurt the worst. He could never talk quite right after that, though some people blamed it on his growing up in the North. The argument had some merit;

everyone knew BJ wouldn't hurt a fly if he could help it.

Old Sven never washed the shirt on which he had so gallantly bled. Eventually he made $40 by selling it to Johnny Ruth. BJ framed it and put it up in their store. Old Sven, of course, developed his own version of the gunfight, so that he hadn't cut his own throat with an ax. Instead, he was hit five times but still kept coming, so that (with Arney's help) the devil woman was finally put down. He finally had his personal legend, and like all of Sven's stories it grew in time.

Arney came out looking pretty good. He had done his peace-keeping thing, and proved once again that Heartbreak ought not to replace him with a night watchman.

Johnny Ruth also did well. Heartbreak Bank, Pawn and Knife Co., had real, honest-to-God bank robber bullet holes all over the front of BJ's custom-made front door. There were even more inside. In an instinctual but splendid marketing move she refused to let BJ fix the numerous holes. Sure enough, hundreds came to see the only visible remains of the gunfight. Johnny Ruth could jiggle and laugh in dozens of intriguing variations as she told and retold the story. She sold her notions and even a few of BJ's custom knives.

The Waterin' Hole Café did best of all. Sally Rae's "Gunfight Fajitas" became a favorite meal after folks worked up a hunger viewing all the sacred relics of The Great Heartbreak Bank Holdup.

THE FAILED HOLDUP WAS A CINCH

"Hello Ma'am, this here's a holdup",
Said the man with the shaky hands.
He ordered her to bag the cash,
And hoped she would go with the plans.

He looked all around the lobby,
He didn't attempt a disguise.
Folks knew he must be dangerous,
Because he surely wasn't wise.

He was ready to grab and run,
But his pants were too loose he felt,
So he laid the gun on the desk,
And stopped to tighten his belt.

A quick teller grabbed the weapon,
The guard pulled his gun in a stance,
The robber said his motive was,
To buy a smaller pair of pants.

Marlene Tucker

THE THEOLOGY OF STARTING A TRACTOR

EMMITT BENNETT IS MY NEXT DOOR
neighbor, less than half a mile away, up the hill from me. He used to be a hard drinking man. After he burned down his house shooting at a possum he sobered up and got religion. Ole Emmitt sang in the choir and told anyone he could make listen to all the particulars of his sinful life. The best I can say about that is, he seldom had to repeat himself. Most people listened politely; we weren't big enough for an AA chapter and no one was willing to actually discourage him from sobriety. Privately, though, most of us were amazed at how little sobriety had improved him. He still had a personality like a trash can bee with hemorrhoids.

Emmitt spent long hours talking with God, first about whiskey, then his plumbing business, then which crop to plant and how many goats to run. Of course, Emmitt told everyone all about these conversations, and how God answered him back. Pretty soon we all got to noticing that if only Emmitt was the one wanting something, after a while God sort of came around.

Anyway, Emmitt had an old Massey Harris tractor he inherited from his father. It had to date back to 1947, but old tractors can nearly always be brought back with enough work and patience. It was a huge rust covered slab of metal, but Emmitt went over every square inch with sand paper, primer, paint, and a sort of love he never could express to his wife or children. He had the starter rebuilt; the generator rewound, and bought a new battery. He even pulled the

260

cylinders and polished them one by one, but the old chunk of metal still would not crank.

I still don't know if God finally gave him an inside tip or if Emmitt figured the next part out on his own, but Saturday morning came and Emmitt had half of Heartbreak out to watch him crank his old massive Massey Harris.

Emmitt wrapped a chain around and around one of those huge iron rear wheels. He held the chain in place with duct tape. The tire was jacked up six inches or so off the ground. The other end of the chain was coupled around his trailer hitch on his new F-350 Ford pickup. Emmitt flipped on the tractor switch, sprayed ether in the air filter, and ran to his truck. He gunned away from the tractor, the chain spinning the tractor wheel. Since the tractor was in second gear, the transmission moved the power to the cylinders –sure 'nuff—the old tractor began to cough and then run. Emmitt looked out his window, proud as if he'd birthed that old tractor hisself.

"Pride commeth before a fall and a haughty spirit before a mighty rear-end whopping," my old Sunday school teacher always said. It was at that moment Emmitt's foot slipped and he gave the tractor one more little yank—and the old tractor fell off the platform and started forward. The first thing that happened was it gathered speed and smashed into the rear of his new truck. That spun Emmitt sideways; so on the next hit the tractor was tangled on the chain and dragging his truck down the hill toward my place. We all scattered. Emmitt found that he could exercise some control by pulling on the rear axle, where his chain was tangled, but his results were uncertain, sort of like a two-headed calf having an argument with itself.

At one point the tractor headed straight for Emmitt and Lizzy's front door. Emmitt might have let the situation get out of control, but Lizzy never would. Her house was less than six months old and there was no way she was going to play hostess to some old tractor passing through her living room. Lizzy stood there in the front doorway with Emmitt's 12 gauge and steadily put round after round into the front grill of the old Massey. Nothing seemed to dissuade it, though; it just kept coming at a steady 8 or 10 miles an hour until she blew out a front tire.That sort of got the old beast turning. In a left-handed present from God the rear bumper finally tore clean free from Emmitt's truck. The tractor rumbled forward. Next it hit the power pole to their new house. A hot line dropped across the diesel tank and blew up sky high, slicker than a Hollywood movie.

All us neighbors clapped. Emmitt *did* know how to put on a show.

Next, the tractor ran over the gas meter, breaking it off and sloshing burning diesel on the natural gas. It blew up, but it would have been sort of disappointing except it was next to Emmitt's hay pile.

We were all developing a grudging admiration for the old tractor—once reanimated, nothing was going to stop it. It was sort of like Frankenstein on steroids; Massey Fergenstine, if you will.

All of a sudden I started getting worried. Though wounded the beast was still dangerous. The tractor ran downhill, those little front wheels following the lay of the land. Downhill was the direction of my house; I realized I had yet another reason that I was sorry for giving up the high ground to the Bennetts.

The flaming tractor tore out 6 or 8 newly-planted peach trees, flattened a wheelbarrow, and tore through my fence as it headed across my place. In a last effort, the front wheels bounced off of a stump and directed the whole thing into my stock tank. There was a mighty hiss, and the fire went out. The beast was dead.

Most of us were sort of laughing, maybe a little nervously, when Lizzy walked up to confront poor ol' Emmitt, who still looked a little dazed..

"Emmitt," Lizzy said, "I want to know, was it the Lord who told you how to start that thing?"

"Uh, I guess so, sorta," he admitted.

"Well, why didn't He tell you how to stop it?"

BEST INTENTIONS LOCKED AWAY

It was her first day of work at New Blessed Church.
It was the position she had always wanted.
She had heard all the stories about bad first days,
So she left for her new job a little haunted.

With her mind made up to make a good impression,
She left early to get some donuts for her boss.
Getting a newspaper might also be thoughtful,
So if he didn't like sweets it wasn't a loss.

In one hand she held her phone and the fresh donuts.
The newspaper box required coins to begin.
While reaching down into the box for a paper,
Her new handbag came off her shoulder and slid in.

The door slammed shut on her purse and best intentions,
The necessary coins were locked inches away.
She dreaded making the call to her employer,
Announcing she'd be late for her very first day.

Marlene Tucker

THE PASSING OF OLD GREY

ABOUT THREE YEARS AGO, I LIMPED into Heartbreak Texas after a terrible divorce. I had nothing with me but my most prized possessions: My daughter, Janey, a few clothes and my tools, and my broken-down pickup, Old Grey. My first stop was The Waterin' Hole Café. I awakened my trip weary daughter, Janey. At 16, she looked like a hurt puppy, all snuggled and asleep against my shoulder, more full of worry, fear and apprehension than any teen ought to be. She needed reassurance. I tried to give it to her, though I didn't feel it myself.

An unusually pretty waitress, Sally Rae, gave me local instruction about how to find the old Miller Ranch. I liked it, and by 10 a.m. I was in a loan officer's office and he surprised me. He made me a loan. My credit was good (or at least my prospects weren't as bad as the Millers,) and by noon, I owned a genuine ranch. Janey and I were moved in by that Tuesday. Fast forward, two years later I married Sally Rae. In large part all this depended on my hard work and the Grey Ghost, my old pickup truck.

The Grey Ghost was a relic when I acquired her. She had 140,000 thousand miles on her when I bought her back in Houston. I put another 60,000 miles on her, but finally one day she would not start at all. I replaced the battery, put in new spark plugs, replaced the air filter, and I even poured 6 gallons of Premium grade in her, but the Grey Ghost would not start.

The Grey Ghost sat in the front yard, almost cranking, but not quite. We put in a new battery, it ran down. I recharged it and bought ether and while Sally Rae sprayed it into the carburetor. I cranked the Grey Ghost. I had the final machine doctor, BJ Elkert, out for a house call. The moment I knew that was coming finally came. He pulled the oil stick and a slimy brown-grey emulsion of oil and water adhered to it. Darn! Old Grey was terminal.

A rancher without a pickup is like a cowboy without a horse and a saddle. It is the most basic tool for the trade and no excuses can work. For about a week, Old Grey sat in our front yard, like a monument to my failure as a mechanic

Our favorite time of the day is when I sit down with Sally Rae at the end of the day. We sit on our porch and talk. We talk. We listen to each other and the sounds of the country woods around us. We recount our victories and our losses. At 62, this is near the top for intimacy. I would have never guessed it. Just three years ago I felt so desolate that no woman could revive me. We helped each other, held each other, sleeping and secure, secure in our mutual hope and trust that rain would come in the drought, that the coyotes would miss this crop of goat kids, that an old grey pickup truck that had lived four times its warranty would get another year. These were my actual days, and these are the moments that will me forward. That was I how we lived.

"Darlin'", I began, "oh my Darlin', the Grey Ghost was about all I brought in the way of assets into our marriage, but she has just about done her 250,000 miles and...."

"Darlin,'" she said, "Oh, my darlin', " and Sally Rae skipped off our porch into her retreat. A moment later she gave me a wad of $20 dollar bills.

"Here it is $2,400 for a down payment on a new truck!" She offered jubilantly.

I felt a major moral alarm. I was taking money from a woman that I was supposed to love, honor, cherish and support.

"This'lll keep us afloat until fall, won't it?"

I answered honestly. "I don't know." Raising goats, I was finding out, was like bucking the house odds in Las Vegas. Never bet against the house.

Then I asked, "Where'd all this come from?"

Heartbreak, Texas

Sally Rae said, "These are just the tips from the courthouse, When the Circuit Court comes here, last Friday of the month, there is always a hungry lawyer or three at the bottom of the stairs ready for lunch. They sit and play poker while they tell each other lies. I guess its cause lawyers love words so much, but they would rather talk than breathe! I serve 'em, and they give me a manilla package of money to take with lunch up to the Judge. He unpacks his lunch, and then he opens the white package and gives me a $200 tip. I DON'T ASK or tell anyone but you."

Three days later, I bought a 1994 Ford, a F150 straight six with only 150,000 miles on it! I'll confess to being "little kid" sort of excited. I seldom got new things in my new life. For three months of Sally Rae's tips and an additional $85 a month, I had a new used pickup truck with less than 50,000 miles on its rebuilt engine. She has red sides and Sally Rae named her "Rosie." The ranch struggled on.

Late at night, things nag at me. I know that lawyers and such count money different than honest ranchers and waitresses like me and Sally Rae do; but $200 for carrying the Judge's brown bag up to him with lunch? Something here stunk to high heaven. I knew Heartbreak's history, at least a little.

I knew we had always had white lightning, prostitution and gambling south of Heartbreak in Quick Fix. I knew we had a mighty courthouse like only county courts have, but that in the 1930's we were down-graded and the new court house moved 20 miles north to Culver City. I knew from teaching civics classes back in Houston that our county was one of the last six in Texas that still used a circuit court.

Another part of me knew I held onto this ranch by the Grace of God and my banker's good will. I lived in a shallow boat on a stormy sea, and if I shook things, the first casualty would be me and my family. Corruption is a dirty word, but I had gave up on courts and justice a long time ago. Big corporations got "justice" if they paid enough millions, but little men like me stayed a lot happier if most things went along without too much examination.

I troubled over it as I rolled about in my sleep, but in the end Sally Rae's courthouse "tips" troubled me less than my broken down fences and Old Grey rusting in the front yard. And like the snake in Eden, the words "poker game" kept going round and round in my

266

mind. I've always been pretty lucky – at least, in cards — and the ranch always needs something else repaired. I drifted off to sleep....

The next morning I was shaving, but my mind was far away.

"Dave, quit thinking, or give up shaving! I'm not ready to be a widder yet!" Sally Rae exclaimed.

I looked in the mirror. Sure enough, I had half-dozen new cuts and I had not felt a thing. Poker was calling to me...

Love My Truck

Friday night after work I was coming home late,
I planned to take my best girl out on a date.
She said she had to stay home and wash her hair.
Drove my truck by to see her but she wasn't there.

I drove down the back roads on my way home,
Looked like I was going to spend the evening alone,
Then I saw the little car of my buddy, Buck.
He was off in the sand and looked like he was stuck.

I found my girl cheating with my best friend,
Years of friendship suddenly came to an end.
I learned I couldn't count on friends or love or luck.
The only thing dependable was my old truck.

Well, I couldn't leave them both standing in the road.
I said I'd take them home but his car could be towed,
Made them ride in the back with the bumps and the buck.
And I thought as I was driving how I love my truck.

Marlene Tucker

THE POKER GAME

NO YEARS ARE EASY IN HEARTBREAK,
but this year was especially bad. My tractor seemed beyond repair; Old Grey, my pickup, had to be replaced, and new bills multiplied faster than the new goats that had to be sold to pay those bills.

Ranching is a high risk game where the rancher has to buy everything retail and sell his product wholesale. A man has to put out a year of work and expense in the hopes that one day at the auction, in under 5 minutes, he can recoup all his losses. Moses' father-in-law was hardly the first man to wonder what happened to him. Anyway, if that tickles you, read Genesis. Jews love Moses 'cause he led them out of Eygpt. I like him 'cause he is the first successful goat rancher in recorded history. Some days, I fear he was the last.

I had multiple ranch problems and I thought I had better resurrect some of my old college skills to get by.

I learned that the lawyers over at the court house had a "friendly" poker game going on the first Tuesday of every month, when the circuit court came to Heartbreak. Basically, a friendly poker game was one where, if you had a bad run of luck, the winners would only take all your worldly possessions and maybe your wife. The winners would leave your children, at least most times.

"Would you guys like another player?" I asked, all friendly like.

A look went around the circle. I was a non-lawyer, not even a paralegal. Perhaps they would have considered me if I was at least a client, but as a non-lawyer they considered me to have diminished capacity. It wasn't personal, lawyers have been dim-capping the public since Venus decided to go into a profession, instead of taking a job. Still, handling it right was important.

A local lawyer, Wes Harday, spoke for his esteemed colleagues. "Well Dave, Judge Bother is about ready to hear our pleadings, so we're just shutting it down for the day."

About then a new face spoke up. I'm Polonius Faulkner," he said, extending his hand.

His hand was tough and calloused, not what I expected from a lawyer. His face was plowed with wrinkles and tanned really deep. His voice was a rough, gravelly sort of drawl that only a lifetime of cigars can bring about.

"Hi Polonius. I'm Dave, and I'm looking for a poker game."

He winked at the group. "I hear tell of one out in Quick Fix next Friday, at Dancers Anonymous. Interested?"

"Sure, I'll be there."

I didn't lie to Sally Rae about all this at all, I just didn't say anything. Sometimes a man has to do what a man has to do to save the ranch. After all, my winnings would be for the family. It's not like I was planning something wrong, or really bad, actually...but a part of my imagination was excited as a teenager going out Friday night with the school's "bad girl".

Meanwhile, I had to get myself a little stake; a poke to get my winnings going. That week I sold six of my culls and two plump little withers at the local auction. I hocked my lever-action Winchester, and, in a stroke of luck, I even sold a spare watering trough to some boys down the road.

A couple of years earlier, I'd had a bad experience at Dancers Anonymous, but I'm not superstitious about such things. I was rarin' to go when the time came. Those guys were gonna get plucked, whoever they were. I was on a mission and my cause was just.

Now even a juke joint like Dancers Anonymous wasn't so blind to Texas law as to have an overt poker game, not even in a wide open place like Quick Fix. I walked in and asked for a shot of "12-year-old Irish single-malt." Everyone in that shabby little clap-board house knew there wouldn't be any alcohol available there more than 3 weeks old, so the bartender knew what I meant and motioned me around to a back door.

I knew I was in the right spot the second I walked in. Cold air and cigar smoke washed over me like a malediction.

Six men sat over the table in deep concentration. Holding their cards, they could have been a meditation group of gargoyles. The air in the dimly lighted room was so thick you could fold it in a pie crust and sell it at $2.75 a slice. The window box-air conditioner breathed out the perfume of old sin and new temptation.

Polonius looked up only long enough to say, "Sit down or move on. We got bidness here."

I sat.

For about the first hour, my luck held. I didn't win any big hands, but I won enough small ones to feel a little confidence. Of course, anyone who has played much money poker will tell you right off that it is a science for the people who play to win. It's a game for people who play to lose. I had to win; my ranch depended on it.

One of the Quick Fix gals brought in a round of drinks. I started to dig into my pocket for some cash.

"Keep your money, big guy, this is on the house."

That right there should have made me suspicious. Quick Fix was famous for ALL kinds of hospitality, but it had scarcely any charity at all. My first sip of the lovely amber liquid in my hand should have been another warning. It really **was** 12 year-old single malt Scotch. Do wonders never cease?

The first thing any novice at poker has to learn is when to take the plunge. If you got 4 Jacks or higher, bet the ranch, as they say, but hold back until you're sure. Meanwhile, the trick is to euchre others into betting when you have a winning hand. Of course, it's never too safe; that's why they call it gambling.

I played for another hour, never getting much ahead or behind. Finally, in a hand of 7-card stud, I got the hand I'd been waiting for. I had 2 Queens showing and another in my hand. My last card down was another Queen. Do tell! Or better yet, keep the poker face and get the table stakes up.

That part was easier than I expected. I had to put almost my last dime to keep up my end of the betting, but I had a sure thing so I was determined to see it through.

Finally, the last man said, "Call."

There had to be close to $2,500 on the table by then. This might seem puny to some folk, but it was just the princely sum I had to have to keep the ranch.

It was time to show. I laid down my four Queens. The stranger across from me laid down four Aces.

All of a sudden I knew what it was like to be sucker punched.

The stranger reached for the pot and Polonius said, "Hold on, mister," and he proceeded to lay down a Royal Flush.

What happened next went fast—real fast.

Gunfire filled the room as the stranger and Polonius shot it out.

I went over backwards. I whacked my head something fierce, but I was back in my right mind in less than a minute. When I stood up, I noticed for the first time that it was full dark outside. I glanced around the little room.

Nothing clears out a place like gunfire.

The first thing I noted was that the stranger with four Aces had a new eye-socket in his forehead. I didn't have to look at the back wall to know his brains were splattered there.

I was ready to run myself when I heard a groan from beside me. It was Polonius, somewhat worse for the wear.

"Oh Lord, I'm gut shot," he moaned.

Well, I didn't owe Ole Polonius a thing. I opened the door to the main room, getting ready to bolt. The main dance floor and bar of Dancers Anonymous was as deserted as Cottonwood Baptist on a Tuesday morning. I took one step, and then Polonius moaned again.

That did it. Yeah, my momma raised a softie, but there are just some things I couldn't do. I couldn't run off and let him bleed out when he might be saved. I walked back into that little den of iniquity and hauled the bleeding man out to my truck.

On the way to the Culver City Hospital, Polonius came round. "Give them this when we get there," he said, and passed out again. He had a blood stained Texas Ranger badge in his hand.

Two days later I visited him in the hospital.

"How you doing, Polonius?" I asked.

"I've been way better. My bad luck. We have been after those guys for most of the last six months. Now someone else will have to start all over."

"By now you probably figured out that I'm no lawyer. Keep quiet about who I really am. Something else, Rube, stay out of gambling halls." He fixed his cold blue eyes on me.

"But I was winning," I insisted, like a fool.

"You did win. You got out of there alive," the Ranger said. "This time and this one time only I'm giving you a free walk 'cause you saved my life. All those others were cheating you, you just couldn't see it. Now, they're all going to jail, except for the one who got a funeral instead. Now get out of here. Go home to your wife. You have no natural gift for sinning. And from now on, stay away from Quick Fix!"

Well, I sure took his advice. I know when I got a good deal.

I also know that when I gathered up Polonius with one arm, I grabbed the table cloth with my other one. Back at home, I had $2,346.18 buried in a mason jar behind the chicken coop. My little ranch in Heartbreak would make it another year.

BOOKING A BET

Roy sat down at the poker table
His friends thought he must wish to be dead
Because if his wife caught him gambling
She would knock him up side of the head

Roy placed on the table his Bible.
The guys asked why he had it about.
He said "My life counts on believing."
They all nodded but still there was doubt.

In all the games Roy was successful.
It seemed he had phenomenal luck.
He was gathering his bonanza,
When the door was repeatedly struck.

The money was stuffed in the Good Book,
Just before Roy's wife bolted in.
He said, "You'll be proud of me, darling,
I've been preaching that gambling's a sin."

Marlene Tucker

Elegiac Reflections

Sometimes you Can't Get It Right

I FLED HOUSTON, LEAVING BEHIND A bitter divorce and an unfaithful (though legally triumphant) wife. Almost two years ago, I came here to Heartbreak, Texas. I arrived with the only things that mattered to me: my daughter and my old pickup truck. I was a refugee, running from my past, running to my future, like the millions who had preceded me.

I'm getting old. I'm overweight. I'm proud of the hairs I have left, and see their graying as a badge of survival. I have a prematurely-aged woman 15 years my junior, my trophy bride. I have an astonishingly beautiful daughter, so beautiful that she would make me doubt my first wife's integrity; except I see so much of myself in my daughter that I know the genetics are true. All in all, I am blessed.

I first arrived near sun-up in a forgotten part of a largely forgettable place, a place where the bluebonnets still have the courage to come out azure, or lavender, or navy blue; where the cows moo from contentment and the people are real in a way most of us have forgotten, if we ever knew.

I went down Heartbreak's only main street, pulled into The Waterin' Hole Café, and a pretty woman with too many miles on her face for her years said "Want some breakfast, honey? We got gravy and biscuits, and a slice of vinegar pie left from yesterday." That was

275

Sally Rae. Two years later I married her; but then, I'm getting ahead of myself.

Sally Rae is not conventionally what you would call beautiful, any more than I'm what some might call handsome. Some might call her worn or plain. I call her God's Gift, and anyone doesn't think Sally Rae's beautiful can meet me around back. Don't expect to come back pretty, either. Neither time nor experience has cut either of us many breaks, but our toleration of events has sweetened every good moment left to us.

I was driving into Heartbreak for a cold Dr Pepper and Vinegar pie break, looking forward to a visit with Sally Rae at The Waterin' Hole Café when I rounded a curve in the road. The sun shined on the dirty window of my old pickup truck when something glimmered, and a deer crashed through my windshield. All of a sudden I had a 12 point buck staring me in the face from the passenger seat beside me!

He came round a little faster than me; I braked and he did what deers do: wagged his antlers and cut my face. I grabbed his antlers with my right hand as I ran through a fence and off into Doc Sam's stock tank. I got stopped with one hand on the wheel, one hand holding the antlers off my face, and water seeping in the floorboard. I decided Mr. Obama was right; *it was time for a change!*

My door opened and I slipped out of the door into the pond muck. Of course, my feet went right out from under me and I went under the green scum that passes for water after cows have done their special thing in it for months of drought.

I decided pretty quick that my life's greatest ambition was not to drown in eight inches of cow muck, so I crawled up the side and around to the back of my old Ford pickup. Every Texan with a pickup keeps a few tools scattered around (except for the big cities, where leaving a tool in a truck assures it'll get stolen).

I reviewed the situation. The poor deer had at least two broken legs and other injuries. His days were up. I popped him on the head with my hammer and pulled him from the wreckage of my truck by his antlers. Just as I got him free, he woke up and began to protest, mightily. Since I was standing in knee deep water, I got both hands on his head and, well, not to put too fine a point on it, I held his snout under the pond scum. It was all I could think of.

About that time Arney, the town cop, drove up.

"Drowning deer out of season, Dave?" he drawled.

"Just this one," I yelled, dodging the deer's hind legs as he fought me. "You won't to give me a hand here?" I asked.

Now Arney could have done several things. Homeland Security had bought him a bunch of shiny new toys and he was down right confused as to which one he should play with at any given time. He could have helped me hold the deer's antlers, he could have shot it, he could have even written me a ticket for drowning deer out of season.

What he did do was whip out his camera and get a series of pictures of me in my struggle. I guess his personal motto was "Preserve, Protect and Record."

"Arney, put that fool camera down and DO something," I yelled, near the end of my strength.

Arney did something alright. He whipped out his brand new Taser and assumed the lawman's stance.

I was standing in water holding the deer. My last words were "NOOOO! It will…." And then I woke up on the side of the pond, coughing out snot and green cow water. The only thing worse than boys and their toys was laws and their toys.

A few days later I served Janey a venison roast.

"Daddy, this tastes wild," she complained.

"Just eat it and hush. You have no idea what I went through to put meat on our table, honey."

It wasn't her criticism, though, that hurt. In front of me, page one of the *Heartbreak Times*, was a full color picture of me standing in the pond. The headline said, "Deer Drowner Hits the Big Time." Small towns can really get starved for news.

That night as I sat alone on my porch, an owl went, OOOo! About 15 seconds later he went, "OOOo!" again.

I went "Oool!"

The owl paused and went "OOOol!"

I tried to copy, but went, "OOo."

Long silence . . . The owl went "OOOol."

Why couldn't I get it right? "OoOol" I tried again.

The owl, disgusted, went silent.

Sometimes you just need to save your breath. You're never gonna git it right.

277

THE BUZZ ABOUT TOWN
(*or* Just Let It Bee)

Young Buster was a budding beekeeper.
The four-page paper in town had no news.
A reporter nagged for an interview,
But the beekeeper would always refuse.

One day Buster ran to see the doctor.
He was covered head to toe with red whelps.
The nurse let it slip to the reporter,
His motto being: "Each little tip helps."

The next day was printed a sweet story,
At least the way the tabloid had it coiled,
It told of a guy who was heartbroken
When elopement with his honey was spoiled.

But the town folk agreed the bold headline
Was the best the paper had ever seen.
It read "Local Spends Time With Royalty"
Page three, "Buster's Short Visit With The Queen."

Marlene Tucker, 2013

ANOTHER DAY

SALLY RAE AND I WERE READY TO settle down into a happy empty nest but a stray cousin dropped off a spare child on us sudden like. The four-year old boy was Li'l' Billy and he is a piece of work. Li'l' Billy is loosely classified as a savant; I know this from my teaching years. At not quite five years he can read English and some Latin. He mostly speaks in quotations and he's a great mimic. Man, is he ever a handful! There is a reason God has us make children when we are all young, in our '20s, hot and bothered, but one thing I have learned is true: Sometimes The Big Guy drops off these children to people other than their natural parents to raise.

Anyway, 62 was a lot different for me than 61. At 62, one knee gave out, my back began to ache in places I'd never heard from before, and the morning coffee that Sally Rae left on my bedside went from being a convenience to a necessity. I had little to say for myself, except that I didn't come with a warranty.

Still, life went on. If I moved slower, it gave me more time to think about which direction I was moving. Moving slower gave me moments of reflection. I remember a time this week; the ranch was dry (of course), I had to get another draw from the bank to see me through to the rains. A goat, No. 243, just bit me as I helped her with her third birthing.

I had shooed Li'l' Billy out from the hornets (again), and my knee ached something awful. I knew Sally Rae was just finishing up breakfast for the Cedar Choppers back at The Waterin' Hole about

279

now. This never put her in a good mood.

One gets to worry about family as often as one wants to, but I looked at myself, my love for Janey, who is all gone off at college. I looked at Li'l' Billy, swatting at the hornets, and I looked at Ms. No. 243, now licking her new kid. Life was work, life was a struggle, but life was good. It was one of those rare moments I felt the Presence of God. I just dropped to my one good knee and I thanked Him for this moment, with the prayer that I could have lots more days just like this one.

It's easy to be dissatisfied with life. Complainers never lack material or proof. I felt pain several places, but I felt gratitude throughout my whole meager soul. I could still work. I had a woman I loved. My beloved daughter was off gaining her own life. None of us knew what sort of life it would be, but I knew she would own that life. I believe in her.

Li'l' Billy, well, he was another story. Too early to tell on most things, but he was a rounder. I figure Li'l' Billy would either be governor of the great State of Texas some day, or on death row. Or maybe a professor of some sort. It wasn't my job to set him on a course of action, but it was darn sure my job to teach him how to pee in a bathroom, to teach him how to judge Laeritie's writings, how to know the difference between right and wrong. Li'l' Billy was a full time job, along with the ranch, the banker, fixing my old truck, and a herd of goats that insisted on dying about as fast as they were born.

Life in Heartbreak Texas is real involved. I love it. I wouldn't take money for it. Beauty is in the eyes of the beholder, and like the Navajos, each morning when I see a new day come up I feel a surge of joy. I don't take life for granted, and now I got joy with my life. I think the Talmud says that a rich man reckons the happiness he has. I know I am rich. How much does it take?

Any way, Li'l' Billy, somewhat predictability, lost his latest fight with the wasps. I took my swelling, crying baby into our old farmhouse and put baking soda on the tad's wounds; I fed him some blacked-peas from yesterday's dinner, and soon he cried himself to sleep. Growing up is rough; no doubt. Growing older is much rougher.

I thawed some beef and set it on fast cook, cut up potatoes and some fresh onions that grow behind the old barn. I threw in some

David Mosley

fresh minced garlic that Sally Rae brought home from The Waterin'
Hole. I dumped in some ingredients into that new bread maker we got
for our wedding; dinner was on.

I went back out to my goat lot for the evening feeding. Most of
my herd came right back in after my first cry of "Ewhie, ewhuie!"
This cry sounds sort of like the Rebel Yell, only in reverse. Slow
goats don't get fed at all, so they all just thundered right in.

Anyway, I put my last opened bag of feed on my shoulder and
poured it out, as I always do, a little in each feeding bin. It's sweet feed
so it sticks together a little bit. At about the fifth bend I felt something
a little different than sweet feed. What I pulled out was a four foot
diamond back rattler who was all caged up in that bag. It was hard to
say which of us were more surprised; him or me. Anyway, I emptied
that rattler into the goat bin and he landed with attitude!

His first move was to strike at my face, but I saw him a second
before and jerked back. I drew my .22 magnum pistol I always carry
on me and I shot him twice in the face. He quieted down after that,
and I fed him as a snack to my favorite hog, Milly.

So, after dinner, Sally Rae and I sat out on our upstairs porch,
our special place. A half moon lit up our faces. It is our special time.

"What went on with you today, my darlin' Sally Rae?" I asked.

"Same old, same old. Big Ben, the cedar chopper boss, asked
for extra fries, fresh from the skillet. When I served him he reached
up and grabbed my right boob. No big deal; I brought the hot skillet
down on his hand and laid it there 'til I raised a blister. I added on
$3.50 to his bill, he paid. Big Ben is getting old and he has something
to prove. How was your day?"

"Same old, same old," I said. "Li'l' Billy got stung a few times,
fighting wasps."

"Why is your right cheek so swollen," Sally Rae asked.

I went inside and looked in a mirror.

"Some dumb rattle snake must have grazed my cheek. I killed
him and fed him to the hogs."

"Oh," said Sally Rae. "You think we'll ever get any more rain?"

"Probably not this week."

After that we went inside. I don't write about that part, but it is
good to be alive. I am blessed.

Hogging the Chores

She started her day with laundry,
Hanging the clean wash out to dry.
She had just stepped in the doorway,
When she saw something running by.

The view was clear from the window,
In the brightness of the sunshine.
Chewing on the sheets she had hung,
Was her husband's small herd of swine,

The woman became so angry,
With a stick she started to yell.
The hogs got tangled in the wire,
When the post of the clothesline fell.

By evening she had the fence fixed,
And the hogs were back in their pen.
When the husband asked for clean clothes,
She turned the hogs back out again.

Marlene Tucker

Dog Days

THE IRISH BELIEVE IN THE SIDLE, A
sort of parallel universe whose reality overlaps with our own, or
shines through, like sunrise behind a parchment curtain. This other
reality is inhabited with faeries, leprechauns, and evil sprites that can
alter one's life instantly in some capricious way.

Many Texans (some of Irish descent) have similar beliefs about an
Old West filled with cowboys, bad men, and a warrior ethic that can see
one through most anything. It's part history and part Hollywood, and
it's lead to the ruin of more poor boys than the House of the Rising Sun.
The legacy of the Alamo is a heavy burden for Texas males.

Personally, I think it's mostly all bull-pucky, except for the part
about evil sprites. You can't live around a ranch very long and keep
up your belief in a benign universe.

I'm not particularly superstitious, but I try not to be stupid,
either. I can't help wondering how much of what we call superstition
or intuition is really some primitive part of our brain processing a
warning system we are too "modern" to completely understand. I
know this: there is a time in the summer when the heat mounts
every day. The wind doesn't blow, and Nature doesn't even send a
fake cloud by to give us a little hope for rain. The nights don't really
cool down. As the last drops of humidity are squeezed from the air,
scents travel further, so the rotting leaves from the creek mix with
the smell of sweet feed on the hill. hat's it, that is the smell of Texas
Summer.

283

On such nights, if you listen closely enough, you can sometimes hear— in all that quiet— the sound of a wild dog baying at the moon. If you ever hear that sound it will prickle the hairs on your neck. Go back inside. Don't drink, keep your wits about you. Turn on the air conditioner, the television, and bury yourself in technology. It's a night when you want nothing to do with Nature.

The heat could wilt the wax candles in my dining room if the air conditioner died. I know, I tried, and the next day 10 beautiful twelve inch tapers from our wedding were all bent over like they had paid final homage to the God of Heat. Humans weren't doing much better. Tempers were short and good sense was even more rare than normal.

Emmitt Bennett's pack of wild curs woke me up so often that week that I sat outside all one night, blowing on my silent dog whistle every time they stopped. I knew I could never convince him to get rid of any, but I hoped, maybe, their constant baying would convince him.

Something new was preying on my goats, and I suspected either a raccoon or a bob cat. Either one can hit 40 pounds, either one can be a fierce predator and a strong competitor in close quarters.

My daughter Janey is usually as sweet as fresh-chilled milk, but that night she smarted off to me six times before Toby picked her up for the Heartbreak Raccoon's game. They were 3-4 for the season, not too bad for a little town like Heartbreak. Frankly, I was glad to share her for a change. God's speed, Toby.

I called Sally Rae. She was almost as short with me as Janey.

"Dave, I told you and told you that Friday's my worst night here at The Waterin' Hole. Just be glad you can afford to sit around and be bored." Click. Wow. I felt about as popular as an empty beer bottle in a church parking lot.

One of my donkeys, Dick, sidled up to my window and began braying with all the reserve lung power God gave that benighted species.I gave him a skeptical look. "I'm feeling for you, Dick, I'm feeling for you, but I can't quite reach you."

Funny, but I believe I really did know how he felt. It really was one of those nights when I could hear the wild dog baying.

I reached for a glass to get a drink and knocked off one of my mother's ceramic nick knacks, destroying one of the last of its kind. Then I choked on the water. This got me coughing and I couldn't stop so I went to the medicine cabinet and popped one of last winter's cough drops in my mouth. Seconds later, my mouth really began to burn. I spat it out. Sugar ants were all over it. Sugar ants are tiny, but even they can deliver a sting, especially in my mouth.

About then I heard the sounds of terrified goats in my barn. I grabbed a bat. I admit it, I was in a foul mood and ready to brain some hapless raccoon for bothering my animals.

I threw the barn door open and there, eating a new-born kid goat, was the biggest mountain lion I ever saw. He saw me right back, too. For a second we both froze, then he headed straight at me about 60 miles an hour. I would have panicked if I'd had the luxury and the time. Instead, I brought the baseball bat straight down and broke it smack across his head! Of course, this just sort of set him back a little. In the next instant we both got incredibly polite. I backed off to one side to give him an easy exit and he sort of tippy-toed away, looking sheepish.

I felt fluid fill my boot. I figured I'd lost control—but to my surprise I saw my pants leg was torn from the knee down and the liquid filling my boot was red. That did it—I filled the other boot with yellow liquid.

An hour later, at Old Doc Bailey's, he had me stitched up.

"Roll over, Dave, I'm gonna give you a shot in your hip."

"Go ahead, Doc; it'll be the high point of my day."

Another hour later, I drove back onto my little ranch. I got my shotgun and a jug of ice cold lemonade. I reviewed the day. First I'd hidden, then I'd charged into action unprepared. I now sat in the dark, sipping lemonade and feeling the welcome weight of the shotgun in my lap.

After a long while, Toby drove in, bringing Janey home. His headlights shined across me and he abruptly leaned over and let Janey out. He was gone faster than a paycheck.

Janey scowled down at me. "Are you sittin' out here just to show your old shotgun to Toby? she demanded. "You scared him off, you know."

"I don't rightly mind if Toby knows I own a shot gun, but no, he's not the reason I have it."

"Well, why ARE you sitting here with a shotgun in your lap?" she demanded.

"I only have this here shotgun because I don't own a machine gun. Now go to bed." Off in the distance, I could still hear that wild dog baying at the moon.

A TEXAS SUMMER CASUALTY

Texas heat pressing in at late summer,
Can sometimes fry common sense to a crisp.
It can turn Lone Star, big haired politeness,
To a senseless, discourteous wisp.

A woman supportive of little league,
Trekked to the park early to get a seat.
She was dressed in shorts and a club T-shirt,
And planned to wait in spite of the heat.

She walked resolutely to the ball fields,
The park crew was cleaning before the game.
They said they had to clean the metal stands.
She quipped she would sit there just the same.

The scorching heat added to the quarrel,
She said "I'm early and I'm gonna stay!"
The men had words they wanted to tell her,
But knew it was more than they should say.

She defiantly sat in the bleachers.
The park workers noticed tears in her eyes.
Their thoughts changed from empathy to justice,
When she walked away with burns on her thighs.

Marlene Tucker

DROUGHT

THERE'S AN OLD SAYING ABOUT THINGS
that seem to go on forever: the last three days before pay day, a bad sermon, and polite Southerners saying goodbye on the telephone. To that list I have to add: Texas summers — especially the ones with a drought. Droughts go on for three months, three years, or even three decades. To a Texan, drought is among the most feared things that can happen.

It doesn't just mean just that your lawn gets brown, or your water bill goes up. It means that you have to sell off the herd that you spent years putting together. Old Nelly, that lead goat that you mothered right special, that you watched mother a hundred kids, gets sold to a dog food company for $29. Or maybe she dies and you don't even get that. Drought means you break all the promises you made to your herd, and it means you break the promises you made to your banker, feed supplier, yourself and (most of all) to your daughter about her college escape — her one chance to not join another generation of Heartbreak women.

Drought means my mind flashes back to one of my earliest memories. My mother had a weak heart and we had a sweet black lady who sort of raised me. When I was about four, we took walks on the old dried lake bed next to our house during the drought of the early 1950's.

I fell into a crack in the lake bed about up to about my shoulders. The goo at the bottom of the hole seemed to suck me down. Mandy put her big, strong arm down into the hole and pulled me out. Far as I'm concerned, that pretty much solved any sense of racial superiority I may have felt. God bless Mandy! I wonder what ever happened to her. I hope she fared well before the Lord took her home.

I think about love as a metaphor for weather. What are the first signs of attraction? A smile from a woman that holds promise, followed by kind word? A wiggle of a hip, meant just for me? A mystery presented? A subtle request for faith in the process?

So what does infidelity look like? Nothing, at first. The smile is gone, and also the wiggle; an avoidance of touch, a sort of disappointment where mystery was presented before. Now, a man into cheating tends to shower emotion all over his family; a cheating gal just sort of disappears.

In Texas, fickleness is a cloud that rains in the next county, a storm front that dies 10 miles to the south, a gift from God that never quite gets to your own parched acres. God is awfully impersonal when He passes out rain and dry spells.

The drought crept up on me. First I noticed it was sort of dry, then, well, nothing. The clouds floated on by; next I noticed there weren't even any clouds. I bought a little extra feed for my stock, enjoyed the times with Sally Rae every trip to town, and just figured I'd make the best of it. You see, every rancher takes his land as his lover, and he (foolishly) never expects betrayal.

I think there are three kinds of optimists all on the road to perdition: gamblers, weathermen and ranchers, in that order. All I know for certain is that there ain't no moss on my rain gauge.

How do you track a real lack of rain? I used to use rain gauges, then pond levels and finally well depths.

The last measure is the amount of equity in my land that I give back to the bankers for permission to work in Hell and just hang on for another season. The real gauge is trips to town for feed (rising), price per pound for live stock (dropping), and my banker asking for a new balance sheet (nagging).

In drought, cactus and good humor wilt, and even cedar dies. I knew I was in a drought when I walked into The Waterin' Hole Café and pecked Sally Rae on the cheek and she snapped, "Yea, so what do *you* want?"

Drought eats away at the core. I even caught myself yelling at my dogs when they ran up to joyously wash my hubcaps. "Put that moisture on the grass where it'll do some good!" I yelled, before I realized how foolish I was starting to sound.

The next week, cedar trees started to turn brown. The week after, poison ivy turned yellow like it does in the fall, and it was only July. We had two more months at least before there was any real hope for significant climate change.

The first year I goat ranched, it rained too much. Snails grew in the fields and the snails grew nematodes, which killed my goats. The first symptom was that my lead billy lay on his back with four feet in the air. I felt sorry for him, but I felt sorrier for myself. I'd spent $2,000 on him and all I ever asked was that he do what billys like to do best.

I'll admit, there were problems before that. He preferred the company of young males over the females. I'm not real judgmental, but this was business. Anyway, he up and died, so I bought another billy, a "rodeo red" that was enthusiastic about his job. But he got all worn down (as billys will) and needed a rest. The unrelenting heat and merciless dryness didn't help him any.

Meanwhile I got Janey to help me with birthing the kids. Janey has little hands and she assisted with difficult deliveries and other problems a lot of times. Imagine this scene lit by kerosene lamp: "Feel left for hooves. If not, feel right. Rotate up and pull."

This was when I read from a husbandry manual by a lantern in a barn and Janey had her arm well up a very unhappy nanny's hind end.

"Do not rotate the hooves. Pull straight out."

Most kids that we helped this way with died in a few hours, but Janey is as game a girl as I ever saw. We tried hard.

Early on I bought a donkey for $200 from a real good man, every one told me he was really good (especially him). But that jenny turned out to be sterile and died a short time later. That was Old Man Storm.

Well, imagine how gifted I felt when I bought another donkey for only $10! Then a friend gave me one, and another guy gave me another. The next day, Old Man Storm showed up with a trailer and said "I know you like donkeys, Dave, so I brung ya some more!"

"Who knows, maybe I charged you a little too much for the first one," he said, as he squealed away in a dust cloud.

All of a sudden, I had six donkeys running all over my place.

I have a confession to make. I am 1/32nd Cherokee. The Cherokee were the most civilized tribe — that is, the easiest to sneak up on. I woke up one dry morning and realized I had been snookered. People were unloading donkeys on me during a drought. Three months later, I had a pasture full of free-loading donkeys and starving goats.

It is a measure of my desperation that I finally had to resort to reverse rustling. I loaded up all the donkeys and drove down to mean Old Man Storm's pasture. I cut his fence, backed up my trailer, and set them free. Being a rancher, of course I fixed the fence — but I also wiped out my tire tracks and worked out my alibi.

Finally, the weather patterns started to break. Rain fell north of us, but died out. Rain blew in from Mexico, but died out short of us. Rain came in from Houston, the air got humid, but the high pressure system that sat overhead deflected it and Heartbreak remained as dry as a penitent AA member.

Pecans started to drop off the trees in my yard. Then the big pecan trees started to shed their limbs. When I heard a real deep, resonate "CREAKkkkkk" and knock, I began to run. Think of a sledge hammer hitting an oak tree. Shortly thereafter, a huge limb would fall to the ground. Anyone caught under it would be dead meat.

I cut firewood for a seasonal job, but of course, every other desperate redneck in Heartbreak was doing the same thing, so we immediately bid ourselves back down to working for free.

Finally, in mid-fall, an arctic air mass bullied through the high pressure dome that had roosted over Heartbreak for so many months. Huge grey clouds boiled over our little city. Lightning struck the iron cross on Cottonwood Baptist Church. All the citizens of Heartbreak came outside as the gusty little winds blew from too hot to too cold. Rain drops the size of grapes suddenly fell from the sky. Dust kicked up in final defiance, but water from the sky ruled the day.

We all walked around like dumb young turkeys, our eyes skyward and our mouths open! God's grace fell from the sky! In moments, the big drops turned into a wall of water. Sheets of rain fell as if to make up for the earlier deficit. All us rain-starved denizens of Heartbreak walked in mad circles, soaked to the skin for the first time in a year! My banker passed by me and he actually smiled at me. It was a day of miracles.

Heartbreak, Texas

The rain finally ended. We got three inches, but not another drop for a month. It didn't really break the drought, but it bent it enough we could hang on a while longer.

Real gamblers don't have to go to Las Vegas. Real gamblers sometimes go to Cottonwood Baptist Church, and we try to earn a living off the land.

Restoring Rain

The dry of summer drug on, leaving dust upon the trees,
While heat sucked all the cool out of every passing breeze.
Momma didn't smile much; her face looked tired and thin.
We never heard her laugh like she used to do back then.

We lost dad and she grieved for the most of two long years.
Like land caught in the drought, she was sad without the tears.
Momma, with no life partner, no love and no best friend,
Took us to Church on Sundays and prayed the drought would end.

It was in late August, I won't forget that day,
I helped Momma with the wash, my brothers were at play.
As she hung out the laundry I handed her the pins.
No one paid attention as the clouds were rolling in.

One loud clap of thunder then large drops began to pelt.
I looked at Momma's face to determine how she felt.
She started with a smile, then a grin and then a laugh,
We all began to giggle as the earth got a bath.

The shower washed the dust off and made the leaves look green.
The air was fresh which gave the feel of life renewed and clean.
As rain had brought us hope that someday the drought would end,
It also gave me faith that Momma's heart would one day mend.

Marlene Tucker

Final Story

OF COURSE, AFTER ALL THAT, THINGS got worse. Sally Rae made some potato salad at the Waterin' Hole Café for the Cottonwood Baptist Church annual picnic and it killed several prominent persons. The State of Texas Health Department shut her down. Gomer, her boss fired her from her place as Chief Cook, Bottle Washer and waitress.

Li'l' Billy burned down the goat barn with most of the herd in it. I got real sick, I mean I felt like was dying...but I get ahead of myself. Keep on reading. Heartbreak is a tough place to live and tough people keep on living.

Dave